Lynna's Rogue

Curse of the Conjure Woman
Book One

KITTY MARGO

This story is a work of fiction. Names, characters, places, and incidents are either products of the author's imagination or used fictitiously. Any resemblance to actual events, locales, or persons, living or dead, is entirely coincidental. No part of this publication can be reproduced or transmitted in any form or by any means, electronic or mechanical, without written permission of Kitty Margo.

First Edition October 30, 2012
Second Edition May 30, 2024
Buttercup Publishing

ISBN: 9780985928025

In Loving Memory of

James Clifford Swaringen
1931 – 2013

and

Bertie Ann Swaringen
1936 – 2013

You will be loved and treasured forever.

Chapter 1

Paris, France 1850

Only a fool would fail to realize that the amount of money being offered to Joshua Jordan would come with a great deal of danger attached, and he was no fool.

Would he be asked to pillage and plunder? Turn thieving highwayman? Bloodthirsty assassin? Kidnap a princess for a king's ransom?

The answer to all these questions stood before him in the form of Nathan Rhodes, a man rumored to be the wealthiest in all of France, and one who appeared most eager to put an end to Joshua's vivid speculations.

"It is quite simple really, Captain Jordan. You will be my daughter's protector," Nathan Rhodes stated, as though it were the only pressing matter in the whole of the universe, for to him it was. "A physical presence each and every moment of the day, until she is safely delivered to my sister in America. Lynna must never be out of your sight, and on this point I would require your solemn oath as a gentleman."

"Why me, sir?" When had he gained the reputation as a highly touted babysitter?

"Because I have it on good authority that not only are you a man of your word, but you are also fiercely loyal to those in your care."

Nathan Rhodes rocked back on his heels and clasped his hands behind his back, as he eyed the much younger man. "I realize that you have never met my daughter, and could therefore feel no such sentiment toward her. However, I also realize that with the proper amount of persuasion, you could at least feel obligated to protect her as though she were your very own sister, and see that no harm befalls her."

Joshua was silent, pondering the man's extravagant offer.

Nathan Rhodes prided himself on being an astute businessman, and paused to allow his words to fully sink in. He was aware that to a man of sound mind, such a proposition would be impossible to refuse.

When Joshua failed to immediately agree to the terms of the contract, Nathan continued, undaunted, a man obviously accustomed to having his way in all matters. "Now, Captain Jordan, if you will give me your word as an officer and a gentleman, that you would be willing to forfeit your own life for the safety of my daughter's, then all that you see before you will be yours."

Forfeit his life? "Now hold on just a minute, Mr. Rhodes." At twenty-nine years of age, Joshua was neither ready, nor willing, to die for a complete stranger. "Perhaps you should enlighten me as to precisely what it is your daughter needs protecting from, sir."

Nathan Rhodes motioned to the money and breathed a pained sigh as he sank wearily down on a chair in front of Joshua's desk. "Over the years, I have amassed a sizable fortune, Captain Jordan. I was visiting here from the red clay of Georgia just after completing my education, when I was introduced to my future wife, and soon entered into a profitable partnership with her father. Without really working to achieve it, the wealth seemed to be deposited in my lap."

Nathan waved a careless hand toward the money bag. "This is but a mere pittance compared to my vast holdings, I assure you. When my wife's parents went to their heavenly reward, I was bequeathed their rather immense fortune, although my wealth means nothing to me at the moment." He cringed, and rubbed the area over his heart as though a great pain had settled there. "Not without my darling daughter to share it."

The haggard man paused, as if expecting a reaction from Joshua. When none was forthcoming, he plowed ahead. "To get to the point, Captain Jordan, I have received numerous death threats against my daughter's life in recent years. There have been two strong armed kidnapping attempts, with the last coming only two days ago. The miscreants came too close this time, much too close. If not for a few minor miscalculations on their part, they might have succeeded in kidnapping Lynna."

The grieving father's voice shook as his eyes clouded with pain. "Only the Good Lord above knows what the reprobates might have done before releasing her. *If* they released her."

Again, Joshua nodded. Odds were great that Nathan would not have seen his daughter again, at least not alive.

The older man snatched a handkerchief from

his pocket and wiped at the perspiration beading his brow. "Even though what I am being forced to do pains me beyond measure, it would be detrimental to my daughter's welfare to remain in France. I must relinquish her until these criminals can be captured and brought to justice. My justice!" he stormed, slamming his clenched fist on the table hard enough to make a few of the coins flip.

Joshua noticed a tear slip from the overwrought man's red rimmed and swollen eyes, as expressions of deep sorrow flickered across his gaunt features. "I have the wherewithal to purchase anything my heart desires, Captain Jordan. Anything in the world I could wish for, except happiness. Not once in my daughter's life have I missed a single breakfast with her, nor spent a night without her peacefully slumbering in the room juxtaposed to mine. If not for the fear of losing her forever, a separation such as this would be unthinkable."

Joshua scrubbed a hand over his face and considered the offer before him; the pros and cons. The pros being the money, of course, while the cons meant being saddled with a spoiled and whiny brat for the entire voyage.

He chose his words carefully as he strolled to the open window, to gaze across placid ocean waters. "Since I have no doubt that you've had the whole of Scotland Yard running a thorough background check of my life, past and present, I'm sure the detectives informed you that the *Windjammer* is a cargo vessel. We only have accommodations for two passengers at most."

Nathan nodded, and Joshua accepted the fact that the man probably knew more about his life, as well as his ship and its passengers, than he knew himself.

He moved to a sidebar and poured two shots of brandy, offering the aggrieved father a glass. "On this particular voyage, both passengers have sailed with me previously. Therefore, I can vouch for their character, as well as my crew, whom I would trust with my life."

"According to my reports, both passengers are upstanding citizens," Nathan confirmed. "However, the female appears to be a bit of a busybody."

"An understatement if there ever was one." Joshua chuckled.

"Each member of your crew has passed inspection as well," Nathan added.

"If one of them had failed the test, I have a feeling he would have missed the boat on the journey home."

"Nothing nefarious," Nathan replied. "He would have simply been given free passage on another sailing vessel."

"Since you have no reservations concerning my passengers and crew, and you have my word that every possible precautionary measure will be taken to assure your daughter's safe voyage, are we in agreement then?"

"Absolutely." Nathan drained his glass, with a look of immense relief on his otherwise miserable countenance, and extended his hand to Joshua. "Thank you, Captain Jordan. I have been assured by your brethren in the seafaring world that your word is your bond."

Joshua savored the taste of the amber liquid

as it slid down his throat, then he returned to the brandy decanter and faced Nathan Rhodes as he poured a refill. "I feel safe in saying that your daughter would have no greater need than a female traveling companion while onboard my ship."

"A female traveling companion!" Nathan Rhodes thundered, leaping from his chair to stand before Joshua like a man possessed of hidden demons. "Have you gone completely mad, man?" His hands on Joshua's shoulders jerked, as though he were trying to shake some sense into a simpleton. "It is their intention to abduct my daughter and hold her for ransom. For the love of God, man, they might even resort to murder if their kidnapping plot were to somehow go awry. A hell of a lot of good a traveling companion would do her."

Joshua stood before the overwrought man in stunned silence, as brandy overflowed the glass and dripped to the floor before he thought to right the decanter.

Nathan Rhodes took slow deep breaths in an apparent attempt to calm his shattered nerves. "Captain Jordan, please allow me to impress upon you the seriousness of this situation. My daughter must have a bodyguard, someone to protect her from any and all adversaries encountered along the way. Someone who will be by her side by day, and especially at night, when the brigands are most likely to strike."

Joshua lit a cheroot, quietly observing his agitated visitor.

Nathan placed his empty glass on the desk and sighed heavily. "Understand this is not a pleasure cruise, sir. If it were, I would build my daughter the most opulent and lavishly bedecked vessel to ever navigate the seas. I would see it equipped with every convenience and have every extravagance known, or even considered in the shipping industry, to take her to any destination her heart desires. Yet, the degenerates would expect her to travel in such a manner."

Nathan closed his eyes and inhaled a ragged breath. "After much consideration, and as you have already alluded to, my discourse with Scotland Yard, we have decided that concealing her on a cargo vessel would be the safest and least conspicuous means of travel."

Joshua nodded in agreement, as the idea had merit.

Nathan's eyes swept over Joshua's muscular frame. "I put complete trust in you, Captain Jordan, to be the gentleman and protector my daughter needs. Nonetheless, should she come to any harm, or should she not remain chaste while in your care..." The tortured father was quiet for several minutes as he gazed out the window at the calm, sparkling water of the bay. His knuckles whitened under the pressure of his clenched fist as he whispered, "May the Good Lord take pity on your soul."

Nathan's eyes locked with Joshua's, and while his words were spoken calmly, they carried an ominous warning. Should any harm come to his cherished daughter while under Joshua's protection, the captain of the *Windjammer* would be signing his own death warrant. He knew beyond a shadow of a doubt that Nathan Rhodes, with the able assist of some of the best detectives in Europe, and possibly a few assassins, would search heaven and hell to see the deed accomplished.

"Do we have a deal, Captain?" Nathan was apparently bringing the discussion to a close. "If you can agree to my terms, may I suggest preparations get underway to sail at your earliest convenience? I wish for my daughter to be out of this godforsaken country on the next high tide."

It had been some time since Joshua had bestowed upon his crew a hefty bonus for their years of faithful service, so he made an immediate decision to accept the man's offer and split the bounty with his crew. "We have a deal."

"Very well." Nathan made to leave, but stopped abruptly and turned to face the man who would hold the life of his cherished daughter in his capable hands. "Before I go, there are a few things I feel obligated to tell you about Lynna's unique and decidedly unorthodox upbringing, Captain Jordan. If you are to understand my daughter, you must first understand her rather exceptional childhood."

Nathan massaged his temples, in an apparent attempt to ease a pain there. "Due to numerous kidnapping attempts, she has lived a sheltered life of relative seclusion.

The man of great wealth found it a truly lamentable fact of the times that even his immense riches could not guarantee his daughter's safety. "The consequences of this sequestered life, are that Lynna knows very little of what goes on in the world around her. The Chateau was her world. A world filled with every available luxury and with every indulgence at her beck and call. Lynna was given everything, except friends, girls her own age with whom to share intimate secrets."

Nathan raked a trembling hand through his thinning hair. "Her only acquaintances were the household staff, who were nearing retirement age when she was born. A few have passed on, but since the day Lynna was born, the servants at the Chateau have doted on her."

Joshua was intrigued by the man's heartfelt story. "Go on."

"There was Gertrude her maid, an elderly native of New Orleans who planted all sorts of supernatural voodoo nonsense in my daughter's head. While the woman should have been fired years ago, she was Lynna's favorite so I kept her on."

"What about her education?" Surely, the child was allowed to flee the geriatric household on occasion, at least long enough to attend school with children her own age. "Did she go away to a private school?"

"Lynna wasn't allowed to leave the Chateau, Captain Jordan. I lived with the constant fear that I might never see her again if I allowed her out of my sight." Nathan shook his head and breathed a defeated sigh as if, for the first time, he might be regretting his decision to subject his child to a life of lonely isolation. "Her schooling came from two of my most trusted friends."

"Let me guess." Joshua quirked a brow. "Old friends?"

Nathan hung his head. "I could not risk allowing outsiders into our private world. We never knew who could be plotting against us."

"In essence, your daughter was reared by, and for her entire life has only known, people who were considerably older."

Nathan nodded. "The few times she left home, which was not often I must admit, she was heavily chaperoned."

"By old men?"

"Yes," Nathan confessed, shaking his head as if to rid his mind of a painful memory. "Lynna's life was never the same after her mother was kidnapped on her third birthday. The bond between mother and child was unbreakable. You rarely saw one without the other." Even after all these years, Nathan's eyes still clouded with pain. "While I paid the ransom within hours of receiving it, my wife's ravaged body washed ashore three days later."

Joshua witnessed the pain and grief that flickered across his face. The man had lost his wife to kidnappers, and now his only child was being threatened with the same fate, and being forced to sail from the only home she had ever known. Joshua was now able to fully understand the father's irrational fear for his daughter's safety.

"I will tell you this, Captain Jordan. If you find my daughter lacking in worldly ways, and I am confident that you will, you must bear in mind that it was through no fault of her own. It was forced on her by my constant fear for her wellbeing."

As Joshua watched Nathan Rhodes' melancholy departure from his cabin, he was reminded of what his own mother had so often told him as a child.

Money makes life easier, to be sure, but it cannot buy happiness, son.

As Nathan Rhodes left the ship to bring his daughter on board, Joshua went on deck to inform his crew of the bonus they would receive after the safe delivery of their precious cargo.

While his mother's words were true indeed, it was also true that the extra coins at the end of this voyage would be the next best thing to happiness for his hard working crew.

Chapter 2

Lynna Rhodes peered from beneath long, sooty lashes as her father clutched her arm the same way a drowning man would clutch the nearest floating object. Her gaze dropped as a sudden wave of guilt almost overwhelmed her. How could she feel so elated, when he was so miserable and forlorn? He reminded her of a man in mourning, or one on the way to the gallows, while her own excitement was impossible to contain.

Due to her father's irrational fear for her safety, not once in her eighteen years had she been onboard a ship, or even allowed to venture to the docks for that matter. She had often watched ships entering the harbor from her daydreaming perch on her upstairs window seat, and longed to sail into the horizon. To set a course for one of the intriguing and far distant countries, that until now she had only visited in books. Her dream was about to become a reality, and she could hardly wait to experience it.

She was destined for an exciting new land, a new home, and a new way of life. Best of all, she was setting sail without the hovering bodyguards that had forever been a perpetual thorn in her side. Just this morning, her father had informed her that she would be traveling without them, or even her maid Gertrude, since they would only draw unwelcome attention. She was to rely on Captain Joshua Jordan for her every need.

She eagerly anticipated hearing captivating tales of his thrilling adventures around the world. There should be plenty of time for storytelling, since the captain was to assume total responsibility for her safety, and they would be spending a surplus of time together.

Still, according to the numerous books she had read, sea captains were an old and dowdy lot, and this one would probably pay little attention to her whereabouts. He would most likely be too busy with steering the ship, or whatever captains did, leaving her to explore the sailing vessel and its passengers at her leisure.

She wanted to run across the deck, laughing and singing to the high heavens, instead she gazed into her father's downtrodden visage and her heart puddled at her feet. She had never felt more torn, as excitement and misery waged a heated battle within.

She consoled herself with the fact that his sorrow would be short lived, since she was convinced that he would soon see the villains captured and hanged, and she could promptly board a ship for her return passage to France. With that thought firmly fixed in her mind, she pulled her eyes away from her father and counted the sixteen sails above her.

Nathan escorted his daughter to the captain's cabin and hugged her close with tear filled eyes. "My darling, you will never know the agony this decision has caused me. You must realize why I am sending you away, and the heartache I feel in doing so. Please, tell me you understand."

"Of course I do, Father." In all her life, Lynna had never seen her distinguished father look so defeated. "We will be together again soon, you shall see. Your men will have those horrid despots caught in no time, and I will be awaiting word that I may return."

"Godspeed, my darling child. Rest assured that I shall send for you as soon as the danger has passed. Now, I must leave before I am recognized. Look to the Captain for your every need until you reach America, where Aunt Judith will be waiting with open arms."

"I shall be awaiting your missive," Lynna cried, around a tight knot that seemed to lodge in her throat. "*Au revoir*, Father. *Je t'aime!*"

Her father's shoulders sagged miserably as he opened the door, and she caught a glimpse of a man casually leaning against the doorjamb. As her father closed the portal, she heard the lock click into place and felt a brief moment of panic. Had she traded one prison for a much lonelier one?

She removed the whalebone hoops from beneath thirteen yards of cornflower blue silk ruffles that made up the skirt of her gown, then she perched on the edge of the bed to remove her soft kid slippers, feeling gloriously unencumbered. She was grateful that her father had never forced her to wear those two foolish contraptions, hoops and corsets, at home.

She heard muffled voices coming from the opposite side of the door as she fidgeted nervously with the hem of her flounced petticoat. Was this ship really about to set sail, with her in it? She could hardly fathom her recent turn of good fortune. Or would her father have a sudden change of heart at the last minute and insist that she return home?

She wouldn't truly believe her first grand

adventure was underway until she heard the wind billowing in the canvas sails of the *Windjammer*.

She took a moment to survey her new surroundings, and found it to be a room much like her father's study, with the addition of an intricately carved four poster bed and a massive sea trunk. Along the walls were shelves lined with delicately shaped trinkets of ivory, glass, and metal.

A large desk took up one corner of a cabin that was cluttered with maps, a compass, a sextant, and a hand carved model of the ship. She had to wonder how much it had cost her father to persuade the captain to give up the comfort of his bed for her convenience.

She swiped at the perspiration that trickled into her cleavage, and considered taking leave of her cumbersome traveling outfit for a more appropriate day dress. It was stifling hot, even though the window in the cabin was open. Surely the ship would soon be underway, and she could feel a cooling ocean breeze on this sweltering day.

She retrieved a fan from her reticule and fanned herself vigorously, before plopping down in the center of the bed to wait patiently for her introduction to the captain of the *Windjammer*.

After Joshua assured Nathan Rhodes for the umpteenth time that he would care for his offspring as though she were his very own sibling, and escorting him off the ship, he strode toward his cabin to console the grief stricken lass. He had put off his duty as long as he could, now he must see to his charge, who would likely cower in the corner when he entered the cabin and scream bloody murder if he so much as looked at her sideways.

Fortunately, there was one other female passenger who might be persuaded to befriend the young recluse and share sleeping quarters with her. He would make a few inquiries on the morrow. No, that wouldn't do. Nathan would have his head if he allowed her out of his sight.

It was a given that the girl would be as dismayed by this situation as her father, after being banished from the only home she had ever known, without so much as her maidservant by her side. After living such a secluded life for so many years, albeit a spoiled and pampered one, she could hardly be expected to be a social butterfly. It was his guess that she would more resemble a painfully shy hermit.

He already dreaded the sleepless nights ahead spent calming the forsaken heiress, but his consolation was that he would certainly be well compensated for any disturbed sleep.

He plastered a cheery smile on his lips, and prepared himself for her caterwauling as he knocked softly and slowly opened the door.

What charade was this?

Had he been duped?

Had he dreamed the entire conversation with her father?

The vision before him was certainly no homesick or grief stricken wallflower, he would bet his ship on that. His jaw dropped to his chest as he stood perfectly still, inhaling sharply as the exquisite creature beamed a radiant smile.

The voluptuous young lady on his bed could not be Nathan Rhodes's painfully shy and withdrawn daughter. Could she? He had to admit that the ravishing beauty looked anything but upset at the thought of leaving her father, and country, behind.

While Joshua had viewed beautiful women in ports all over the world, Lynna Rhodes far surpassed them all. She had been blessed at birth with smooth creamy skin and breathtaking vivid blue eyes that sparkled up at him, moist pink lips, a dainty upturned nose, and waist length feathery golden curls that hugged her enchanting curves. She was far from shedding the tears Joshua had assumed would be flowing at the thought of putting an ocean between herself and her sire.

"You must be Captain Jordan. I am Lynna Rhodes, although I'm sure you already know who is occupying the cabin in your stead." She giggled as she tumbled from the bed to offer her hand. "I can hardly wait to set sail, will it be very much longer?"

Joshua was shocked to the roots of his hair as he accepted her delicate hand, and her sparkling azure gaze held him captive. As if she had read his mind and sought to fulfill his wildest fantasy, she moved into his arms and pressed her soft, and very luscious, curves against him.

"Thank you, Captain, for giving up the comforts of your bed. I was dreading the very idea of sleeping on a hard bunk. I trust your new quarters are suitable?"

With her soft breasts pressed against his chest, Joshua's pulse quickened as a powerful surge of blood shot toward his lower anatomy. Was he expected to hold her curvaceous body in his arms and not feel anything?

Only if he had a desire to continue living.

He took her by the shoulders and stood her an

arm's length away, trying desperately to think mundane thoughts.

Indeed, his quarters were quite suitable. Where had she gotten the erroneous notion that he would be abandoning his cabin? Her father had given strict orders that he was to share a cabin with her, sleeping on a hard cot in the corner of course, but always within sight of his precious daughter. Surely, Nathan Rhodes had not been remiss in sharing this knowledge with his beguiling offspring.

Once again, his eyes strayed to the body of a woman who seemed to possess the innocence of a child, a hazardous combination to be sure. Her embrace was a cordial display of affection, nothing more. No coy flirtatious, move designed to send a man's blood racing and have him drooling at her feet.

In fact, he would bet every coin Nathan Rhodes had deposited in his safe that his daughter did not possess the slightest notion of how her affectionate hug would affect him, or any other member of the opposite sex for that matter. Her father's words repeated over and over in his mind. *"If you find my daughter lacking in worldly ways, Captain Jordan…"*

"Oh, Captain Jordan, I am terribly excited about this voyage." Her sapphire blue eyes danced up at him. "Still, if I am being perfectly honest, you are not at all what I expected."

"An understatement if ever there was one, my lady." Joshua leaned against the door to observe the enchanting imp at his leisure. "Pray tell, what did you expect?"

She turned her exquisite head to study him with a furrowed brow. "Um… someone much older, saltier perhaps, and more rugged. Yes, that's the word I was searching for, more rugged, from many years spent on the deck of a ship."

"I've spent many years on the deck of the *Windjammer*, to be sure." Joshua chuckled. "As for my age, I don't believe I am ready to be put out to pasture just yet."

"Neither do I, sir. At any rate, I must confess that all my knowledge comes from books. While I have never been to your country, I have read much about America. Our journey should be an eight-week voyage. Is that correct?"

"If we have good winds at our back."

"You will tell me what to expect when we arrive, *oui*?"

Joshua watched as a tiny trickle of perspiration slid down her neck to the valley between her breasts, her full, creamy breasts. What he wouldn't give to....

Why was he even thinking such ludicrous and life threatening thoughts? Not only would Nathan Rhodes have his head, he would mount it and hang it on his office wall, as a daily reminder of the man who had the sheer audacity to dally with his daughter.

He raked a trembling hand through his hair as he tore his eyes from her lovely cleavage, and spent the next several minutes perusing a tiny speck of dirt on the toe of his boot. He had been hired to protect this girl, just as he would his own sister, but damn Nathan Rhodes all to hell.

The man should have warned him of what a truly delectable creature his daughter was, instead of rambling on and on about her supposed lack of social graces. There was not a red blooded man alive, be he

French, American, or any other nationality, who would not be caught completely off guard by the stunning beauty of Lynna Rhodes. "I came to see to your comfort, and you look extremely... um... comfortable. If all is to your satisfaction, I will return to my duties."

Lynna motioned toward the inviting four poster bed. "I could not have asked for more comfortable quarters."

"I'm glad you approve," he choked out, swiping at the perspiration that beaded his brow. "I will bid you good day, and endeavor to return in time to share the evening meal with you."

"Good day, Captain," Lynna whispered to his retreating back, as he closed the door softly behind him. Her brow creased as she sat down on the bed feeling *something*. Heavenly days, the captain was certainly a different sort of man than what Gertrude referred to as the stuffed shirts in her father's employ.

The captain was tall, at least six feet two inches, with black wavy hair that fell carelessly across his forehead, and skin tanned golden from many hours spent on the deck of a ship. His teeth were pearly white, and she was sure they would sparkle were he ever to attempt a smile.

Her thoughts meandered back to the impulsive hug she had given the captain. She had felt, what was it she had felt... exactly? A strange, yet, entirely delicious sensation in the pit of her stomach.

The feeling had begun as butterflies in her midsection, and rapidly spread to all parts of her body, leaving a noticeable sensitivity in her breasts and at the apex of her thighs. She brushed her hands across her bodice and remembered, vividly, the feelings that had awakened in her loins when she pressed against his broad chest.

Of course, she had felt twinges in that area while bathing with a soapy cloth, but nothing compared to the sensations that erupted when Captain Jordan's hand softly caressed her flesh.

She knew one thing for certain. Captain Jordan was unlike any other man she had ever before encountered.

Chapter 3

Lynna was humming, so she didn't hear Joshua's knock when he entered the cabin a short while later. As she turned, clad only in a scanty cream colored chemise of the finest lace money could buy, his eyes feasted hungrily on the alluring view of long shapely legs, only a few feet from his own.

"Oh, Captain Jordan," she cried, snatching her dress to hastily cover herself. "You should have knocked, sir. I am not dressed to receive company, and I certainly hope you do not make a habit of barging into a lady's bedchamber unannounced."

"Not as a general rule, no. Normally, I'm... invited." Joshua was much chagrined as he hastily backed out the door to stand in the hallway like a chastened lad. "Please, forgive me. I will wait outside until you are suitably attired."

Several minutes had passed before she called for him to enter, and the embarrassing incident had apparently been forgotten. "Will our meal be served soon? I find myself quite famished."

"The meal should be delivered any minute now." He sat at his desk, and opened his log book.

Lynna smiled brilliantly, without an apparent care that her gown remained unfastened in the back and was in danger of slipping from her shoulders.

The sight had not gone unnoticed by Joshua, and although he fought it, his eyes feasted on the satiny bosom rising and falling above the lace of her chemise, beckoning him from an arm's length away. In one simple motion he could have her in his arms, have his mouth on her inviting pink lips. No!

He closed his eyes and issued a silent prayer for strength. Was he going stark raving mad? He was a gentleman for crying out loud. A gentleman who not less than one hour ago had sworn an oath to protect this enchantress with his very life, and now every fiber in his being yearned to seduce her?

"Captain Jordan?" Lynna whispered, as concern etched her delicate features.

His tongue finally untied itself and he was able to speak. "Supper should be here soon." He was about to make a hasty retreat before making an even bigger fool of himself, when his feet simply refused to move.

While he was far from being over the trauma of having her enticing front side so near, she presented him with her back. "Before you go, Captain Jordan, will you fasten me, *s'il vous plaît*? I fear I am rather lost without my Gertrude."

"Dear heavenly Father above," Joshua silently implored, "if ever I needed your strength, it would be now." He was thankful that her back was turned, so she wouldn't witness the trembling hands that moved at a slug's pace toward her back, sorely afraid that to touch the velvety skin would be his undoing.

"Captain Jordan?" Lynna wondered at the delay, after several long, fumbling minutes had passed. "Is there some difficulty?" As she waited, she fiddled with a tiny locket that hung from a delicate gold chain around her neck. "I fear my dear father has sent me away grossly unprepared. I cannot possibly fasten and unfasten the stays at my back, nor do I feel comfortable asking you to assist me morning and night, but what other choice is there when I have no other acquaintance onboard this ship."

Pity for the girl was strong inside Joshua. Had her father not been sorely vexed at the thought of sending his daughter across the ocean, the fact that she would need a maid to accomplish these menial tasks would not have slipped his mind. "No difficulty at all," he croaked the lie.

As his hands reached for the dress, his fingers made powerful contact with her bare skin. He glanced out the window to see if a storm was brewing, after feeling a jolt of lightning shoot through his fingers and exit the top of his head.

Did she feel the tremor that coursed through him, or the heat that leapt from her body to scorch his hands?

As he reveled in the feeling of her satiny flesh beneath his fingers, he was suddenly aware of a thumping noise from seemingly far, far away. The sound grew louder and louder, until it penetrated the fog that swirled through his brain.

"Are ye in there, lad?" Sam, the ship's cook, shouted. "Yer meal is getting cold, and I don't intend for my victuals to sit outside the door and be consumed by rodents, so open up."

Sam's shout succeeded in gaining Lynna's attention. She grabbed a nearby shawl and draped it over her shoulders, hastily tying it in front.

While Joshua shook his head to loose the cobwebs, Sam had called several more times before

he could make his way to the door. The impulse was
strong to stuff a chicken leg in the cook's mouth and
inform him that food was not what he hungered for.
Instead, he opened the door and allowed the grinning
man to enter.

Both men knew the menial chore of
delivering lunch trays fell to the cabin boy.
Normally, Sam would consider the task far beneath
him and be greatly affronted if instructed to carry it
out, so why the hell did he lower his standards today?

Joshua was fully aware that the older man's
curiosity had overridden his pride, and he wished to
see firsthand if the gossip making the rounds of the
ship was true.

"I'm happy to see that for once the rumors
have merit, for you are a bonny lass, indeed." Sam
smiled broadly at Lynna as he marched into the
cabin. "A winsome one for sure."

Lynna's beaming smile brought a twinkle to
the seasoned sailor's eyes. "You are most kind, sir,
and a welcome sight as I find myself quite ravenous."

"At your service, milady." Sam was not one
to waste time chatting, and having seen what he had
come to see, was ready to depart. "Now, if you will
excuse me, I have forty more starving mouths to feed
on this vessel. Enjoy your meal, lass."

After Sam's departure, Joshua sat back and
watched as Lynna ate heartily of the fine fare spread
before her. She paused long enough to glance up and
ask in between bites of crispy fried chicken, "Will
you not join me, Captain? I thought you were
hungry?"

"Maybe later." He poured another glass of
wine and peered over the rim. "Would you care for a

glass of port?"

"No, I don't... um, yes." *What would it hurt to try it?* "Thank you, Captain Jordan."

Joshua watched her sip the wine, and make a small purr of pleasure before downing the entire glass. "How delicious." She licked a drop from her moist lips, causing his pulse to skip in an erratic manner. He refilled her glass as she speared a succulent potato and pushed it past dewy lips.

Ten minutes later, she untied the shawl and tossed it on the bed. "It has gotten rather warm has it not, Captain?" With the back of her hand, she swiped at a trail of perspiration as it disappeared into her décolletage.

"Perhaps you've had enough port. You wouldn't want to drink overmuch and miss leaving the harbor." He slid the bottle out of her reach and went to pour her a glass of water, when he was interrupted by a tapping at the door. Thinking it was Sam again, he flung the portal wide, only to find his first mate.

"We are ready to set sail, Captain. Will you be wantin' to steer us out of the harbor?"

"Yes, of course." Joshua turned to his slightly tipsy cabin mate. To his surprise, he found that he rather enjoyed the lady's company. "Enjoy your meal, Lynna. I will return shortly."

Chapter 4

When Joshua entered his cabin almost an
hour later, Lynna was nibbling on a square of
buttered cornbread as she reached for the nearly
empty bottle of port. He was taken aback by her
apparent thirst for wine. Was the lady a lush? Some
women would be falling out of their seats after
consuming an entire bottle.

Lynna wasn't exactly falling out of her seat,
probably because she had a death grip on the edge of
the table with her right hand. Her left hand was
pouring the few remaining drops of port into her
plate, while missing her glass entirely. She dropped
the bottle sideways on the table and took a bite of
apple cobbler, smiling up at him.

"Port is *sreally* very good, Captain Jordan. I
was never allowed to have it at the Chateau. Father
said ladies should not par... part... partake of
spirits."

"Now you tell me." Joshua shook his head at
his vast stupidity. Some protector he was, the girl
was drunk before they left the docks.

"It does make my head feel... *frunny*." She
hiccupped loudly, and daintily covered her mouth
with a lace handkerchief. "I need fresh air." Lynna
gazed with longing toward the open window, as she
stood and cautiously made an unsuccessful step
toward it.

Joshua reached out to catch her just as she fell

into his waiting arms, causing her gown to gape open and reveal things that could be detrimental to his continued health and longevity. "Here, Miss Rhodes, please, allow me to fasten your stays. It appears that I have been remiss in my duties."

"Thank you, Captain *Jerden*."

He inhaled a steadying breath, stood erect, and once again reached for her back. Nope. He couldn't do it. He knew better than to touch her. Her father would demand his heart on a silver platter. "Please, have a seat until I return. There is one other female passenger who should be able to help you dress. I will fetch her."

"*Non*, I want you, not a stranger helping me dress." Lynna waved an unsteady finger at him. "My father ass... ass... assured me that you would see to all my needs. I am to *thrust* no one else."

She made a good point. He could do this. He casually opened his hands to see the task completed, when his thumb accidentally caressed the softness of her back. Her skin was silky to the touch. Smooth as glass. Radiating heat. So soft. What would be the harm in allowing his palms to caress, for the briefest of moments, the velvety softness?

With his blood simmering on a low boil, he was unable to comprehend a single harmful consequence that might result from such an action. He placed his hands on her back and closed his eyes, savoring the heady feeling of having her smooth skin beneath his calloused palms.

As the rest of his body immediately responded to what his hands were feeling, he was quick to realize what a grievous error in judgment it had been to touch her. His hands now moved of their own volition across her back, and toward the gentle rise and fall of her breasts.

She should turn around any moment and land a resounding slap to his cheek, and he would welcome the pain. Better still, he prayed she would draw up her enticing knee and deliver a fierce jab to his privates. Anything to clear his befuddled head, and put a halt to his roaming hands before it was too late.

Sadly, the thought of slapping or kneeing Joshua never entered Lynna's spinning head. In fact, she didn't benefit from a rational thought at all, as her mind was currently swimming through a murky lake. Her blurry eyes saw two Captains standing before her, and it was so hot. She was wholly convinced that if she didn't soon remove every stitch of her clothes, she would perish from heat stroke.

She drew a stuttering breath when she felt his rough hands on her unclad skin. His touch felt glorious, absolutely sublime. So sublime, in fact, that her entire body seemed to melt beneath his touch. The very skin where his hands rested felt singed by flames as they left a trail across her heated flesh.

Every nerve in her body seemed to be centered under the palm of his hand. Now those hands were moving around her sides slowly, much too slowly. Her breasts ached, no throbbed, with each and every beat of her heart, pulsing against the thin material of her chemise as her nipples strained against the fabric.

She had never experienced feelings of passion such as these at the Chateau. Not once. Was it the wine? Is that why her father never allowed her to drink it? Could this ship be enchanted? Was she under the influence of a magical spell? Was the captain a wizard perhaps?

She knew about sorcery and bewitchment from the books she had read, and Gertrude quite frequently consulted Tarot cards when Lynna's father wasn't around to witness the Celtic spread. Why, the elderly woman even possessed a voodoo doll, made to the likeness of the woman who had pilfered Gertrude's betrothed away. She would viciously push pins into the doll, nightly, while chanting an unknown tongue.

Lynna felt his hands fluttering at her sides and knew exactly where she wanted them. She recalled frequently hearing her father say to his associates, *"If you want something, go get it. Odds are great that it won't stumble and fall into your lap."*

Perhaps he had not meant for his words to be taken quite so literally but, in that moment, she knew that having Captain Jordan's hands on her breasts would be tantamount to dying and floating off to heaven on a wispy bit of cloud.

While she was at a loss to explain the intense craving, having never felt it before, she saw absolutely no harm in fulfilling the desire. Without a care for the consequences, she placed her hands on top of his and tugged them around to cup her breasts. *Oh.* The sheer bliss of having his hands on her sensitive flesh caused every nerve ending in her body to jolt to life.

She vaguely heard the captain mumble her name as she pressed back against him, and she had never known such rapture existed as when his hands kneaded her breasts.

Her head rolled limply on his shoulder as a soft moan of uninhibited ecstasy slipped from her parted lips. She felt herself being spun around in his arms, as his mouth lowered to hers in a kiss that she felt in the very pit of her stomach.

His hands slid over her flesh, causing every muscle in her body to tense with anticipation as he slowly caressed her hips and buttocks, before coming to rest on her heaving bosom. Then he lifted her gently and carried her to bed.

Lynna hiccupped loudly as Joshua lowered his mouth to drink deeply of her honeyed lips. He eased the gown from her shoulders, and stroked the inside of her lips with his tongue until her mouth opened to him.

Molten lava coursed through Lynna's veins. She wished to cry out at the loss of his lips, as they left a burning trail down her throat and over the pulsing hollow between her breasts. She inhaled sharply when his tongue sent flames of desire fanning out in all directions, before coming to rest on a rosy peak.

As his soft lips cherished her breast, her mind centered around the intensifying need that threatened at any second to explode and set fire to her lower region.

He continued his lustful assault, running his tongue along the tender underside of her breast to send shivers of pure ecstasy coursing through her. Surely one could go mad from such exquisite torture.

She took his head between her hands and returned it to her swollen peak. "Oh, Captain Jordan," she whimpered, "I need…"

"Lynna, would you not agree that under our

present circumstances, you may forgo the formalities and call me Joshua?"

She was unable to answer, as the throbbing inside her intensified until she writhed on the bed in search of relief. Her legs fell open of their own accord, wanting, needing, pleading, "Please, release me from this torment."

Joshua would have given all his worldly possessions to make love to the tempting seductress. Yet, her virginity was not worth the loss of his life, and he had no doubt that Nathan would seek a physician's reassurance that her maidenhead was intact when the ship docked.

He winked seductively as his mouth fell to her breast, and his hand traveled to the space between her legs. "I will be happy to release you from your torment."

He spread her legs wide as his finger massaged her most sensitive spot, while his lips suckled her breast, sending her to a climactic finish that rocked her to her toes and left her gasping for air, while crying out his name over and over.

Later, when her breathing had returned to normal, Lynna released a contented sigh, and stretched her arms over her head in an innocent pose of satiated bliss, and slept.

Thinking she would probably sleep until noon the following day, Joshua went on deck and took matters into his own hands before his lower anatomy exploded. He had no clue that he possessed the herculean willpower required to leave a gorgeous, and naked, enchantress alone in his bed.

Only the thought of having a man like Nathan

Rhodes, hell bent on his rapid demise, was sufficient to cool his ardor.

As weariness seeped into his bones, he made his way back to his cabin and lay down beside the intoxicating and intoxicated creature. He drew her into his arms, surprised by the feeling of contentment that enveloped him as he joined her in slumber.

Chapter 5

Lynna's first day at sea dawned clear and bright, with white fluffy clouds prancing across the horizon. She was dressed in a fashionable day dress of aqua silk that buttoned in front and was trimmed with dark blue ribbon. Her hair was left to hang to her hips, and held back from her face with the same ribbon.

She strolled the deck after a light breakfast of fruit and coffee, pausing to lean against the mahogany rail and breathe deeply of the salty sea air. She closed her eyes and smiled, thankful for the opportunity to experience this daring new adventure with the dashing sea captain.

Thoughts of the captain made her glance toward the wheel deck, to find him looking devilishly handsome in the bright rays of morning sun. His lips curved into a knowing smile as he tilted his head her way.

Her eyes were immediately drawn to his lips. Why did the sight of his mouth cause her to suddenly remember a tongue drawing circles around a taut nipple?

Was it her nipple?

She remembered her erotic dream from last night and felt a blush stain her cheeks. It had seemed so real. She recalled each and every sensation, vividly, as a mouth suckled her breast. Of course, it didn't really happen. It had been nothing more than a delicious dream caused by too much wine.

Wasn't it?

Her stomach tightened into knots and her nipples grew rigid just thinking about it. Then a hand had moved down... down... down... and touched her... there. Dear Lord above, it *had* happened? Just the memory of his lips and hands caused her lady parts to throb.

While the captain went about his duties, Lynna's lower region set up a steady thrumming. She ignored the kiss of the warm ocean breeze on her face, and the water that splashed against the hull of the ship to spray her with tiny droplets. She lifted her golden locks to pile on top of her head in hopes of feeling a cooling breeze on her overheated neck.

"What a lovely day it is with blue skies, calm seas, and a gentle morning breeze," a woman startled her by saying.

"*Oui*, it is a glorious day," Lynna agreed absently. She lifted her skirt and swirled it around her legs, hoping a bit of cooling air might find its way to the area of her body that was in desperate need of cooling.

"I fear I shall miss the sea when I return home, for I am certain this will be my last voyage. Oh, but where are my manners? My name is Natalie Johnson," said a heavyset lady with a ponderous stomach, and hair of the brightest orange Lynna had ever beheld. "And your name is..."

"Bridget," Lynna answered cheerily, using the fictitious name that must always be used in the presence of strangers. Thankfully, after all her flapping and fanning of skirts, her body heat seemed to have dropped to a more normal temperature.

Since Natalie Johnson loved nothing more than juicy gossip, she glanced around to be sure no one was eavesdropping. "Tell me, Bridget. I can't help but notice you are traveling alone, without the benefit of a husband or companion. Why is this?"

"I am not married, and the captain is my only traveling companion," Lynna answered dutifully. "He is allowing me the use of his cabin during the voyage." She pulled a lace hankie from her pocket and wiped at a light sheen of perspiration that lingered on her forehead.

"The captain?" Natalie gasped, seeming to take umbrage at her words. "Where is he sleeping."

"In his cabin," Lynna unwittingly offered, before clamping her lips shut. The woman could probably guess from her blazing cheeks exactly what had transpired last night.

"Well, I honestly never," Natalie spluttered indignantly, turning her back on Lynna to converse with the seagulls. "No unmarried young lady of decent breeding would even entertain the notion of entering a gentleman's cabin without a chaperone. Why, it is simply beyond the realm of decency. What is to become of this younger generation? No morals. No morals at all."

"Excuse me?"

"What? Oh, nothing," Natalie said. "I was but clearing my throat."

Lynna had never before heard anyone use practically the entire alphabet while clearing their throat but, at the moment, her eyes were once again drawn to the tall figure at the ship's wheel. "Oh, there is the captain now."

Natalie smirked. "How long have you been

acquainted with our illustrious captain?"

"Not long at all. He is escorting me to America to visit relatives."

"How nice of him, I'm sure." The woman heaved a dramatic sigh and gazed across the rolling swells, seeming unwilling to discuss anyone other than herself for long. "As for myself, I am returning to America. Virginia actually, after a rather upsetting first visit to France."

"I'm sorry you did not enjoy your stay in my country." Lynna felt personally responsible for the woman's distress.

"Oh, it was not the country, but rather my ill-bred niece."

"I see," Lynna replied, although she honestly did not. "Ill-bred?

"Perhaps I shouldn't air my dirty laundry in public," Natalie continued with her scuttlebutt. "Although, I'm sure you would never repeat it to a living soul."

"Not if you do not wish me to."

"Definitely not." Natalie gasped. "Why, it would be positively scandalous."

"Scandalous?"

"Yes, the whole sordid affair is rather onerous for me to even discuss. You see, one of my unmarried nieces was foolish enough to fall for the oldest ruse in the book."

"The oldest ruse?"

"Of course, Bridget. Men have used the trick forever," the lady huffed. "The simple ploy to get a woman drunk and have his way with her."

A ruse?

To have his way with her?

Natalie Johnson was just getting started. "Anyway, the scoundrel got my niece in the family way back in the states. Her parents were horribly ashamed, as they should be, and asked me to accompany her on a voyage to France, to live with her grandparents until the child is delivered and can be placed in an orphans' asylum."

The woman swiped at invisible tears, using her handkerchief. "My niece didn't wish to leave her lover, one of the lower dregs of society, I can assure you. The dear girl cried incessantly during the entire voyage, until I was concerned for my sanity."

The woman paused for a quick breath and continued, "Quite frankly, I was glad to be rid of her. If my friends back home ever found out that I, Natalie Johnson, had a niece who would behave so immorally, why the shame would be outside the constraints of toleration. I can only pray that they never learn the disgusting and shameful truth." She glanced toward Lynna, waiting for a response to her tale of doom and gloom.

"I'm so sorry," Lynna murmured, as her entire world proceeded to crumble around her.

"Anyway," Natalie huffed, "as you well know, that is precisely what happens when a young lady allows a man to take advantage of her. Even the most uneducated imbecile knows that it takes only one night of illicit pleasure to instill a baby in a woman's womb."

One night of pleasure to instill a baby? Of course, she had learned that from the books Gertrude had slipped her. Yet, with Joshua, she hadn't been thinking clearly at the time, because of the wine, or perhaps it had been his hands, or his… lips.

Natalie bristled before continuing with her diatribe. "I am mortified that a niece of mine would succumb to such indecent liberties."

Lynna shuddered as the bright and sunny day lost most its cheer.

Natalie sighed forlornly as she laid a limp hand across her forehead. "It has been humiliating for the entire family, and her dear father is bereft. He was always so proud of her, and now this? A disgrace. That is what it is, a disgrace. Any man who would seduce an innocent young girl doesn't give a fig about her to begin with."

Lynna was going to be sick. She clutched the rail and inhaled deep gulps of briny sea air.

"Are you feeling out of sorts, dear?" Natalie asked. "You seem awfully pale of a sudden."

"I'm fine," she lied, feeling terribly lightheaded. She wished the sea would open up and swallow her, as she was unable to endure another second of the woman's vitriolic tirade against her poor niece and other young ladies of questionable virtue, such as herself. What had she done? What had *he* done?

Pelicans dipped in the ocean, scouting for their midday meal as seagulls cawed and swooped overhead. Deck hands were busy hoisting sails and scouring the deck, as the tempting smell of fried fish drifted from the ship's galley.

Lynna closed her eyes and held onto the rail as her hair fanned out behind her. What if she *was* with child? With a disgusted glance toward the captain, she hurried across the deck and down the steps to her cabin.

Joshua watched Lynna's every move until her slim figure disappeared from view. Why was she in such a hurry, and why did the sight of her fully clothed cause a quickening in his loins. He yearned to feel her velvety softness beneath him, caress every silken inch of her lovely body all over again, but therein lay the problem. The lady was dangerous, to the point of posing a very real threat to his existence.

It would be best for all concerned if he kept her at a safe distance until they docked in Charleston. Not an easy task, due to the fact that they shared a cabin.

Lynna sat in the center of the bed and contemplated a dismal future. Natalie Johnson wasn't the only one to offer her a brutal lesson on the facts of life. She had also heard Gertrude speak numerous times on the fact that it only took one episode of illicit pleasure to conceive a child. "Even allowing a gentleman under your skirts for five minutes can bring utter disgrace to your poor family," she had warned.

A disgrace? Scandalous? Why, she had never even been within spitting distance of scandal.

She didn't move when the cabin boy brought her lunch tray, and she hadn't budged hours later when Joshua returned. She cursed the fates as she gazed out the window and admired the seagulls their carefree existence.

"Are you coming out of the cabin this afternoon?" Joshua's deep voice startled her. "Clouds have moved in to cover the sun and it's quite pleasant on deck."

Lynna glanced up, exposing eyes that were

red rimmed from her afternoon of crying. She leapt from the bed like a woman possessed, to pummel his broad chest with all the force she could muster. "How could you?" she sobbed, as scalding tears of hurt and humiliation streamed down her cheeks.

Joshua grabbed her small hands and held them to his chest, to still her fluttering. "How could I what, Lynna?"

"You know very well what. Do not pretend ignorance with me, Captain Jordan."

He released her, and picked up the brandy decanter to pour himself a drink. "No, Lynna, I can assure you that I do not. Pray tell, enlighten me."

"You used the oldest ruse in the book on me."

"The oldest ruse?" He chuckled, and sat down behind his desk to light a cheroot. "What would that be, lovely lady?"

"You intentionally got me drunk and had your way with me."

"I did what?" Joshua was totally flabbergasted by the unwarranted accusation. "What on earth are you babbling about? If you will recall you were drunk, of your own accord, when I returned to my cabin last night."

"You offered me the port," she was quick to accuse. "I never asked for it."

"I offered you a glass of port with your meal, Lynna. I had no idea you would drain the entire bottle in my absence."

"I will be a disgrace." She wept, heartbroken. "My dear father will be humiliated. He will turn me away, unable to witness my shame."

"Turn you away. Surely you cannot be serious?" For the first time in Joshua's life, he was actually dumbfounded. "You honestly believe that your father, who worships the ground you walk on, would turn you away in shame because you had too much to drink?"

"Of course not, don't be obtuse. I am talking about the *enfant*!" she shrieked, covering her burning face with her hands. "I am speaking of your child that I most likely carry in my womb."

"My child?" Joshua drained the contents of the glass and poured himself a double. "In your womb?

"*Oui*, your child," she whispered, switching from madwoman to tortured child in a matter of seconds. "Oh, Captain Jordan, how could you do this to me? It will be ever so disgraceful, and you do not give a fig about me in the first place. My dear father will be so hurt and ashamed."

"Lynna, calm down, I give you my word that you won't be humiliated."

"But what if I am carrying your child, Captain Jordan?"

Joshua was unable to hide his puzzlement. Did something happen during the night that he was unaware of? Of course not, if he had made love to the delectable ingénue he would definitely remember it.

"Please, I beg you, don't even joke about it." He was fully aware that Lynna could not possibly be carrying his child. "Can you imagine the hurt Nathan Rhodes would visit upon my head, if he even suspected I stole your virginity?"

"You? You! Is that all you can think about at a time like this? You? And what my father might do to you, which I can assure you will not be pleasant." Lynna was beyond furious as the smooth lies slipped from his lips. "What about me?"

Joshua turned to her with a bemused frown. "When did we make love, Lynna?"

"Don't pretend that you don't remember taking indecent liberties with me. She turned away to hide her furiously reddening cheeks. "I remember what happened last night."

Joshua shrugged. He had pleasured her, and left with a severe case of blue balls. Surely the sheltered recluse didn't believe a female could become with child simply by having an earth shattering climax.

"Oh, Captain Jordan," she cried, completely heartbroken. "How could you singlehandedly bring about the ruination of my entire life?"

"Lynna, if you will recall, I did nothing against your will."

"It was the wine," she murmured, ignoring his protests. "I was never allowed to drink wine at home. You knew I was not responsible for my actions and you took advantage of me." She stopped, blushing a most becoming shade of pink as she recalled the series of unfortunate events that had been bestowed upon Natalie Johnson's niece.

"My *tante* will turn me away when I arrive on her doorstep, ponderous with child, and without the benefit of a husband. I will have no place to go. Our *enfant* and I will be roofless vagabonds, forced to resort to a life in back alleys. Our only recourse will be to sail back to France, where my baby will be stripped from my arms and placed in an orphans' asylum."

"Orphans' asylum? Nathan Rhodes' daughter living in a back alley?" Joshua sat on the bed and crossed his booted feet at the ankles, wondering if his ship had veered off course and was currently sailing through the Devil's Triangle. "Lynna, I did not force myself on you last night. Truthfully, I was a perfect gentleman, so it is physically impossible for you to be carrying my child."

Lynna closed her eyes and exhaled slowly, remembering the pulsing contractions of sweet ecstasy that had convulsed her lower region when his hand caressed her there. Why, her nipples puckered at the thought. She would never forget his touch as long as she lived.

They had made love, of that she was certain. Why was he lying? Of course, because he was terrified of her father's wrath. Who in their right mind wouldn't be?

She sauntered over to Joshua with a look of pure innocence, drew back her hand, and slapped him across his divinely handsome face. Although, she would be the first to admit the slap was woefully late in coming.

"You, sir, are a liar."

Chapter 6

Lynna kept her door latched in the weeks that followed. Her monthly curse was late. It had been well over two months, and each new day found her sinking deeper and deeper into the gaping jaws of depression.

If Joshua so much as poked his head around the portal she proceeded to convulse into a fit of screaming. She was inconsolable, allowing only Sam to bring her trays and enter the cabin to inquire about her well-being. Joshua had been none to happily relocated to a bunk in the cook's cabin.

She placed a quivering hand on her still flat stomach every few hours, searching for any evidence of growth. So far, it was still blessedly flat. *Merci,* God.

Her ruminations often fled across the sea to the Chateau, and her father. Her loving father, who had been so proud of her. She recalled his face radiating with pride as he stood with the staff during one of her many ballet or piano recitals. He was always near with applauding hands, and cheering words of praise for her smallest accomplishments.

Now, when she returned as soiled merchandise with a bastard child, he would be too ashamed to claim her as his own. The scandal would sweep across Paris like the pox. His business patrons would refuse to do business with him. She would discredit his good name and, far worse, she would break his heart. How could she bear to live with the shame? She collapsed on the bed as hot tears of humiliation shook her slender frame.

After three weeks, with only an occasional glimpse of Lynna strolling the deck after the sun went down, Joshua knocked softly. When there was no response, he slowly pushed open his cabin door to step inside, and was left stunned by her shocking appearance. She appeared fragile and pale, and so alone.

He had vowed to protect her with his very life, yet there was nothing he could say to ease her heartache. She would require proof, and he had none.

It was obvious from her bloodshot and glassy eyes that she had been crying. He wanted nothing more than to take her in his arms and gently kiss away her sorrow, prove to her that she was being irrational. Almost without realizing it, he moved toward the breathtaking vision curled on his bed.

"*Non.* Stay away from me, Captain Jordan," she warned, as tears glistened on her lashes. "You may be the captain of this deplorable ship, and stand there with your smug expression, confident that your crew will not turn a hand against their beloved captain. However, I promise you that your expression will be dramatically altered when my father learns of your deception. He hired you to protect me on this voyage, not molest me."

"Molest you," Joshua stormed, before realizing how profound her heartache was and lowering his voice. "I never made love to you, Lynna. How many times must I tell you this?" He turned to the door with a look of tired defeat. "If your father, and Scotland Yard, put their trust in me, why can't you?"

For answer, she picked up an expensive glass figurine and hurled it at his head. "Get out!"

Three weeks later, Lynna was sitting in the center of the huge bed, regarding the dolphins that frolicked alongside the ship, when Joshua entered the cabin. Her eyes were smudged with dark circles, and she appeared even thinner.

They had been at sea for eight weeks, and her monthly curse had apparently deserted her. That was all the proof Lynna needed to confirm that she carried this man's child in her womb.

For the one hundredth time on this voyage, she yearned to have Gertrude by her side. She would know how to handle a crisis that Lynna had mulled over and over in her head until it ached.

With no family, friends, or a confidant with whom to discuss her troubles, she had arrived at the most crucial decision of her life on her own. By now, she was certain that she was *enceinte,* and could arrive at only one resolution to the problem of being unwed and with child. Having no other recourse, she gathered her dwindling courage and forced her gaze from the window. "Will you marry me, Joshua?"

Her heart sank to her feet as she watched a myriad of emotions play across his handsome face, from surprise, to shock, and finally anger. He had no intention of making an honest woman of her. She was alone in her plight. While she agonized over the birth of his child, he would be off on another voyage, perhaps instilling the same predicament on another young innocent.

"I will have to decline your tempting offer, my sweet," was his callous response. "I will not be forced into marriage with a woman who despises me."

He was refusing to marry her, after deflowering her? Somehow she had known this would be his answer, even before he uttered the selfish words.

"What kind of low, depraved, black hearted seadog are you? You planted your seed inside me without a care for the consequences, and now you refuse to take the responsibility of seeing your child reared?"

Was marriage to her such a loathsome prospect? Who did this man think he was? For the love of all that was holy, she was the daughter of Nathan Rhodes, a man who had clawed his way out of the red clay fields of Georgia to become the powerhouse he was today. Where was her backbone?

"Rest assured, Captain Jordan, that you will not be forced into an unwanted marriage with me. In your perpetual quest for pleasure, you acquire females as if their virginity was another novelty to store in your sea chest, without regard for the fact that no respectable man would marry a soiled woman."

Joshua's nerves were almost at the breaking point. Lynna would convince Nathan Rhodes that he'd had his way with the man's daughter while under his protection, which could only set about a chain of events with a disastrous outcome.

With his jaw set and his eyes smoldering, he ground out, "At the time I was pleasuring you, I don't recall hearing any grievances uttered from your side of the bed."

As her sharp gasp echoed around the cabin, Lynna wanted nothing more than to wipe the smug smile from his face. "I will hate you until my dying day for the agony you have caused me. I can only pray that my father tracks you down, and we both know that he will. I also pray that he shows no mercy when he finds you. Now get out. I never want to see you again. Ever!"

Joshua tried reasoning with her. "Lynna, believe me, you are working yourself into a dither for naught."

He was so calm, when her entire life was in shambles. He would have no trouble turning his back on her and walking away without a care.

She could only glare at him with her feelings accurately mirrored in her sky blue gaze. He had performed the vacuous act of sex with her, plain and simple, just as any man would. Then, he had the audacity to lie about it, leaving her to suffer the consequences of his depraved actions alone.

It was a pale and drawn Joshua who brought Lynna's dinner tray two weeks later. His haggard appearance validated the fact that he'd had little sleep during the past several weeks.

This thrilled Lynna to the very core, almost making her giggle. Heaven knows she would laugh at anything today. After a wretched night of painful cramps, and the wonderful discovery that she was not with child, her entire world seemed brighter and filled with new and exciting possibilities.

Yet, she could not allow her happiness to show. Joshua might witness her sudden merriment and guess the truth, when he deserved to suffer. She faced the window to conceal the light she knew must be dancing in her eyes.

"Lynna, I have decided to return to my cabin," Joshua announced, immediately upon entering. He turned his head, so she wouldn't see his extreme relief upon the discovery that she was back to her cheerful self again. She was almost giddy.

"*Non.* You will do no such thing." With her hands on her hips and her breasts thrust forward, she presented a most alluring sight. "I must decline the invitation of your company, sir, for I can assure you that you and I shall never again occupy the same living quarters."

"Oh, contraire, my pet." Joshua enjoyed having the upper hand, for once. "I feel that I must insist. Since you obviously carry my child, I can find no logical reason for us to remain apart. The damage has been done, as they say, so we have naught else to fear. We can make love to our hearts content. You requested that we wed, did you not?"

When she failed to answer, Joshua continued, "Therefore, I have come to grant your most fervent wish. Upon our arrival in Charleston, we will be married and spend the remainder of our days as husband and wife. You, me, and our adorable offspring. My parents have beseeched me for years to present them with at least a dozen grandchildren, so they will be thrilled beyond measure when I bring home a bride."

He burst out laughing at her look of stricken horror. "I can be very persistent, Lynna, and I assure you that there will be no changing my mind on this point. I have given the matter careful consideration,

and decided that I cannot see my child raised without a father. I shall go now and have my belongings returned to my cabin."

"*Non!*" she almost screamed the word. She could not allow him to return to his cabin, and risk a repeat performance of their first night together. "That will not be necessary, as I have recently discovered that I am not *enceinte.*"

"Would you care to apologize for calling me a liar?" his voice was cold as ice as he eyed her with disdain.

"No, I would not, as I still believe you to be a heartless fabricator of lies. I was simply fortunate that the seed you planted did not sprout."

"Believe what you will, Lynna." Joshua shrugged. "I have long since tired of trying to convince you of the truth."

"You have taught me a great deal during these past few weeks, Captain Jordan. For that much, I am grateful. I feel certain that I can now face my new life, and any obstacles or hardships I might encounter along the way, after this journey with you." She paused to gaze across the calm ocean toward her homeland. "From this day forth, I will know to steer clear of a rogue like you."

Lynna ambled across the cabin to stand before him as her cerulean blue eyes locked with his, her moist lips inches from his own. Before she knew what was happening, Joshua had her in his arms and his soft lips found hers. She wanted desperately to respond to his embrace, to give free rein to her rising passion and enjoy the ecstasy that she remembered so well, but she could not.

She refused to grant him forgiveness, and risk

living through the hell of the last several weeks again. Instead, she slapped him soundly across the face and watched his lust swiftly change to anger. "Don't dare touch me again, you despicable cad."

"Don't trouble your pretty little head." Joshua rubbed his reddening cheek as he turned toward the door. "If I ever touch you again, it will be because you begged me to."

"Beg you?" Lynna laughed. "I pray that I never lay eyes on you again after I depart this ship."

"You will get your wish, fair lady, as we will be docking in Charleston within the hour." Joshua opened the door and whispered, "Au revoir, Lynna."

Then, he walked out of her life.

Hopefully, forever.

❧ *Chapter 7* ❧

Three Years Later
Charleston, South Carolina
1853

Joshua leaned over the rail, peering into the swirling fluorescent water as it lapped against the hull of the *Windjammer*. It was a lazy slapping sound, and one that had lulled him to sleep many restless nights. Now the sound was bittersweet, for after today there would be no more salty sea breezes. No more moonswept nights listening to the wind fill the billowing sails, and no more late night walks on deck, where he would spend countless hours gazing into the constellations. He was going home.

Home. Where instead of being surrounded by a brilliant sea and sailing to exciting new destinations, his feet would be firmly and permanently anchored on dry land. He realized that it might be years before he felt the deck rolling with the easy swells again, and had left the job of sailing the ship to his first mate, as he went on deck to contemplate his future.

He gazed across the ocean that he loved so dearly, convinced that the best years of his life were behind him, a part of his carefree past. His parents needed him, and that was where he belonged. He blinked several times as his eyes misted at the thought of his beloved parents, Jeremiah and Patricia.

His boisterous father, tall, robust, and the picture

of health, had always enjoyed life to the fullest. His love for pranks was well known throughout the plantation, especially by his wife, who was the recipient of the majority of his shenanigans. Joshua couldn't have asked for a happier childhood, or better parents.

He had not learned of the tragedy until the previous Christmas, when he returned home for the holidays after an extended sea voyage. He remembered galloping up the dusty road toward home, filled with excitement at seeing his family after a rough year at sea, but something was amiss at Sea Grove. He had sensed it even before entering the silent house.

No sounds of children's gay laughter echoed from the quarters. It was as quiet as if the plantation was in mourning. Mourning? "Mother!" he shouted, taking the stairs two at a time.

It was too still. Too quiet. No joyous Christmas hymns filled the air. No freshly cut Christmas greenery entwined throughout the staircase balustrade. No mistletoe hung from every doorway, and the heady scent of cedar didn't perfume the air.

Flossie, his childhood nanny, met him halfway up the stairs and gave him a warm embrace. "You sho' is a sight fo' so' eyes, Mist' Joshua." She sniffled into her handkerchief. "We is mighty glad ta have you home."

"What's wrong, Flossie?" He held his breath as his heart hammered against his ribs, already fearing the worst.

"Go on up ta yo' pa's room," she whispered, wiping at a torrent of tears. "You jes' go on up an' see yo' pa."

A cold sheen of sweat covered Joshua's body as he slowly climbed the curving staircase, with apprehension building with each step until he finally stood outside his father's bedroom. Even though he had tried to prepare himself for anything he might encounter at the top of those stairs, it would have been an impossible feat.

Nothing could have prepared him for the sight of his father's stump of a body, deathly pale, with his eyes open but seeing nothing. The sight had sent a shockwave through Joshua that left him chilled to the marrow of his bones.

In a flash, he recalled how his father's laughing eyes would twinkle with mischief when he chased his daughter around the yard with a harmless green snake, or when he was slipping a June bug down his wife's bodice. He remembered, as a youngster, when his father would hitch him over his broad shoulders and carry him through the fields, explaining the intricacies of growing cotton.

In the past, his father had loved to dance at the numerous Balls held at Sea Grove, with every family in the county attending. Now, he didn't even have legs. There would be no more dancing at Sea Grove.

Whether his father was joking with friends, or grabbing his wife in a hug that lifted her clear off the ground, Jeremiah always had laughter in his eyes. Now those eyes were dull and lifeless, staring blankly at the ceiling.

Joshua's mother had risen from her seat beside the bed, a woman whose appearance had aged several years in the short span of twelve months. Dark circles lay under her eyes, and her shiny brown hair that had once been the envy of many, had turned the color of snow. Still, what disturbed Joshua most was her dramatic weight loss. She was almost skeletal.

"My darling son, you have come home at last," his mother had whispered quietly as she ushered him into her adjacent room, where she proceeded to fill him in on the gory details of the accident.

His insides churned as he listened to his mother tell the story of how his father and several of the slaves had been cutting the winter's supply of firewood. They were chopping in an area often referred to as the *voodoo woods* on that ill-fated morning.

Having spent the greater part of his youth clearing fields with his father, Joshua knew Jeremiah was an expert at felling trees and always steered well clear of their intended path. However, on that fateful day, with no thought for his own safety, he had rushed into the shadow of a giant falling oak, after spotting a little girl standing precisely where the tree would land. While Jeremiah had moved with a speed that surprised even him, he was not fast enough.

He barely had time to shove the child to safety, before a blinding pain struck as the massive oak splintered around him. He never saw the child again, and they never recovered her body, but he swore that when he placed his hand on the child's shoulders, his hand passed clear through her skin.

One of the branches knocked Jeremiah to the ground and crushed every bone in the lower half of his legs. As blessed darkness washed over him, Jeremiah was certain that he was going to meet his Maker.

Instead, he awakened a fortnight later with both

legs amputated from the knees down, wishing
fervently that he had.

He did have an occasional good day. When
Jeremiah was awake and lucid he talked endlessly of
the beautiful little girl, always concerned for her
safety. At night he would wake everyone in the house
as he pleaded with the child to, "Run! Get out of the
way!" The bewildering part was that no one else,
none of the eight men working side by side with him
that day, had seen the little girl, only Jeremiah.

The slaves were a superstitious lot, and swore
that the spirit of the long gone *conja woman* had
cursed the child, making the angry haint haunt the
voodoo woods. They firmly believed that not only
had her spirit caused Jeremiah's accident, but she
was still roaming the forest in search of her next
hapless victim.

No matter how many threats were issued, the
slaves adamantly refused to go near the voodoo
woman's house, or return to the patch of woods
where the accident occurred. They often visited the
current conjure woman, Amari, seeking amulets to
protect them from the sinister specter.

The sight of his mother's face would be forever
etched in Joshua's mind. He would never forget the
dark circles under her eyes that contrasted with her
too white skin. She rarely ventured into the sun, as
her days and nights were spent in a darkened room,
sitting quietly by her beloved husband's side as she
prayed for a miracle.

Jeremiah was a proud man, and Joshua knew his
mother worried that he would no longer have the will
to live. A small glimmer of hope had shone in her
lifeless green eyes when her son entered the room. A

hope that the responsibilities of running a cotton plantation the size of Sea Grove could be lifted from her weary shoulders, thus allowing her to devote her time and energy to making her husband see that life was worth living again. She hadn't found it necessary to ask for her son's help, he was there when she needed him most.

While it had been impossible for Joshua not to return to sea after the Christmas holidays, having several binding commitments to fulfill, he had hired Jake Almond to oversee the plantation in his absence.

"Land ho!" The first mate shouted from the crow's nest, bringing Joshua back to the present.

He gazed across the gracefully rolling swells to see the barely visible landmarks of Charleston in the early morning fog, with Saint Michael's steeple towering majestically over the waking city.

They would be docking in a few hours. After battening down his ship for a much needed rest, he would bid farewell to the *Windjammer* and his old way of life, and plant his feet on solid ground.

Chapter 8

After thanking each man personally for his years of loyalty and faithful service, Joshua strode below deck to his cabin to pack. Memories flooded him as his eyes fell on souvenir pieces from various countries he had visited over the years.

He lifted the teakwood box that contained his most treasured possession, Lynna's locket.

Her locket had been lost under his bed during their only intimate encounter, and contained a likeness of Lynna's mother. Looking at it was akin to looking at Lynna herself, since both women possessed the same unique beauty. Joshua held the tiny locket close to his chest as he recalled the tiny wisp of a girl who had stolen his heart.

He had lay awake many nights and wondered *what if*. What if he had wed Lynna Rhodes when she was convinced that she carried his child? Would he be settled on his family's cotton plantation, bouncing a baby on each knee? Would he have Lynna in his arms each night, instead of only imagining her there? Enough of rehashing the past, he had done more than his fair share for the past three years.

No one since, and there had been many in his futile attempts to banish her from his mind, had come close to igniting the passion the little lady stirred in him. He returned the locket carefully to the box and stored it with the other treasures in his sea trunk. Now these pieces would serve as his only link with the past. He forced his mind to concentrate on the business at hand, as he completed his packing and left the ship.

Nothing had changed. The Battery was still a noisy beehive of activity, with ships loading and unloading their cargo, peddlers hawking their wares, and drunken sailors returning to the ship after a night on the town.

To Joshua's well-traveled eyes, Charleston was still the most beautiful city on earth. He had found nothing in his journeys to rival the stately mansions, picturesque homes, and colorful gardens.

He steered his horse along the cool shade of Church Street, where towering oaks and magnolias stood alongside stately palmetto trees. A gentle breeze that blew inland from the Cooper River caused the leaves to sway.

The loud clip clop of horse's hooves could be heard as he steered the steed down cobblestoned Chalmers Street. The cobblestones had been brought to Charleston as ballasts on English ships, unloaded, and replaced with cargos of indigo, rice, or cotton.

A wide grin split his rugged features as he thought back over the many memorable evenings spent in this area, in what the more religious sect referred to as the houses of ill repute, or Mulatto Alley.

As he rode through town, a nagging thought struck him as he passed by a milliner's shop and caught sight of a very immodest, bright pink satin ballgown on display in the window. He envisioned a slim body draped in that gown, or one very similar to it, but could bring to mind neither a name or face to go with the body. He dismissed it as trivial. If the lady in question had appealed to him in the slightest, she would not have been so easily forgotten.

Once he reached the outskirts of the city, he spurred his horse to a full gallop, eager to be home. He breathed deeply of the pleasing smell of low country soil as he rode for hours, allowing his mind to wander until it reached the same destination it had for the past three years.

Lynna.

When the sun had reached its zenith, he stopped to rest his horse and drink from a bubbling stream. Though he tried to dismiss it, worry gnawed at him as he neared home. He dreaded having to relive the pain he felt at Christmas, after finding his once hale and hearty father bedridden.

A few miles from home, he steered his horse up the avenue of cedar trees that led to Cedar Hill, a neighboring plantation. Whether a wish to be welcomed home by old friends, or simply postponing the inevitable, he couldn't be sure.

He brought his horse to a halt in front of the towering white columns and leapt from his steed to grab Beth, who dashed down the steps to greet him.

"Joshua, I'm so glad you're home." She laughed gaily as he lifted her off the ground and spun her around. "We have missed you so much."

"I'm glad to be home, little bit." He winked slyly, knowing she detested the nickname he had tagged her with as a child. "You have grown even lovelier than when I left."

"We were wondering when you would show your ugly mug around here," Beth's husband Samuel bellowed, coming around the side of the house from the direction of the barn. "Unhand my wife, sir."

"There's the rutting scoundrel who stole my one true love whilst I was away at sea, and could not fight for her," Joshua accused a grinning Samuel, as he held a giggling Beth in the air.

"Oh, Joshua, you are incorrigible," Beth smiled affectionately. "Put me down."

"Admitted." Joshua grinned. "But you love me anyway. Now that I have retired my seafaring ways, you can divorce this dirty dog from Georgia who wormed his way into your affections and married you behind my back. Come to Sea Grove where you belong, my sweet Beth."

"Over my dead body," Samuel rumbled.

"Very well." Joshua released Beth to clasp Samuel's hand. "Choose your weapon, sir."

"Hush all of this nonsense about weapons and come inside for a cool drink." Beth looked upon both men fondly.

Beth's mother had died giving birth, leaving her to be raised by her stern father. He was a good man, but overly strict where his only child was concerned. Beth had envied the carefree and loving family life at Sea Grove and spent a great deal of her youth visiting with Joshua's sister Malinda, her best friend. Joshua had watched over both young girls with a keen eye, dismissing any number of unsuitable suitors as they grew into charming young ladies.

Joshua glanced over Samuel's shoulder as his vision was drawn to a slight movement on the verandah, and a long forgotten memory came rushing to the surface. She was the girl in the pink satin ballgown, now he remembered. She was Samuel's sister, but what was her name?

She really was quite lovely, but try as he might he could not attach a name to the face. He climbed the steps and took her extended hand, bowing low to plant a soft kiss. "Good evening..."

"Suzanne," she furnished somewhat crisply, after seeing that her name had altogether eluded him. She batted her lashes demurely and changed her tune completely. "Surely you haven't forgotten little ole me, Captain Jordan."

"A man never forgets a beautiful lady." She was pretty enough, but not exactly what he would consider beautiful. He reserved that title for only one.

Suzanne's face fairly glowed with excitement, and she was on the verge of fishing for more flattery from the fine male specimen, when Beth rudely interrupted her.

"Joshua, I realize how eager you are to be home with your family, but surely you can spare us a toast to your homecoming."

"Have I ever been able to deny you anything, little bit?"

"No, and I dare say you never will. Oh, how I have missed you, Joshua," Beth whispered, hugging him close. "It hasn't been the same without you."

"Would you two rather be alone?" Suzanne whined.

"Don't be ridiculous, Suzanne." Beth gave her sister-in-law a quelling glance. "Joshua is the brother I never had."

"Well, I do hope he won't be inclined to feel brotherly toward me," Suzanne purred, thoroughly embarrassing her brother and his wife, evidenced by Beth's reddening cheeks and Samuel's disconcerting frown.

Joshua chose to ignore her brazen remark as he entered the house and took a seat on the settee, stretching his legs to relieve the cramps from the long ride.

Much to his surprise, an overzealous Suzanne plopped down beside him, almost on top of him. Her actions made him remember why he didn't particularly care for the frivolous female. She was too forward by far, and he had a definite aversion to overbearing women.

Suzanne's perfume reminded him of the night of a Christmas Ball, when she had made it known to one and all, that he was her intended catch of the day. If he remembered correctly, she had been visiting her brother then also.

Joshua had been shrewd enough to realize, within mere seconds of making her acquaintance, that her innocent demeanor was little more than a facade. She had wasted no time in adding his name to her dance card.

No sooner had they reached the dance floor, than she proceeded to press her feminine curves against him in a most seductive and inviting manner, oblivious to the stares and heated gossip her brazen actions stirred.

"You dance divinely, sir," she had whispered softly against his ear, as her tongue darted out to caress his earlobe.

He was momentarily taken aback by her bold behavior, and drawled, "That's not all I do well."

"Why not let me be the judge of that?" had been her saucy retort, not at all put off by his boldness.

Never one to deny a woman, Joshua had escorted the shameless hussy across the dance floor, through the open French doors, and outside into the moonlit night. He led her through the garden gate, and took her in his arms under the sweeping branches of a weeping willow tree.

For a man like Joshua, who had been with more than his share of willing females, he was left completely shocked by her amorous response. She behaved like a woman starved, as her hands raked through his hair and grabbed handfuls. She moaned deep in her throat as she kissed him passionately, until she broke away and proceeded to unbutton his trousers.

"Damn!" she swore softly, upon hearing her brother call her name from only a few feet away. "We will continue this later," she promised, pausing long enough for one last lingering kiss. "To be perfectly honest, I'm sorely tempted to ignore my brother's rather persistent call, since I have no doubt that a tumble in the grass with you would be well worth a few lectures on propriety. Then again, it might be best not to press my luck."

She could only push her brother so far before he sent her home.

"There should be plenty of time to become better acquainted with you, Captain Jordan. After all, this is the season of Balls, and I will be attending them all, especially now that you are making the party circuit." She hurried back into his arms for one last kiss, before darting through the garden and into the house.

She would be greatly affronted to learn that Joshua had not given her so much as a fleeting thought since that night.

"Joshua, dear, you haven't heard a word I said," Beth chided.

"I'm sorry," he apologized. "Please, forgive my rudeness. I suppose I'm more tired than I thought. What with docking the ship, packing, and the ride home, I could fall asleep right here."

"Well, then, you should." Suzanne leaned toward him with hard to conceal excitement. "Beth has oodles of beds in this big old house. You could sleep here and get a fresh start in the morning. Or better yet, I could ride home with you, since I have been intending to visit Malinda but can never seem to find the time."

"Joshua knows without being told that he's welcome to visit us whenever he chooses, Suzanne." Beth cast a stern glance at her overzealous sister-in-law. "I'm sure he's anxious to inform his family that he has arrived home safely. Malinda was here just yesterday, and informed us that her parents were eagerly awaiting their son's homecoming, so we cannot expect to monopolize all his time. Although, I seem to recall that you complained of a simply vicious headache, and didn't venture downstairs once during his sister's visit."

Beth rose, giving Suzanne a pointed look. After one last welcoming hug, she escorted Joshua to the door. "You won't be a stranger now, will you? I'm sure they'll be keeping you busy over at Sea Grove, but do stop by to see us whenever you can."

Joshua clasped her small hands to his chest. "You just try keeping me away, little bit." He shook Samuel's hand, and asked, "Could I impose on you now and then for advice, since I may be a bit rusty on plantation affairs?"

"Call on me anytime." Samuel had intended to walk him out, but after a meaningful glance from his sister, he bid Joshua good night at the door and escorted an exasperated Beth back inside.

Beth marched straightway to the window and pulled aside the curtain. "Samuel, Joshua is tuckered out and would most likely prefer not to be bothered by your sister's simpering ways tonight."

Samuel drew his wife close in an attempt to soothe her ruffled feathers. "Joshua is a big boy, honey. If he doesn't care to be bothered, I'm sure he won't hesitate to tell my sister as much."

Joshua turned to bid Suzanne good night, and found her draping a lacy shawl over her shoulders. "I believe I shall take a stroll through the garden, since it's such a pleasant evening."

"Enjoy your walk, Suzanne. I'm exhausted, and headed for home." A cool night wind blew across the land as he walked toward his horse. He turned when he felt her small hand on his arm.

"What's your hurry? If I remember correctly, you and I have unfinished business to attend to."

A few more hours without sleep wouldn't kill him, Joshua surmised, and she might prove a pleasant diversion from plantation life in the weeks to come. "At your service." He slipped his hands around her tiny waist and attempted to pull her against him.

Suzanne inhaled sharply, and took a nervous step backward, glancing toward the parlor window. "Why, surely you can't be serious. I have a reputation to uphold, and unless I miss my guess, Samuel and Beth are peering through the curtains at this very moment like some peeping Toms. At times,

I think Beth is just looking for a reason to send me packing." Her pulse raced, and her skin burned where his hand had rested on her waist. "I'm afraid we must show some discretion. Shall we meet later tonight?"

Joshua climbed into the saddle and peered down at her with sea green eyes that sparkled. "Name the time and place."

"Midnight, down by the pond." She smiled up at him with pouty lips, just before turning to bolt into the house.

Joshua grinned as the door slammed shut behind her. She had certainly turned nervous and jittery upon finding him a willing subject. While he had every intention of keeping their rendezvous at the pond tonight, he doubted Suzanne would show, not after witnessing her hasty flight into the safety of her brother's house.

Joshua arrived home just before dusk. After a heartfelt welcome home complete with hugs, kisses, and tears of joy, he quietly climbed the winding stairs to enter a room that reminded him of death. He immediately noticed the absence of the sickly sweet smell of infection that had assaulted him upon his last visit.

He both feared and anticipated this reunion with his father. He was sorely afraid that he would be unable to control his emotions, and allow pity to slip into his voice, an emotion his father would hate. He took a calming breath and opened the door, only to be left standing with his mouth gaping open.

Was that really his father propped up against the headboard of the bed, as he shuffled through a neat stack of papers? From the waist up he resembled the man Joshua remembered.

"You are looking exceptionally well, Father." He couldn't keep his amazement at his father's rapid recovery hidden. What could have brought about such a drastic change, when on his last visit the man had appeared to be within a hair's breadth of slamming death's door behind him?

Jeremiah was engrossed in his work and hadn't heard him enter. He looked up with a broad smile playing across his still handsome features at the sight of his son. "Good to have you home, son. Good to have you home." His deep voice echoed through the house. "Even though your mother assures me you were home at Christmas, I can't say that I remember any of it."

Joshua was astonished by his father's cheerful demeanor as he took a seat beside his bed. "I must confess that I'm left speechless by your recovery from then, until now."

"It goes without saying that I feel much better, son. I guess anyone can see that. The truth is, I moped and pouted and just plain felt sorry for myself for months on end, and where did it get me? Nowhere. Then one day I realized that my life was far from over." Jeremiah glanced out the window at the fluffy fields of snowy cotton that stretched as far as the eye could see. "I've had ample time to come to a conclusion, as to how I intend to live the remainder of my life, son."

"What was your conclusion?"

Jeremiah placed his papers on the bed and looked directly into his son's eyes. "The Good Lord saw fit to take away my legs. I don't question his logic, nor do I ask why, for in exchange he gave me a double dose of willpower to continue living. He gave Jake the knowledge to build that fine chair with wheels, and a wooden ramp, so your mother and sister have no difficulty pushing me outside to feel the warmth of the morning sun."

He smiled, a completely serene smile. "God has His master plan already laid out. It is our choice whether to accept it, or waste precious time fighting it. I chose to accept it."

"So, my worry was for naught?" Joshua examined the sturdy wooden chair with wheels. "I should have known, since nothing can keep a Jordan down for long."

"Truer words were never spoken." Jeremiah laughed heartily. "Sit a spell, son. You look tired. By the way, Jake is a fine overseer, just fine." He handed Joshua a stack of papers. "I have been over his record keeping with a fine tooth comb, and having talked with the man at length, I have no complaints. Although, I would confess a desire to see the fields. Not that I don't trust him completely mind you, I do. Still, seeing is believing, and I'd like to tour the fields and talk to the hands myself."

"First thing tomorrow morning, I'll hitch up the buckboard and we'll ride through the fields." Joshua was eager to speed his father along the road to recovery. "Are you up for that?"

"Fine, son. That will be fine." Jeremiah fought to keep his heavy eyelids open, but found the task entirely too difficult. "I look forward to it."

Joshua quietly rose from his seat as the sun was sinking low on the horizon, and left the room in a much better humor. He heard his father's soft snores as he closed the door, and chuckled to himself. He knew from years of living under his father's roof that his snores could rattle the windows.

Shortly after midnight, Joshua silently crept from the house, heedful not to wake his mother. He would hate to lie to her about his destination. Some things were better left unsaid.

The night was bright under the full moon, causing a wicked smile to play across his lips. Good. He liked to see what he was getting, if she showed up.

He laughed out loud into the peaceful night,

startling the nocturnal inhabitants of the quiet woods and causing a rabbit to scamper across the road.

Surprisingly, Suzanne was in attendance as promised, floating near the water's edge with a smile of dreamy anticipation. He could just make out her naked figure under the rippling waves created by her kicking feet. She could not be called voluptuous, lacking the curving slopes he found so irresistible. Yet, she had one advantage over every other woman in Charleston tonight. She was here.

"Come join me," she urged, after watching him watch her for several minutes. "The water is heavenly."

"I wasn't sure you would come." Joshua removed his clothes and waded in to join her.

She darted just out of his grasp and swam to the other side of the pond.

Please, spare me your coquettish games.

He was tired from a long day, and had no patience for her pretenses of being the coy virgin, when they both knew the complete opposite to be true.

Joshua calmly treaded water as he beckoned her with sensuous green eyes that the majority of women, including the one in the water, were powerless to resist.

Suzanne swam back to him and stopped an arm's length away, as their eyes locked, with his having the power to melt her like candle wax beneath a flame. She slithered into his embrace and slid her arms around his slippery neck, as her mouth found his lips.

As their nude bodies molded together, she trembled from the sheer force of contact as his hands on her buttocks pulled her close. His tongue explored every crevice of her mouth before leaving a searing trail down her neck to her small breasts. Her head fell back as his teeth nibbled and gently tugged at the rigid peaks, until she thought she might expire if she didn't soon find release from this exquisite torture. "Take me now, Joshua," she cried. "Please."

Joshua was happy to oblige, and wrapped her legs around his waist as he entered her. He had not expected a virgin, and he did not find one. Instead, he found a woman well versed in the art of lovemaking. They were so caught up in the moment, they slipped underwater and came up gasping for air.

He carried her to the pond's edge, to lie on a soft green carpet of moss. "A person could drown out there if they weren't careful," he whispered against her hair.

"But what a way to go." Suzanne smiled seductively before climbing atop him. "Oh, Joshua, what a heavenly way to go."

As the sun was beginning its daily ascent into the sky the following morning, Joshua headed home. After a rather adventurous night, for Suzanne Fletcher was definitely an adventure, they had slipped contentedly into a satisfied sleep under a brilliant moon, as a chorus of bullfrogs played their nightly concert in the background.

Joshua was more tired now than he had been the previous night, but he would get no respite today. He was eager to take his father on an inspection of the fields, and this wasn't the first night he had forfeited sleep for the sake of a willing female. "One must keep the ladies satisfied," he mused, urging his steed toward home. Unless he missed his guess, the female he just left was definitely that, for the time being at least.

He strode up the steps of the verandah, to find his sister Malinda sitting in a rocking chair sipping her morning coffee. She glanced up with a frown wrinkling her pretty brow as Suzanne's perfume assaulted her.

She released an irritated breath and blew on her coffee to cool it. "You are making a colossal mistake, big brother."

"A mistake?" Joshua smiled. "Care to elaborate, Sis?"

"Suzanne."

"Suzanne?"

"Do not feign ignorance with me, Joshua Jordan." Her porcelain skin flushed crimson. "I know where you were last night and... what you were doing. I only hope you have the common sense not to fall for her feminine wiles."

"I have the common sense not to fall for any female's feminine wiles, and of a certainty not Suzanne Fletcher's." Joshua grinned broadly as he took her cup and drained the coffee. "You should have more faith in your big brother than that."

"Oh, I have faith in you, it's Suzanne that worries me. She has made her purpose crystal clear to me, and anyone else who will listen when she chatters, which is constantly. She plans to marry you, Joshua. The shameless strumpet has even confessed to having no intention of waiting for the sanctity of the marriage bed to.... um... to... well... you know."

"Enough about me." Joshua could not tolerate having a conversation about sex, of all things, with his baby sister. "Will I be allowed to run this plantation in peace, or will I be too busy banishing eager young suitors from our door?"

"I can't imagine there will be an excess of banishing going on, but keep in mind that unlike my errant sibling, I am particular about who I spend my time with."

"Touché, dear sister." He hoped to set the record straight once and for all. "Please, don't worry overmuch about me, Malinda. I am a grown man, no cataracts blurring my vision, and fully capable of seeing the lovely Suzanne for who she truly is."

"I am relieved to hear you say that, Joshua, because Suzanne Fletcher is trouble waiting to happen."

Joshua pulled his sister to her feet for a heartfelt hug. "I have missed you, Malinda, and don't be such a worrywart. How many times has mother warned you that frowning causes wrinkles?" With a sly wink, he added, "Have a little faith in your big brother, would you?"

"I'll try. You just be careful." Malinda reached for the silver coffee pot and refilled her cup. "That girl is poison, for any man foolish enough to fall victim to her simpering ways."

Chapter 10

Savannah, Georgia
Three months later

The sight of Magnolia House nestled among the fresh spring greenery brought a loving smile to Lynna's lips. She sat on a stump at the edge of a forest fragrant with pine, cedar, oak and magnolia trees lost in thought, until Suzanne's rather unladylike bellow from the balcony shattered her reverie. "Lynna, would you be a dear and come up here, please?"

Lynna abandoned her dreams of a land far, far away and walked the short distance to the house, wondering what Suzanne wanted this time. She paused inside the door, where the bright morning sun reflected the labors of the household servants, who had waxed and buffed the floors until they shone.

She ran her finger along the edge of a polished carved oak table, and knew there was not a speck of dust to be found. If there was, the person responsible for leaving it would have to deal with the wrath of Jasmine, self-proclaimed *ruler of dis heah roost*, and none of the household servants relished that prospect.

The focal point of the house was the gently curving staircase. Rich mahogany banisters wound endlessly upward past a shining crystal, wedding cake chandelier, with hundreds of candles, imported from China. To the right were twin parlors of gold and rose.

After dinner, the ladies would be escorted to the rose parlor for tea, while the men enjoyed their cigars and brandy in the gold parlor.

Lynna had seen it all hundreds of times, yet she never failed to be amazed by the beauty and simple elegance of the great house each time she entered it. It was worlds apart from her home, the fortress like Chateau in Paris.

Home.

The thought brought scalding tears to her eyes. Was her father still alive? If so, why didn't he send for her? Or, better yet, why didn't he come for her himself?

In three years, she had not received a single letter, if indeed one had been penned. While she had dutifully kept her promise not to contact him for fear of discovery, it was proving to be a promise that tormented her, and became more difficult to keep with each passing day.

Had her beloved father simply forgotten that she existed?

Had he moved on to live his life without her, after sending her thousands of miles away to live in a tiny cottage with her aunt Judith, simply to be rid of her? Yet, the one question she had pondered over and over in her head until it ached, was why he hadn't sent funds to make their lives easier as he had so faithfully promised?

"Lynna! For heaven's sake, how long does it take you to climb a simple flight of stairs?" Suzanne's irritated voice drifted down the mahogany stairs.

She snatched up her skirts and tried to hurry, she

really did, but thoughts of the Chateau brought heartache and worry over her father, which set off a chain reaction. Her eyes were filled with tears, her heel caught in the hem of her dress, and she tripped halfway up the stairs.

"Lynna!" Suzanne's shrill voice vibrated through the house, sending the upstairs servants scurrying lest they fall victim to her foul temper.

Suzanne's bedroom was a lovely shade of robin's egg blue. A massive four poster bed, surrounded by a sheer lace canopy, graced the center of the room. Beside the bed, a pair of Chippendale wing chairs stood on either side of a piecrust tea table. On the other side of the room was a full length cheval glass, in which Suzanne currently stood on a stool admiring herself, while a young servant girl fanned vigorously with a peacock feather.

Lynna's aunt Judith was on the floor at her feet, attempting to pin the hem on Suzanne's gown, which wasn't an easy task due to her constant preening. As Lynna entered the room, Suzanne spun around so fast she almost fell off the stool, which would have thrilled the servant girl immensely.

With a look of stern vexation, Suzanne quipped, "Lynna, whatever took you so long? My goodness, but you certainly do dawdle. Why, I... never mind." Her mood could change swifter than most women change their bloomers. "How do you like my gown? Is it not positively divine?"

Lynna had to admit the gown was most becoming. Cut from light turquoise watered silk, and fashioned with a low pointed waistline back and front, the full skirt was embroidered with dozens of tiny rosettes. Rosettes that Suzanne hardly noticed, while Lynna and her aunt had spent countless days and nights stitching the tedious handwork. A delicate row of fine lace edged the daringly low cut bodice, with three rows of the same lace falling from the back to form a short triple cape.

Judith was the seamstress for Magnolia House. Over the years, she had stitched clothes for Silas and Mary Fletcher, and their two sons Samuel and Daniel, on the rare occasion when she wasn't sewing exclusively for Suzanne, their spoiled only daughter. Lynna and her aunt shared a small cottage on the plantation grounds.

"It really is beautiful," Lynna said. "As all my aunt's gowns are."

If the truth be told, the gown would rival Lynna's own gowns back home, made by the finest dressmakers in all of Paris. Gowns that mice had most likely built nests in, and were raising their offspring by now.

"I agree, but this gown is special. No one could fail to notice me when I wear it." Suzanne released a quivering sigh, and absently curled a lock of hair around her finger. "Not even Captain Joshua Jordan."

Once again, as it did each time Suzanne breathed his name, Lynna's heart set up a noisy clamoring in her chest. She clutched at her bodice with trembling hands, surprised when the others in the room didn't hear the clattering racket behind her breastbone.

If Suzanne ever found out the truth about what had transpired between her magnificent Captain Jordan, and Lynna, not only would her shame be almost unbearable, but Suzanne would be livid and possibly have murderous intent. Lynna prayed that this infatuation, as the majority of Suzanne's obsessions were, was short lived.

"Don't you agree, Lynna?" Suzanne huffed out a breath when she was forced to repeat her question.

"Oh, yes… certainly," Lynna stammered. "He cannot fail to notice you in such a marvelous creation."

Lynna had heard precious little but the praises of Captain Jordan since last Christmas, when Suzanne had met him at a ball while visiting her brother in Charleston. She wished desperately to warn Suzanne of what a vile, wretched, black hearted womanizer the sea captain truly was, but she could not.

To confess to her horrible blunder would bring humiliation and scorn to herself, and possibly loss of employment for her aunt. If Suzanne ever found out the truth, her revenge would come swift and hard, and she wouldn't care who she hurt in the process. Lynna could only listen silently as Suzanne prattled on and on about the sea captain with the raven locks and dashing good looks.

A man she remembered all too well.

The young servant girl, with perspiration dripping from the tip of her nose, undoubtedly shared Lynna's sentiments. When Suzanne spun toward the mirror, and the girl was facing her back, her eyes rolled toward the heavens. Her actions caused Judith to move close to the hem of Suzanne's gown, to keep from laughing and sucking a mouthful of pins down her throat.

Surprisingly, and to their astonishment, Suzanne dropped her favorite subject and moved on. "Now, for the reason I summoned you, Lynna. Be a dear, and undo my fasteners."

"What?" Lynna's defiant stance, with her hands planted firmly on her hips and her blue eyes flashing, almost betrayed her true station in life. "You called me up here to unfasten your gown?" An arched brow from her aunt ceased her impending rebuke. No one must learn the secret of her birthright that she, her aunt, and Joshua Jordan shared.

A withering glare from Suzanne begged the question; *What would be the error of my ways if I had? Must I remind you that you are both employees of my father, and reside in a cottage graciously allocated by him?*

Instead, for reasons that altogether eluded her, Suzanne chose not to speak her mind. She simply was not feeling argumentative today. "Of course not, silly goose. I would but ask you to model this gown for me. If I see it on you, I can better form an image in my mind of the accessories that would best offset the gown. You know, pretend you are a dressmaker's dummy." Suzanne giggled at her own rare attempt at humor, and removed the gown to admire her slim figure in the mirror as Lynna disrobed.

Lynna closed her eyes and released a contented sigh as the soft folds of silk fell caressingly around her body, and marveled at the long forgotten feeling of having expensive material against her skin.

Judith moved behind her to fasten the gown and tugged, pulled, and shifted to no avail. "Lynna darling, you seem to have.... um.... expanded in certain areas. For the life of me I cannot fasten the gown. Why, up until this very summer, I relied on the exact same measurements when sewing for the two of you."

Judith peered over Lynna's shoulder to see a

mortified Suzanne, who's face flamed at the sight of Lynna's bosom spilling over the low cut bodice. She had insisted the gown be cut daringly low, but witnessing the sight of Lynna's overflowing cleavage only served to infuriate her.

The servant girl's fanning increased a degree as she savored the high and mighty Miss Suzanne's burning cheeks and flaming neck. Suzanne most thoroughly enjoyed humiliating others, yet it was a rare occasion when she received the same treatment in turn.

Lynna witnessed the rush of blood to Suzanne's upper extremities, and the rage glistening in her eyes, and quickly removed the gown. "It looks much better on you, Suzanne."

"That goes without saying," Suzanne snipped, studying Lynna with narrowed eyes and unkind thoughts. True, Lynna's measurements had blossomed in the past year, whereas her own had remained virtually the same. The girls were a study in contrast.

Lynna's hair was the color of spun gold. The sun's rays shining through the open balcony doors added a glowing luster to her waist length golden mane. Suzanne's hair resembled a raven's wing, so black the same sun reflected gleaming blue highlights.

Their eyes were no less different. Lynna's eyes were shimmering pools of summer sky blue crystal that changed with her every emotion. They sparkled like brilliant diamonds when she was happy, shone with sadness in their glistening depths, and snapped with defiance when angry. Suzanne's eyes were brown with green flecks, admittedly not one of her best features.

Both girls had been blessed at birth with the pearly white skin so cherished by Southern women. They protected their skin from the ravages of the sun with parasols, hats, sunbonnets, and nightly applications of buttermilk. Suzanne chose to avoid the sun entirely, venturing outside only in the early morning or late evening hours.

A wicked and triumphant smirk spread across Suzanne's pretty features. Lynna may be more generously endowed, that was painfully obvious, but she could tell by the girl's reddening nose and pink cheeks that she had been outside again, dreadfully unprotected from the harsh rays of the sun. Be patient, she thought callously. A few more days in the sun and the careless girl would have skin that resembled shoe leather.

Feeling much better about herself, Suzanne thanked Lynna graciously for her assistance and climbed into bed for her afternoon nap, thus dismissing them.

No sooner had Judith closed the door, than Suzanne's head filled with the remembrance of strong arms crushing her against a hard body, as moist lips lowered to hers. A shiver passed over her, even though the afternoon heat was atrocious.

Sleep was a long time in coming, as a pulsating and persistent ache settled into a tight knot of desire in the sensitive spot between her thighs, and she reached to remedy it.

Darkness was falling over the plantation when Lynna arrived back at her aunt's cottage.

While helping Judith shuck corn for supper, she

couldn't resist asking about Suzanne's new gown. "Is there an occasion for the new gown, or did she simply open her chifforobe and discover empty space?"

"Oh, there is an occasion." Judith sighed. "Suzanne is returning to Charleston to visit Samuel, yet again. She explained to her parents that she wished to spend time with her brother, and her adorable niece Bethany Breanne. Naturally, they agreed without question, but we both know Suzanne cannot long tolerate Samuel's daughter or any other child for that matter. Need I remind you of the true reason behind her visit?"

"No need," Lynna gushed, affecting Suzanne's simpering whine. "Captain Joshua Jordan. Why, how could I *evah* forget him?"

She would remember the heartless scoundrel until the day she drew her final breath.

"Precisely." Judith laughed. "As you know, she was simply devastated last winter when she failed to add him to her collection of beaux. I must confess that I'd like to meet this paragon. The first man I'm sure who has ever successfully resisted Suzanne's abundant charms."

Lynna was confident that Joshua had long since sampled whatever charms Suzanne had to offer, abundant or not. The same man who had stolen her virginity and taken her on a round trip journey to hell and back, when she was convinced that she carried his child, and refused to marry her. Suzanne could have the despicable rogue, with her blessing.

Suzanne floated down the steps in a snug violet traveling outfit. Her hair was swept off her neck under a matching sunbonnet, with the brim pulled low to protect her face from the harsh sun. The carriage was piled high with numerous trunks and hat boxes, more than she could possibly require for a short stay in Charleston. Even given the fact that she changed her dress three or four times daily, there was still an excess of baggage strapped to the conveyance.

It crossed Lynna's mind that Suzanne was planning an extended visit this time, and scolded herself for being pleased at the thought.

She recalled Suzanne's parting words. "Oh, Lynna, this is going to be the most memorable trip of my entire life. Joshua is coming home, you see. His father had that awful accident, well, actually it was a rather fortuitous mishap, since Joshua is returning to oversee the plantation. In fact, he should be back home at Sea Grove by now."

How could Suzanne be pleased with the fact that a man had lost both his legs? Her appalling lack of compassion for anyone other than herself never failed to astonish Lynna. "Give my love to Samuel," she called, in a determined effort to distract Suzanne from her unending discourse of Captain Joshua Jordan. Her ploy failed miserably.

Suzanne's excitement continued to bubble forth as she motioned for Lynna to come closer. "Lynna, I have a confession to make. For the first time in my life, I am truly in love. I intend to become the wife of the esteemed Captain Joshua Jordan in the not too distant future. I cannot wait to see your face when you meet him for the first time next month, when you all attend Bethany Breanne's birthday celebration. Why, he is just too handsome for words, and filthy rich as well."

While Lynna and her aunt indeed had plans to accompany the Fletchers to South Carolina, to visit Samuel and celebrate his daughter's birthday, she had no intention of going within a mile of Captain Joshua Jordan while she was there. She pasted on a fake smile, thrilled to see Suzanne finally on her merry way.

Rest assured, Suzanne.

He knows me... intimately.

✴ *Chapter 11* ✴

With Suzanne in Charleston, Judith and Lynna's workload was cut drastically. They had kept late hours, in order to complete several day dresses, and two fabulous ballgowns for Suzanne's trip, and now found themselves with rare free time on their hands. Lynna recalled Mary's stunned expression when questioning her daughter about the darling day dresses and extravagant ballgowns she had requested from Judith.

"Mother, whatever do you mean? Why, of course I could not be seen in the same dress twice while in Charleston. What would people say? Would you have Captain Jordan think us penniless, and all but destitute?" Suzanne clutched her chest while uttering the offensive words, as though she were on the verge of succumbing to one of her frequent attacks of vapors. "Why, I could never show my humiliated face in the finer homes of Charleston again."

Mary had left the room mumbling to herself, but Judith didn't complain. Suzanne was her livelihood.

Lynna and Judith quickly adapted to the much slower pace by taking leisurely strolls by the river, stopping to have a quiet picnic lunch, or just sitting on the front porch listening to the birds sing, bees buzz around the flowerbeds, bullfrogs croak from the pond, and crickets chirp. The entire plantation breathed an audible sigh of relief during Suzanne's absence.

Long after the sun had dropped below the horizon, Lynna settled back against a cushion on the old porch swing to enjoy the sight of a full moon and starry night sky. She pushed with her bare feet, to set the swing in motion, and allowed her mind to wander. Her fingers twirled a fat sausage curl as her thoughts drifted to Charleston.

Suzanne was probably having a marvelous time in the Holy City, flitting from Ball to Ball in the fabulous gowns she and Aunt Judith had designed, and painstakingly stitched into the wee hours of the morning. She most likely had all the young bucks vying for her attention, including Joshua Jordan.

She simply would not permit herself to think about him, or what he and Suzanne were doing on this beautiful moonswept romantic night. She froze when she heard a rustling noise, and peered into the shadows, ready to bolt if her uncle appeared.

She and her aunt Judith were grateful, and gave thanks nightly for their peaceful evenings alone. Her uncle had not forced his company on them in over a fortnight, which meant they were due a visit any day. Judith's husband knew she received her wages on the first day of the month, and he would show up at the door with his hand out.

Tobias Mathison was a drunk. A nasty drunk. He was short and heavyset, with carrot colored hair, a pudgy screwed up face, and the meanest of dispositions. After quenching his constant thirst at the local tavern, and spending his last coin for a night with one of the local harlots, he would return home on a hunt for more whiskey money.

"It's only me, Lynna, don't be frightened. I was hoping you would still be awake."

She was relieved to hear Suzanne's brother, Daniel Fletcher's familiar voice. She patted the swing, inviting him to sit with her. "Aunt Judith went inside, but it's such a marvelous night I decided to sit outside for a while. Come join me."

Daniel sat beside her and breathed deeply of the fragrant night air as fireflies cavorted about. He smelled clean, of soap, and earth, and tobacco. "I remember when Suzanne was a little girl, she would pull the hind portion of a firefly off, the part that glowed, and place one on top of each finger. They still glow when severed from the body, you know. She would waltz around with the body parts shining on her fingers and pretend they were sparkling jewels."

"How awful," Lynna cried, feeling sorry for the mutilated insects.

"Suzanne didn't bat an eye when she killed the bugs, dozens each night." Daniel shook his head. "Jasmine always said you could tell a person's true character by the way they treat animals. I wonder if the saying holds true for insects."

"If you ask me, cruelty is cruelty no matter the species. If I recall, you and Samuel also had a penchant for such deviltry," Lynna reminded him. "Remember when you would chase down a June bug, then retrieve a length of Aunt Judith's sewing thread to tie around the June bug's leg? The poor insect would fly madly around and around your head, trying to free itself of the string until it collapsed from exhaustion."

"I suppose you're right," he lamented. "They left

a nasty smell on my hands, too."

Lynna was quiet, enjoying the sweet smell of honeysuckle and sweet bubby bushes scenting the night air. She enjoyed sitting outside at night, watching the beards of Spanish moss drip from the trees and dance on a gentle breeze.

Daniel turned to face her with a look of steely determination, and stood. He took both her hands, and pulled Lynna to her feet to gaze into her eyes. "You know how I feel about you. How I have felt for a long time." He paused, as if gathering his courage. "Will you marry me, Lynna?"

She had no clue what to say, or how to say it. Even though she had been expecting him to propose for months now, when it actually occurred she was caught completely off guard.

Daniel drew her in his arms, as his lips lowered to hers for a demanding kiss that was filled with years of pent up passion. When he reluctantly pulled away, his fingers went to where his mouth had been to gently outline her lips.

Lynna felt no emotion from his kiss, certainly none of the overwhelming passion that she knew simmered inside her. She didn't feel anything really, except sadness, and regret. Still, she refused to hurt Daniel by allowing him to see that his most ardent kiss failed to elicit even the slightest response in her. She would try another kiss, and this time *make* her body respond.

She slipped her arms around his neck, and touched her lips to his in her most passionate kiss; and she had been taught kissing by a master. Still, she felt nothing, not even the slightest twinge in her nether region. She heard Daniel's sharp intake of breath, not realizing he was undergoing the same feelings she had experienced after being the recipient of Joshua's first kiss.

She dropped her arms from around his neck and went to stand solemnly at the edge of the porch, watching moths flutter around a sputtering candle.

After several minutes of pained silence, she turned to Daniel, and could only surmise that he was awaiting a reply to his proposal. She had to stall for time, until she could think of a way to refuse his request without shredding his heart in the process. "Daniel, this is so sudden."

He seemed flushed, and it would seem that his groin area had been beset by a terrible itch. When he finally found his voice, it was scarcely above a whisper. "It's not sudden on my part. You know how much I love you, Lynna, since the first day you appeared on our doorstep as skinny as a rail, and looking as if you had lost your only friend in the world. Please, make me the happiest man alive by saying yes."

Surely there was a way to be truthful, while sparing his feelings at the same time. Save him from suffering the same torment she had been forced to endure, after Joshua so callously tossed her offer of marriage back in her humiliated face.

"Daniel, please give me time to ponder this issue at length. Why, I couldn't possibly give you an answer tonight."

Daniel exhaled a sigh of relief that she hadn't turned him down flat. "How much time do you need, darling?"

"Why, I'm not sure. Marriage is much too serious an institution to be hastened into." She prayed that he could somehow find it in his heart to understand. "When I marry I want it to be perfect, and last forever."

"I realize your feelings are not as strong as mine, Lynna, but given time you would grow to love me. I know you would." He encompassed the plantation and its thousands of acres with a sweeping hand. "I long for you to stand by my side as my wife, and future mistress of Magnolia House."

It was obvious to Lynna that in his mind, no woman could turn down such an advantageous proposal. When in truth, the plantation and all of its acreage was but a drop in the bucket compared to her own inheritance, if she still had one.

"I do love you, Daniel, but I don't know if I am ready for... marriage. I need more time. Please, I beg you to give me that time."

Daniel's white grin flashed in the darkness. "I will give you until morning."

"Oh, you are incorrigible." Lynna laughed, thankful that he was able to joke about the matter.

He held her face and tilted her chin up." I will be eagerly awaiting your answer but please, I beg of you, don't postpone the agony any longer than you have to." He placed a tender kiss on the tip of her nose and ambled down the porch steps.

Lynna watched him walk toward the big house with his shoulders hunched, defeated. What was she holding out for? Why not accept his offer of marriage, and move her scant belongings into the grand plantation house?

Daniel was a handsome man, of average height and build, with his father's black curly hair and his mother's cheerful disposition. A man who would love her and be a splendid father to her children. Just as her own father had been, once, a long time ago. Daniel was a man any woman would be proud to call her own.

Lynna could find only one fly in the ointment. She didn't love Daniel, and she would never hurt him by marrying for any other reason. When she stood before God and pledged her vows, she would mean every single word.

Chapter 12

When Lynna was certain that her aching bones could not withstand being jostled for a second longer, Mary announced they were only a few miles from Cedar Hill. She, along with the other exhausted travelers perked up, eager for baths, clean clothes, and a soft place to rest their much abused behinds. They had undertaken a dusty journey on plush cushioned seats that had long since begun to feel like wooden planks beneath them.

The weary group departed the carriage, and were making their way to the steps when the front door burst open. Samuel Fletcher bounded down the steps two at a time, followed by Beth and their charming daughter Bethany Breanne. After greeting his family, Samuel turned to Lynna with a mischievous grin. "Well now, just look what a gorgeous young lady you turned out to be." He turned to his wife and winked. "Perhaps I shouldn't have been so eager to leave home."

Lynna was fearful of what Beth's reaction might be to Samuel's teasing banter, and lowered her eyes.

Beth hurried to take her arm. "Never mind him, Lynna. Samuel always was the worst jokester, but I don't need to remind you of it, do I?"

"He always teased me mercilessly." Lynna remembered well Samuel's penchant for tomfoolery. "You never knew what mischief he had up his sleeve."

His mother smiled fondly. "Or what bug he had in his pocket to chase and terrorize you with."

"He is still that way to this day." Beth winked at her husband as she led the ladies into the house. "I'll show you to your rooms where you can freshen up before dinner. I'm so glad you could come a few days early, since we're having a special dinner guest tonight. Suzanne has invited our neighbor and dear friend Joshua Jordan."

Lynna jerked her hand from Beth's to clutch at a heart that threatened to fly out of her chest.

Joshua Jordan?

Here?

"At last." Mary affected an exaggerated sigh. "We finally have the honor of meeting the irresistibly charming, unspeakably divine, astonishingly handsome, and just plain perfect Mr. Joshua Jordan."

Everyone laughed at Mary's facetious remarks concerning Suzanne's often heard descriptions of Joshua, except Beth and Lynna. While Beth realized that each description fit Joshua to a tee, except maybe the one about being perfect, she chose to keep mum and allow each of them to discover his numerous attributes for themselves.

Lynna, on the other hand, found absolutely nothing about the man to be worthy of laughter. She felt the urge to throw up, sob hysterically, and walk every step of the way back to Magnolia House.

What would she do? What would she say? What would *he* say? He was such a vile despicable bounder. Would he relish watching her squirm, before happily informing Suzanne and the others of their... acquaintance? She should never have come.

Good Lord, she should never have come.

After being shown to her room, Lynna poured water from a floral pitcher into a matching bowl and sponged her body, washing away the light film of grit that settled over her during the seemingly endless carriage ride. How she longed for a hot soothing bath to soak her weary bones, yet, there was no time. Company was coming to dinner in the form of a black hearted sea dog, and she was expected to hurry downstairs and pretend to greet him for the first time. She would love to greet him with an uppercut to his finely chiseled jaw.

Perhaps she could send word that she had an upset stomach, and planned to retire early. How discourteous would that be, when she hadn't been sick a day since she stepped off the *Windjammer.* Plus, a sudden ailment would only cause her aunt unnecessary worry. It was best to get this ordeal over with. Besides, with the amount of women Captain Jordan had most likely bedded in the past three years, he would be hard pressed to even remember her name.

She felt revived after her sponge bath, and sat at the dressing table to pinch her cheeks until they turned a becoming shade of pink. She then gathered her heavy mass of golden hair atop her head and surveyed the results from every angle. She decided against an updo, and dropped her hair to trail down her back and fall in shimmering curls of spun gold. She pulled the sides back, and held her hair in place with tortoise shell hair combs as bouncy tendrils fell to frame her face.

Suzanne had often chided Lynna for wearing her

hair in such an unfashionable style. *Hair should always be swept off your shoulders for effect, Lynna.* Unlike Suzanne, Lynna had never conformed strictly to the fashion of the day.

With her toilette complete, she chose her favorite gown of sea green dotted muslin. The dress was cut fashionably low, with off the shoulder puffed sleeves and a velvet sash at her waist. The hem flounce, sleeves, and neck border were appliquéd with double rows of creamy French lace that Mary Fletcher had been considerate enough to supply. She added matching kid slippers, and stood in front of the cheval glass for a final inspection.

Satisfied with her appearance, she braced herself for the drama that was surely about to unfold, as she descended the stairs to the sound of robust laughter drifting from the parlor. That laugh. She would recognize it anywhere.

Joshua.

She couldn't face him again. The pain of her heartbreak on the *Windjammer* was still too fresh.

She paused midway down the stairs, suddenly struck by the notion of how foolish it would be to face a man who had the power to completely destroy her reputation, simply by telling the truth. She couldn't risk it. She turned to flee to her room, when her eyes were drawn to the unmistakable physique of the man standing with Silas and his sons. It was him, standing only a few feet away. Even with his back turned, Lynna recognized the captain of the *Windjammer*.

At the same moment, Joshua felt eyes like simmering coals burning into his back. He turned slowly and, from where he stood, he alone saw the breathtaking creature poised on the stairs like a goddess about to take flight.

That face, that body, those eyes, could it be?

Of course not. He must have overindulged in Samuel's fine stock of Jamaican rum, for the exquisite beauty perched on the stairs held more than a passing resemblance to... no... it couldn't be.

He placed his glass on the mantle and scrubbed both hands over his face, before again looking toward the stairs.

It was her.

The very vision that had haunted his dreams for the past three bedeviling years, and she was even more breathtaking now than when he had first witnessed her stunning beauty onboard the *Windjammer*.

Lynna.

He hardly realized that someone was speaking his name, or that anyone else was even in the room, as he found himself silently moving toward her. He had no idea he had left Samuel in mid-sentence, to peer after Joshua with a puzzled frown. He came to a halt at the foot of the wide staircase as his eyes fused with a familiar crystal blue gaze.

Lynna clutched the banister for support as his eyes slowly caressed every square inch of her slender frame. If she should dare take a step, her quivering limbs would surely cause her to tumble headfirst down the stairs to land in a crumpled heap at his feet.

She was stranded, as she could not trust her legs to flee the man's presence by running either up or down. What a humiliating quandary.

Breathe, just breathe. He is but a man, a flesh and blood man. She fought to still her racing heart and out of control pulse, before blood shot from her ears.

She was determined to ignore him, as it was her only hope of enduring the night without making a complete fool of herself. She moved on trembling legs, with slow and careful steps, so as not to trip on the hem of her petticoat before safely reaching the bottom of the stairs. Far from snubbing him, she found herself unable to free her eyes as they were being held prisoner by his searing gaze.

"Lynna, I see you have met our dinner guest." Samuel coughed, and repeated the words that neither of them had heard the first time. He had noticed Lynna's obvious distress and hurried to her side.

"N… no," she stammered, pleading with her eyes for Joshua not to yield their secret. "I have not yet had the pleasure."

"Then allow me." Samuel turned to Joshua. "This ravishing creature is Lynna Mathison. Lynna, this is Captain Joshua Jordan."

Only after Joshua's eyes had leisurely traveled down, and then back up her fully rounded frame to rest on her face, did he extend his hand to take hers and bring it to his lips. He turned her hand over and pressed his warm mouth to her palm. "It is indeed a pleasure to make your acquaintance, Miss… ah… Mathison." He flashed a smile that seemed to light his entire face, and cause his sea green eyes to sparkle. He would have to be very careful, for he had almost called her Miss Rhodes.

Lynna's hand tingled, *burned*, from his touch. When his lips placed soft kisses on the tender skin of her palm, hot liquid fire traveled from her hand to all parts of her anatomy to leave her stunned and breathless. She again clutched the banister to steady herself. Then, drawing a shaky breath, she gratefully took the arm Samuel offered and allowed him to escort her into the parlor, where the others were waiting, and watching, especially Suzanne.

Joshua did not fail to notice Lynna's quaking reaction, and was pleased to note that he had not been so easily dismissed from mind either. In retrospect, he hadn't changed in the last few years, whereas she had blossomed into an even more captivating beauty. He turned to Silas and remarked, "You grow simply stunning women in Georgia, sir."

"I will be the first to admit that there are some gorgeous women in our fair state." He beamed proudly. "But few to rival Lynna and Suzanne."

"Why, Joshua, honey," Suzanne quickly left her seat and almost collided with Beth as she grabbed Joshua's arm, whilst wheedling for a compliment. "I'm sure some of the young ladies you have met during your travels abroad, fair put Lynna and little ole me to shame."

Joshua ignored an infuriated Suzanne, and looked straightway across the room at Lynna with a most besotting smile. "To be sure, I had the privilege of meeting some exotic females in my travels, but I said it then, and I will say it now. I have never seen one more beautiful." As an afterthought, he added, "Than the two of you, of course."

Joshua was tempted to reach out and touch Lynna, to see if she was real or only a figment of his imagination. He had dreamed of her so often, dreamed of her standing in front of him just as she was now, dreamed of her sweet lips and smooth satiny skin.

He took a cautious step toward her, unaware of his true intentions until Beth rushed to grab his arm.

"Shall we go in to dinner, Joshua? You must be starving." Beth had known her reaction would have to be swift, in order to avoid a scene, and what a spectacle Suzanne would have created had Joshua succeeded in his mindless endeavor to embrace Lynna. After witnessing Joshua's reaction to Lynna, Beth realized her sister-in-law was in for a rude awakening. Heavenly days, she already dreaded that drama.

Lynna turned toward the dining room, when she felt a warm hand pressing her elbow, and relaxed. She needed Samuel's calming presence and reassuring touch. She clutched his arm and breathed deeply, leaning against him for support as she attempted to still her racing heart.

"Of all the nights I have dreamed of you," Joshua's whispered words caressed her ear. "I find you practically in my own backyard."

Where did he come from? A second ago Beth had him firmly by the arm and was leading him into the dining room. Why, the odious oaf. Did he expect her to fall breathlessly into his waiting arms again, as she had on the ship? Did he imagine her to still be the young naiveté, who had capitulated heedlessly to his lustful advances after a few glasses of port?

He would soon learn that she was no longer the dewy eyed eighteen-year old she had been on his ship, unversed in the ways of the world, Her uncle had forced the harsh realities of life down her throat shortly after her arrival at Magnolia House. Now, hearing Joshua's smooth southern drawl so close to her ear, caused the memories of *his* callous treatment to return in a rush. Lynna froze for a second, before jerking away from him faster than a duck after a June bug, and lambasting him with her eyes.

"Is anything amiss, my sweet?" he questioned guilelessly.

She moved a few steps away to a more respectable distance, and chose to disregard his question and ask one of her own. "I am certainly not your sweet, Captain Jordan, and shouldn't you be escorting Suzanne? You are her dinner guest, are you not?"

He once again flashed a disarming smile that sent her heart to flutter wildly. "I have terrible manners, to be sure. You see, I almost didn't come tonight." He moved even closer, as his hand slid down her arm to rest on the small of her back. "I realize what a grave error in judgment that would have been on my part, because I wouldn't have missed this night for the world."

She attempted to remain aloof, and gave him a withering glare as she calmly moved out of his reach. "Sir, you forget yourself. Please do not attempt to besmirch my reputation by forcing your unwanted attention on me."

Joshua threw back his head and laughed uproariously, before leaning toward her to whisper, "I have never found it necessary to force myself on any woman." With a sly wink, he added, "As you should well recall."

Lynna's outraged gasp drew the attention of everyone in the room, including Suzanne, who shot daggers from her blazing eyes. She hurried to the table, and was relieved to find her place between Daniel Fletcher and her aunt Judith, who observed her with studied interest.

Suzanne had made a point of being seated next to Joshua. Yet, try as she might, she was unable to gain the man's full attention. He dutifully answered her questions, while his gaze remained firmly fixed on Lynna. It was Silas who was finally successful in gaining Joshua's attention, with a question about Sea Grove.

With Joshua's head turned to answer Silas, Lynna took the opportunity to peruse him more closely. He was just as she remembered, not a hair on his head had changed, and she remembered everything about him so... well.

She watched as he carelessly brushed a lock of raven hair from his forehead, and noticed that his eyes sparkled when he laughed. She was just getting to an inspection of his firm jaw, pearly white teeth, and broad muscular shoulders when he turned, and their eyes locked.

She couldn't breathe. Her lungs refused to push air in or out. Thankfully, her neck muscles still worked, and she was able to pivot her head toward her aunt, but not before seeing his gaze dip purposefully to her breasts.

Her cheeks flushed crimson as she realized the man had lost none of his brash effrontery. She was determined to ignore him as she placed a trembling hand to her throat, in hopes of slowing her erratic pulse, which now seemed to pound in her temples like a jackhammer.

She decided that under no circumstances would she look his way again, and focused her attention on Daniel, until Samuel drew the rapt attention of everyone in the room.

He tapped on the side of his glass, and addressed Lynna with a broad smile. "Lynna, darling, rumor has it that you have accepted my brother's proposal, and I may soon have the honor of claiming you as my sister."

❧ *Chapter 13* ❧

Lynna nearly choked on a dill pickle as her aunt thumped on her back. When she could breathe again, she took a sip of Madeira and turned to Judith, who seemed as completely befuddled by Samuel's startling announcement as she was.

His sister? This night was taking disastrous turns by leaps and bounds. How dare Daniel. He had informed Samuel that they were engaged, when she had certainly not accepted his proposal? One glance at Daniel's apologetic expression assured her that he was every bit as stunned by Samuel's remarks as she herself had been.

So, she asked in as calm a voice as she could muster under the circumstances, "May I ask where you gathered this information, Samuel?"

Samuel had known Lynna long enough to realize that even though her temper was rare, she was indeed in possession of one. He could also tell by her sparkling eyes, that the anger she was trying so desperately to hide was threatening to spill forth. "Perhaps I was misinformed, and a bit hasty in my eagerness to welcome you into the family fold."

His apology did not appear to appease Lynna's ire in the least. "Now don't go getting your feathers all ruffled. As usual, Suzanne was the purveyor of the gossiped word." He glanced askance at his sister, who only shrugged. "She was so overjoyed at the thought of becoming your sister that she had to tell someone. You know she could never keep a secret."

"It's true." Daniel cast his adoring gaze at Lynna, and took the opportunity to set the record straight. "I have asked Lynna to become my wife, that is no secret. While she has not yet consented, I intend to keep trying until I eventually wear her down. I don't mean to cause undue pressure, but if the matter were left solely up to me, we would be man and wife before the sun sets this very night."

"Perfect timing," Samuel joked.

"Lynna, darling, pay no heed to my sons. You take all the time you need." Mary smiled, giving Samuel a chastising glance for his off color remark. "Daniel will simply have to be patient. Why, I myself have always been partial to fall weddings."

Lynna lowered her eyes, feeling wretched. How could she tell Daniel's mother that after tonight, after the effect the handsome sea captain was having on her emotions, she was more sure than ever that she couldn't marry her son?

Suzanne jumped in feet first to make matters worse. "Oh, Mother, honestly. We all know Lynna and Daniel will eventually wed, you and I have discussed it for months now. So why not proceed with the festivities, since we haven't had a decent party in ages." She glared at Lynna with a fake smile, and eyes brimming with contempt. "Why, their wedding would be the social event of the season."

Lynna marveled at whether she was to have any input whatsoever on the subject of her own betrothal.

Mary hushed her outspoken daughter with a stern glance. "Suzanne, you don't make a decision as important as marriage simply because it is the social season. Whenever they decide to marry, it will be reason enough to celebrate."

Joshua held his breath during most of their conversation, fearing Lynna might consider accepting Daniel's proposal. When he caught her eyes, and witnessed the pain reflected in the sorrowful blue depths, he knew he had nothing to fear. She had no desire to wed Daniel Fletcher. Yet, Daniel's family, each of them it seemed, was trying to pressure her into holy matrimony.

Lynna loved Mary and Silas deeply, and hurting them was what she least wanted to do. It broke her heart to know that if she refused their son, they too would feel the sting of rejection. It was a hopeless situation, with no easy way to avoid someone's feelings getting trampled.

A deep voice speaking her name brought Lynna out of her reverie. "How long will you be visiting Charleston?" Joshua asked, as he bit into a chunk of savory venison.

It was some moments before she found her voice, as his green eyes held hers. "I'm not sure, exactly." She didn't miss the sparks that shot from Suzanne's eyes at his soft words. *If looks could kill.* "Samuel and Beth were kind enough to invite Aunt Judith and I, and we certainly hope not to overstay our welcome."

"Impossible," Samuel assured her. "You and Judith are family, and as such you are more than welcome to stay as long as you wish." He turned to his wife. "Wouldn't you agree, darling?'

"Absolutely." Beth's warm smile convinced them that her words were sincere. "Our home is your home."

Lynna was grateful that Daniel had been so

engrossed in conversation throughout dinner, that he hadn't noticed Joshua's unwavering attention toward her. She didn't dare hope that Suzanne had overlooked it as well.

She had glanced up from toying with her food several times, to find Suzanne watching her with untold volumes of hatred shining in her squinted eyes. The message her eyes conveyed was clear. *He is mine. Stay away.*

After dinner, during which Lynna had been unable to take a single bite of food, for fear her fork would fall clattering to her plate, or she would choke on a mouthful of turnip greens, the group adjourned to the parlor. Lynna went to stand by the open side doors to breathe the cool scented breeze, as flashes of lightning began to play across the sky and distant thunder rumbled.

Mary seemed quite taken with her daughter's latest beau. "Joshua, Suzanne tells us you are the captain of your own ship, but you have docked the vessel to oversee your family's plantation."

"That is correct, madam." A hint of sadness crept into his voice as he gazed at Lynna with undisguised longing. "The *Windjammer* will be forced to weather her storms without me for the foreseeable future."

Hearing the name of the ship caused another flood of memories to assault Lynna, leaving her visibly shaken.

Ever observant, Joshua didn't fail to notice her reaction.

"That is certainly admirable on your part," Mary offered. "Still, after all your years on the open sea, do you worry plantation life will be a drastic change, and perhaps even a bit boring?"

"Don't go feeling sorry for Joshua, Mother." Samuel grinned as he slapped Joshua on the back. "It is without warrant, I assure you. Captain Jordan has enough memories stockpiled to last the average man a lifetime."

Once again, Joshua's eyes sought Lynna. "I have many treasured memories from the *Windjammer*, true, but only one that routinely torments my dreams."

Every person in the room witnessed the passionate exchange. It was then that Mary gave up all hope of ever having Joshua as her son-in-law.

Her daughter refused to accept defeat quite so gracefully. She rushed to take Joshua's arm and press her bosom against him, as she fluttered her lashes wildly, successfully embarrassing her family. "It's such a beautiful evening, Captain Jordan. Would you care to take a round through the garden?"

Lynna felt the need to be away from Joshua's suffocating nearness, and Suzanne's persistent whining. "It has been an exhausting day," she said to Beth. "If you will excuse me, I will retire for the evening."

Joshua snatched his arm from Suzanne and left her positively livid, as he hurried to Lynna's side, who feared his purpose was to seduce her then and there. "I hope to get a chance to visit with you again before you return to Georgia," was mercifully all he said.

She glanced over his shoulder and cringed at the unbridled rage in Suzanne's eyes, and her greatest desire was to be as far away from both of them as she could be. She yanked her hand from Joshua's and bid everyone good night. before heading toward the stairs and the safe haven of her room.

Why did she come here?

She slipped into a pale pink nightgown and fell breathless and numb on the bed, with her mind a chaotic jumble. If only she could return to Georgia tonight. Why did Joshua have to live nearby? Why did her skin burn where he touched her? Why did he smell so good? Why, oh, why did he have to be so sinfully handsome? For these and other questions, she had no answers.

She accepted that sleep would be a long time in coming, as she stood on the balcony to watch lightning flash in jagged forks across the sky. A gust of wind blew across the land to rustle the leaves and cool her heated skin as she leaned over the balcony, breathing deeply of the unmistakable smell of rain. The cloud cover parted briefly to allow the moon to cast its golden glow over the earth, lending to it a rosy hue as a multitude of insects struck up a lively chorus.

"Good night, my sweet," Joshua's sexy Southern drawl drifted to her on a warm breeze. "I fear sleep will abandon me tonight as well." He didn't miss Lynna's muffled gasp.

As one hand flew to her mouth, the other clutched her gown more tightly around her bosom. Suzanne had apparently failed in her effort to secure a private audience with him.

His deep laughter echoed through the still night air. "I don't suppose you could be persuaded to come down and take a walk with me?"

The very idea.

"You   should   have   accepted   Suzanne's

invitation, sir. I can assure you that I have no desire, or intention, of ever spending time in your presence again." Incredulous, she spun around and rushed into the room, confident that if she ignored him he would go away.

After waiting for what seemed like an eternity, and hearing nothing, she tiptoed to the balcony and peered over the railing.

"Just as I feared." He grinned a rakish grin before blowing her a kiss. "We will have our walk soon, my sweet." With those words he turned, and Lynna heard him whistling softly as his horse trotted into the dark night.

You had your walk, Captain Jordan, and so much more.

Joshua spurred his horse forward as fat drops of rain splashed him to quickly soak his clothes, and lightning flashed across the sky to illuminate the heavens in a brilliant display. A triumphant grin spread across his lips as he raced across the field toward home at a full gallop.

The pouring rain would prevent Suzanne from going to the pond. The girl was too demanding by far. He had been with her almost nightly for the past month, and she never seemed satisfied. Hell, he doubted if one man was even capable of such a herculean feat. No doubt there would be hell to pay when he put a halt to their nocturnal rendezvous, but it must be done.

Suzanne was a thing of the past. He had every intention of spending his future with Lynna.

He could hardly believe that Lynna's Aunt Judith was employed by the Fletchers, and that

Lynna had been living with her on Suzanne Fletcher's family plantation since leaving his ship in Charleston. He had received frequent letters from Suzanne, pleading with him to visit, which he had promptly dismissed. Had he known Lynna was in residence, he might have been a frequent visitor to Magnolia House and worn out his welcome months ago.

The mystical Lynna had certainly woven an enchanted spell over him. Many nights he had lain awake in his lonely cabin and brought her clearly to mind, often wondering if she was safe and out of harm's way, while at the same time longing for the feeling of her soft curves against his burning skin. He had been content with his dalliance with the insatiable Suzanne, and his many gratifying encounters with the provocative upstairs maid Juanita, until now.

The memory of his passionate encounter with Lynna was as fresh as if it had happened only yesterday. He laughed out loud, remembering how his heart had thundered in his chest at dinner, when Samuel had inquired about her marriage plans. His galloping heart had returned to its normal rhythm, only after realizing the lady had no desire to speak her wedding vows anytime soon. That left the door wide open for him, and he had no intention of wasting a second chance with her.

They could make a fresh start, for after seeing her tonight, Joshua could no longer deny his feelings. Lynna ignited a fire in his loins that no other woman could come close to smothering, and if she spoke her wedding vows to anyone, it would be him.

"Will you marry me, Joshua?" she had once

asked.

If she were to ask that question of him today, she would get a very different response. With his decision made, he arrived home soaked to the skin, and feeling better than he had in… three years.

Suzanne sat by the pond in a glorious rage. Her hair was plastered to her head and her soaking wet clothes clung to her shivering body. Somehow, she had known Joshua wouldn't make an appearance tonight. He had met her almost nightly for the past several weeks and now, after a treacherous slut arrived, he neglected to meet her?

Oh true, there was a torrential downpour at present, but had it detained her from coming? Hell, no. If he was as eager to be with her as she was him, would a little rainfall deter him? Of course, not. She was certain of one thing. Joshua was not at fault here.

Lynna was.

The shameless trollop had practically thrown herself at the poor man at dinner. What red blooded man wouldn't have been sorely tempted by such an openly wanton display? Lynna wanted Joshua, that much was obvious. Why, any fool could see it.

Suzanne closed her eyes and took a deep breath to calm her building rage. She vowed that if Lynna got her hands on Joshua, it would be after *her* cold dead body was rotting in the grave.

Chapter 14

The rain poured down steadily throughout the night, drumming on the tin roof and settling the occupants of Cedar Hill into a peaceful slumber. By morning, the lawn was standing in several inches of water and turning the oyster shell driveway into slush. Still, the rain continued to fall over the hushed plantation.

Lynna went to her balcony door and noticed the storm had set in to stay. The sky was a leaden ominous grey, draping an eerie cloak of darkness over the land as far as she could see, and with the promise of more rain to come. She dressed in warm clothes, against a damp chill that had invaded the house, and proceeded downstairs in search of a steaming cup of coffee. She also had in mind to sample the country ham biscuits that smelled positively divine.

"Lynna," Bethany Breanne chirped from the dining room. "Will you sit beside me at breakfast?"

Lynna scooped the darling child in her arms and tickled her ribs, sending her into peals of joyous laughter. "I can't imagine anyone I would rather sit next to."

"I can," Suzanne sneered. "While you may hope to entice Joshua with your flirtatious ways, let me assure you that you will not succeed. I noticed, as did everyone else, how you batted your lashes throughout dinner and dallied with him like the common white trash strumpet that you are."

Lynna felt blood rush up her neck to stain her cheeks. Suzanne was jealous and spiteful, that was painfully obvious. "None of your accusations are true, Suzanne. If you will recall, I was not the one making overtures last night. It was your Captain Jordan who seemed to have some difficulty keeping his groping hands to himself."

Suzanne gasped, incensed. "Why, you devious little twit. You never had any intention of marrying Daniel, did you? You were just toying with him until you found a man with a wealthier purse, and you think my Joshua is that man. Be warned, Lynna, he is mine."

To make matters worse, Bethany Breanne announced, "Joshua called Lynna *his love* last night. The thunderbolts woke us, and Lucy and I went to my balcony. He was talking to you under your balcony during the storm, wasn't he, Lynna?"

Suzanne's blood simmered on a low boil as she mentally counted off the ways she could cause Lynna a slow and painful death, just as a betraying blush stained the tramp's cheek. Of all the nights she and Joshua had made love until sunrise, he had never once used that or any other term of endearment with her. She spun on her heels and fled the room as humiliation caused her cheeks to flame.

So, the little brat had heard Joshua's sickening words as well as that prying bitch, Lucy, her nanny. Suzanne knew Lucy would giggle and gossip about the incident for days, causing all the housemaids to snicker behind her back. She had to put a stop to this nonsense before it got further out of hand.

After a few days of warm sunshine and steady breezes, the ground was dry enough for Lynna to venture outside. She vowed that she couldn't tolerate one more day of being cooped up in the house with the insufferable Suzanne, and skipped down the steps in search of Daniel, hoping to persuade him to go riding. She would gladly face his pressuring questions of matrimony, in exchange for the opportunity to flee Suzanne's veiled barbs for a few hours.

Yet, the days of forced confinement had left Samuel's chores backed up, and Daniel had volunteered to help his brother.

Before Lynna could reach the stables and ride off on her own, which she would have dearly loved, Suzanne came traipsing down the steps in a midnight blue velvet riding habit. She had a matching sunbonnet tied under her chin, with three feet of streaming satin trailing down her back, and the brim pulled low over her face. "Are you two going riding?"

"Lynna is," Daniel replied. "I was just coming to find you, so the two of you can go together. I promised to help Samuel today, and I would prefer that she not ride alone."

"Daniel, honestly, I am quite capable of riding without a chaperone tagging along for heaven's sake," Lynna admonished, unwittingly striking a most alluring pose with her hands on her hips and her blue eyes flashing. Daniel had successfully sent her pleasant day to hell in a handbasket.

"Don't be a goose, Lynna. I don't mind

accompanying you." Suzanne tilted her pert nose and rushed past Lynna into the stables.

She returned leading two chestnut mares. "If I have to remain inside that house for another second I shall go stark raving mad."

It would be a short trip, Lynna thought sourly. She didn't question Suzanne's sudden mood change. She was too happy to be outside and enjoying the glorious sunshine.

They saddled up, and cantered down the path behind the house at a leisurely pace. Lynna held her face to the sun, soaking up the rays as a warm breeze caressed her skin and fanned her hair behind her. She felt lighthearted and carefree, and yearned to feel the wind in her face.

She glanced at Suzanne, who refused to allow her horse to move at a pace above a trot, lest an errant breeze muss her elaborately styled coiffeur. So, throwing caution aside, she raced with the wind and left a preoccupied Suzanne in her dust.

She was some distance ahead, and galloping at a speed most would consider risky on a sidesaddle, when she spotted a lone figure watching her from the shadows of a sycamore tree. She immediately recognized the black hair and broad shoulders. Must he be at every turn? Her first impulse was to turn the steed and rejoin Suzanne, but Joshua's horse was already trotting toward her.

"Hello, Lynna," he greeted. "You look radiant this morning."

When she ignored his compliment, he grinned. "It would seem that wishes do come true, as I was wondering how I might have a private moment with you, and you magically appear."

The man's arrogance knew no bounds. "Captain Jordan, it would seem that you either suffer from hearing loss, dementia, or a sad combination of both. I have told you in English, as well as French, that I do not wish to have a private moment with you ever again. I made a colossal mistake once, but I have put it behind me. I would be eternally grateful if you would do the same."

"What was your mistake, my sweet?" He smiled, what some might consider a simply devastating smile. "We had a pleasurable encounter, but unless you have been intimate with another man, you are still very much a virgin."

Could what he was saying possibly be true?

"It has been three years, Joshua," Lynna pleaded, with tortured eyes. "Please, tell me the truth of what happened that night. It is a question that has tormented me for too long."

"Nothing happened, Lynna."

"How can you say nothing happened? I remember…"

"You remember a pleasurable experience that was very memorable, my love. However, I did not take your maidenhead. On this, you have my word as a gentleman."

Lynna knew his words were true, she felt them in her soul. She had leveled untrue allegations against an innocent man yet, surprisingly, he held no animosity toward her.

Joshua witnessed the relief in her eyes as she finally accepted the truth.

"I'm sorry, Joshua," she breathed. "I remembered feeling your hands … on…"

"All is forgiven." In an effort to ease her

discomfort, he flashed a brilliant smile that caused her pulse to quicken. "Now that we have that matter settled, would you care to ride down by the river?" His dancing eyes dimmed as Suzanne appeared from behind a thicket of trees.

Suzanne positively glowed upon sight of him. She snatched her bonnet off after noticing Lynna's golden locks flowing past her waist, and yanked pins haphazardly from her hair to shake it loose, in what she hoped was a provocative manner. "Why Joshua, I certainly didn't expect to see you this morning. What a pleasant surprise."

He smiled lazily, lighting a cheroot and sending smoke to circle around his head. "I was just asking Lynna if she cared to accompany…"

"Why, we would love to. How very considerate of you to ask," Suzanne interrupted, having no qualms with including herself in the invitation. "I might very well take leave of my sanity, if forced to remain shut up in that dreary house with that bothersome child for another day. It simply baffles me why children feel the incessant need to prattle on and on about such inconsequential things."

Suzanne surreptitiously steered her horse next to Joshua's. "Why, I might become as famous as Mr. Eli Whitney and his cotton gin were I to invent a muzzle for little girls." She laughed gaily, totally dominating the conversation and leaving Lynna to follow behind, which suited her fine.

From this angle, she could observe Joshua at her leisure, without him ever knowing, and hopefully not get caught in the act this time.

Joshua knew he was being watched when the hair on the back of his neck prickled. He smiled broadly, leaving Suzanne with the mistaken impression that he truly delighted in her company.

The land was fresh and green after the rain, and the fields were a gay riot of wildflowers. With Joshua's every thought focused on Lynna, instead of steering his steed he left the horse to choose his own destination, which was a familiar path.

"Ouch!" Lynna cried, as a limb in front of her that was bent back by Suzanne, whether intentional or not, slapped her sharply across the face. She rubbed her stinging cheek and could already feel an ugly welt rising. She clenched her teeth and muttered under her breath as she drew back, allowing them to proceed some distance ahead of her. Suzanne could be a royal pain in the derriere, especially when she was jealous, and the green eyed monster was perched front and center on her shoulder today.

They left the forest and entered a clearing dazzled by iridescent sunlight. Lynna was about to dismount, when strong and deeply tanned hands gently lifted her from the saddle. She glanced toward Suzanne and noticed her mouth forming a perfect O of outrage.

Joshua was totally unbothered by Suzanne's infuriated stance, and instead of releasing Lynna, his hands remained tightly clasped around her waist. The pressure of his hands brought back such unsettling memories, that Lynna had to struggle against the urge to brush her lips against his as he gently lowered her to the ground.

Why did this man's touch affect her so? The feeling was so strong as to be almost impossible to resist. She could almost taste his lips on hers. Thankfully, Suzanne was only a few feet away, or she might have succumbed to the unrelenting urge to taste them again.

"What about me?" Suzanne simpered, sounding on the verge of a childish temper tantrum. "Would you have me break my neck by taking leave of this huge beast unassisted?" The high color in her cheeks gave witness to her mounting fury.

Ever the gentleman, albeit with great reluctance, Joshua released Lynna. As she bent her head, he noticed the vivid red welt rising on her cheek. He guessed correctly that Suzanne was to blame for marring her porcelain skin, and walked over to wrest her rather unceremoniously from her steed.

"Well!" Suzanne hissed. "I would have been better off falling from the blasted creature."

Lynna couldn't suppress a giggle, which she quickly tried to cover. Too late, it only served to infuriate Suzanne, and cause her eyes to blaze with smoldering fury.

Joshua released a seething Suzanne, and returned to Lynna's side to take her hand and lead her to the pond. "Allow me to put cool water on your face, perhaps it will take away some of the sting."

Lynna opened her mouth to reply, when she felt herself being drawn down to the water's edge. She watched as Joshua dipped his kerchief in the water and caressed her cheek with a feathery touch. His touch was soothing, and left a tingling sensation that rapidly traveled from her face, to her midsection, and parts beyond.

Joshua watched the passion flare in her eyes, and his willpower altogether deserted him. The world around them ceased to exist as his hands moved behind her head and through her silky hair, and his mouth slowly descended to hers. Her lips were so close he could feel her warm breath on his cheek when a splash, followed by a cooling spray of water, made them both glance up.

Lynna's hands flew to her mouth when she noticed Suzanne cavorting in the pond, without a stitch of clothes, as her small breasts bobbed in and out of the water.

Suzanne laughed derisively at Lynna's shocked expression of dismay. "Lynna, honey, close your mouth before a dragonfly flies in, and come join me." Then she turned to Joshua with her most seductive grin. "The water is heavenly, sugah. It's much warmer than it was last week when we got chilled to the bone…"

"Enough, Suzanne," Joshua warned.

"Oh, don't be silly, darling. She knows how we feel about each other, don't you, Lynna? We don't have to hide our true feelings around her."

"I said that was enough." Joshua's voice was cold, and as hard as steel.

Lynna wiped water from her face and started toward her horse, intent on fleeing Suzanne's humiliating display, when she was stopped by Joshua's hand on her shoulder. "Don't leave, Lynna. I don't expect you to remove your clothes and join her."

"How very generous of you." She shoved his hand away and continued toward her horse. "But I have no intention of being witness to Suzanne's appalling lack of morals."

"Please stay." Joshua took her hands and held them to his chest, seemingly not at all shocked by

Suzanne's lewd behavior. While that should have been some indication that the man was accustomed to viewing Suzanne in all her glory, Lynna was too besotted by his devastating smile to think rationally. "Let's take a walk until she cools off."

Reasoning that Joshua couldn't be blamed for Suzanne's disgraceful conduct, any more than she could, she allowed him to take her elbow as they moved toward the shadow of the trees. After all, he was an innocent bystander to Suzanne's revolting escapades, and his dreamy eyes were coming closer and fusing with hers, his moist, soft lips were inches...

"Joshua, honey, are you coming in?" Suzanne called, standing temptingly so that her bosom jutted out of the water. "We haven't been able to meet in days because of the rain. Surely, Lynna could be prevailed upon to leave us alone for a short while, couldn't you, Lynna?"

"Certainly." She was incensed by Suzanne's words and snatched up her skirts.

Joshua had brought her to the very spot he and Suzanne had their trysts?

When she realized Joshua was behind her, offering to help her mount, she roughly brushed his hands away. How could she have been so blind? Such a naïve fool? Of course they were lovers. His arrogant attitude should have warned her that he was accustomed to having any woman he desired, just for the asking.

It was painfully obvious that he had tired of Suzanne, and was ready to discard her like yesterday's stale bread and start anew with her. What a fool she had been. She mounted her horse and raced from the clearing, without a farewell to either of them.

A dark scowl crossed Joshua's handsome features as he watched Suzanne's dripping body leave the water and amble slowly toward him. She eased her slippery arms around his neck and pressed her wet, naked curves against him, as she attempted to pull his lips down to hers. Having had his fill of her insatiable lust, Joshua pushed her away more roughly than he had intended.

"Is there a problem, darling?" she whispered, wanting nothing more than to feel him deep inside her. "I knew you would appreciate me getting rid of *Little Miss Prude* so we could be alone." She reached for him, only to be left frustrated when Joshua once again sidestepped her intended embrace. "It has been such a long time, Joshua. I know you are as eager for my touch as I am yours."

"Appreciate it?" he stormed incredulously. "Appreciate the fact that you behaved like a common whore?"

"Whore?" Her face flamed as she took a step back, as though she had been struck. "If I behave like a whore, it is because you made me one."

"Not by a long shot, Suzanne. Your wares had been sampled long before I sailed into your life," Joshua was determined to set the record straight. "I was but one on a long list of many."

Suzanne's cheeks grew red as her outraged gasp echoed across the water.

With Joshua's temper somewhat abated, his voice softened with the hope that they could end the affair on amicable terms. "While it was enjoyable for us both while it lasted, our little fling is over."

"Fling? What are you saying? Over? You can't mean that. You love me, Joshua. I know you do. Why, I have been patiently awaiting a proposal of marriage."

"Marriage?" Of all the fool notions. "You were dreadfully mistaken, Suzanne. I never promised you anything other than a good time, and unless I miss my guess, I have fulfilled my end of the bargain."

With rising despair, Suzanne watched him mount his steed and ride away, leaving her naked, dripping, and humiliated beyond words. He was leaving her to go in search of his little trollop no doubt. Lynna had ruined everything.

Suzanne closed her eye, and visualized Joshua's hands roaming over the slut's more ample curves, while whispering sweet words of devotion. That must never happen.

She would not lose Joshua, especially to poor white trash like Lynna. Why, the penniless waif wouldn't have a single coin to fill a dowry with which to bring to her marriage. Besides, Joshua was the only man in her entire life that Suzanne had ever truly coveted. She refused to give him up without a fight.

Lynna arrived home completely distraught, and unobserved. She was able to slip quietly into her room and throw herself on the bed as she silently gazed out the window, missing her father to the point of tears.

It was over an hour later, when Suzanne came bouncing in the house with a satisfied smirk, and made her way straight to Lynna's room to gloat.

"Lynna, why on earth did you leave in such a fired up tizzy?"

Lynna could only glare at her, unable to hide her disgust. "I saw no reason to stay and watch you degrade yourself."

"Degrade myself?" Suzanne's laughter was keen as she waltzed around the room. "You never cease to amaze me, Lynna. Why, I didn't feel degraded at all, quite the contrary. By the way, you have perfect timing. After you left, Joshua joined me for a swim. Then, we lay in the sun to… um… dry."

"Are you saying that you paraded around in front of him without your clothes?" Lynna tried to conceal her shock, as nothing Suzanne did should surprise her anymore.

"Lynna, dear, when will you lose your childhood naivete and realize that it's difficult to satisfy a man, especially one as lusty as my Joshua, while still fully clothed. A real man likes to see what he has in his hands."

Lynna was appalled by her words. "Suzanne, your behavior is like that of a common whore in the red light district. I can't believe you have so little respect for yourself."

Suzanne's hands clenched tightly by her sides, and her breathing became shallow as Lynna called her the very same slur Joshua had used earlier. It would never do for the harlot to see how upset she was. She must convince Lynna that she and Joshua had spent the better part of the afternoon happily ensconced in each other's arms. "Respect is boring, Lynna. I choose to spend my life in pursuit of more amorous endeavors. With a man like Joshua, what more could a girl ask for?"

Suzanne began to undress, shedding her gorgeous day dress in a careless heap on the floor. "He was magnificent today, by the way. I would have been happy to remain in his strong arms until morning." She picked up her dress with a contented sigh, and headed toward her room in her chemise. "I'm going to take a nap now. Joshua insists that I meet him by the pond again tonight, and I have no intention of disappointing him. The man simply cannot get his fill of me."

As Suzanne closed the door, Lynna could summon only pity for the girl. She sympathized with anyone foolish enough to fall in love with the likes of Joshua Jordan.

Chapter 15

The following afternoon, as the birthday celebration was in full swing, the front door slammed and all eyes turned to see a glowing Suzanne traipse into the room. Lynna's heart sank as she witnessed her satisfied smile.

"You almost missed your nieces' party," Beth chided her thoughtless sister in law.

"I take it you found Joshua," Samuel remarked.

Without sparing one glance for her adorable niece, who had somehow smeared birthday cake into every single strand of her hair, Suzanne turned to Lynna with an expression of pure bliss. "Actually, we found each other."

When everyone's attention had returned to the birthday girl, Suzanne leaned close to Lynna's ear to whisper, "Come to my room."

When she could slip away, Lynna climbed the stairs with mounting dread. Why did the thought of Suzanne and Joshua together rip at her heart?

When she entered the bedchamber, Suzanne rushed to close the door and flung herself on the bed. As if in a trance, she fabricated a detailed lie solely for Lynna's benefit, and reveled in the immense pain she knew it would cause her lovesick nemesis.

"I was riding by the river this afternoon, daydreaming about which material to choose for the next ballgown you will make me. I had just gotten to the bodice, and was debating over whether it should have lace trim, ribbon, or batting, when I noticed Joshua repairing a fence. I quietly slipped from my horse and went to join him. Honestly, almost before I knew what was happening, he was pulling me into his arms and kissing me like a man starved. Why, to be honest, even I was shocked by his ravenous behavior, especially since we've been together practically every night for the past two months."

"I could care less what you and Joshua do, Suzanne." Lynna used her most convincing tone, when they both knew she was lying through her teeth.

"Oh, Lynna, he was so forceful. I love nothing more than being wrapped in his strong arms, but today he was just so... so... Joshua." Suzanne clutched a feather pillow to her breast. "I am convinced the man is madly in love with me. He could never make love to me with such passion if he wasn't."

"Of course he could." The words left her lips before Lynna even realized she had spoken them out loud. "Any man could."

"You're just jealous," Suzanne spat, leaping from the bed to stand before her with eyes blazing. "You always have been. You want Joshua for yourself, everyone knows that. Why, a blind person could see it, but take these words to heart. You will never take him from me."

Lynna opened the door to leave, feeling nothing but pity for the besotted girl, yet she refused to make her exit without one parting shot. "I imagine the field hands heard your little display of temper, Suzanne, but be advised of one simple truth." She had taken so much abuse and insult from Suzanne over the past three years, now she had the perfect opportunity for a little payback and she was actually angry enough to mete it out. "Consider yourself fortunate, because we both know that *if* I wanted your Captain Jordan, I could easily have him."

With that said, she casually strolled from the room, having finally succeeded in delivering to Suzanne her comeuppance and, for once, leaving her at a loss for words.

Lynna's eyes flew open as her aunt shook her from an afternoon nap. "Lynna, honey, wake up. Captain Jordan was here with an invitation for dinner."

"What? Why, we cannot possibly attend a dinner at his... house." Just the thought of spending an evening with the man caused her entire being to quake. How could her betraying body react in such a way, when she knew him to be nothing more than a heartless philanderer who used women, then tossed them aside without a care? She had no intention of becoming his next conquest. "You go ahead without me, please. I don't feel up to visiting today. I would rather remain here, and keep Bethany Breanne entertained."

"Nonsense." Judith's hand on her face forced Lynna to meet her eyes. "Your chances are as good as Suzanne's, probably even better."

"Aunt Judith, what on earth are you prattling on about?" Surely, she had not heard her correctly. "What chances?" She slowly sat up to rub the sleep from her eyes and wonder if perhaps she dreaming. Her aunt could not possibly know her true feelings, could she?

"Why, Captain Jordan, of course." Judith grinned broadly as she reached into the armoire. "He is a very handsome man, dear, and I've seen the way your eyes light up at the mere mention of his name. No one can deny his attraction to you either." Judith brought out a lovely gown of peach silk and carefully spread it across the bed. "If you want him go after him, and don't let anyone stand in your way."

By anyone, did she mean Suzanne? "I don't... want him, Aunt Judith."

"Of course you do, darling, any woman would," Judith countered stubbornly. "Now hurry, before your bath water grows tepid."

Lynna replayed her aunt's shocking words over and over in her mind as she soaked in a hot tub.

Afterward, she sat at her dressing table and brushed her hair until it shone, still unsure as to how to style it. She pulled it atop her head and tied it loosely with a velvet ribbon. That should do. On impulse, she added a small amount of kohl to her eyelids and gazed at her reflection in the mirror. What was she doing? She must truly be mad.

She slipped into a sheer lacy chemise after completing her toilette. Next, she stepped into the peach colored gown trimmed with ecru lace that she and her aunt had only recently completed. The delicate folds of material enhanced her every curve.

When she was satisfied with her appearance, she knocked on the adjoining door to her aunt's room. "Aunt Judith, would you fasten my gown, please?"

Would you fasten my gown, please? Those remembered words took her back to the cabin on the

Windjammer, and left her shaken.

Judith and Lynna descended the staircase together, greeted by a chorus of whistles from Daniel and Samuel. "I must say, you ladies look ravishing."

"Are there any compliments left for your own sister?" Suzanne floated down the stairs in a cloud of gold chiffon. Her hair was also pinned atop her head, but unlike Lynna's shimmering curls, Suzanne's raven locks were straight and refused to hold curl, lacking the added effect of the short bouncy tendrils falling to softly accentuate her face. Brilliant emeralds dripped from her ears, as she gloated in the knowledge that she would outshine Lynna one way or another.

As Silas and Mary joined them, Daniel asked, "Father, would you agree that we have the pleasure of escorting four of the loveliest ladies in all of Charleston tonight?"

Daniel smiled bravely for Lynna's benefit, but Suzanne knew his soul was tortured. She recalled their conversation from earlier in the day as they sat on the verandah sipping sweet tea.

"Of course, you realize that Joshua has developed an apparent infatuation for Lynna, don't you, Daniel?"

Daniel failed to respond, choosing to focus on the swirling tea leaves in his glass.

"Believe me, the fact leaves me quite mystified, when he could have me instead. I'm sure his choice leaves you as puzzled as it does me, dear brother. Nonetheless, if you continue to behave like such an incompetent wimp, Joshua will succeed in

snatching Lynna out from under your nose, leaving us both in the cold."

"Nonsense, son," Silas was saying. "Their beauty encompasses the entire South."

"What about me?" Beth's musical laughter drifted from the top of the stairs. "I distinctly heard you say the four loveliest ladies, Daniel Fletcher." As she descended the stairs, she counted off the ladies of the house on her fingers. As she neared Silas, he shammed for her ears only, "You, Beth, are by far my most lovely daughter-in-law."

"Well, thank you kindly, sir," Beth beamed at the compliment.

Their laughter flowed like water through a stream as the ladies draped lacy shawls over their shoulders, and the gentlemen helped them into the waiting carriage.

"I am your only daughter-in-law," Beth squealed, as she realized the jest.

Lynna sat in a corner of the carriage and twiddled her thumbs nervously, until Beth announced, "This is where our land ends and Jordan land begins."

The boundary was evidenced by a white fence bordering the road on both sides, and winding through woods that soon gave way to snowy fields of King Cotton. Beyond the fields could be seen a wide avenue of live oaks festooned with Spanish moss.

The view through the trees was breathtaking, as both sides of the road featured small ponds bordered by towering cypress and gaily colored flowers. An enchanting bridge with lattice work sides rose over the water. At the end of each bridge, nestled in the shade, sat a charming gazebo with the same wood carvings as the bridge.

Lynna was duly impressed by the pure and simple elegance surrounding her. Then Sea Grove, with its huge white pillars and elegant landscape loomed proudly before her.

❧ *Chapter 16* ❧

The house was magnificent, with the upper balcony spanning the entire length so that each room opened onto it. While Lynna had expected a home on a much smaller scale, Sea Grove was a plantation to rival Magnolia House.

Her scrutiny of the house was halted abruptly when she observed the chiseled features of a man casually leaning against one of the columns on the verandah. He was unspeakably handsome in his fawn cut-away tailcoat over a crisp white linen shirt and form fitting breeches. He stood next to a man in a chair with wheels, with a blanket draped over his lap.

As the carriage drew up to the verandah, on closer examination she found the man in the chair to be a slightly more mature version of his son, with the same sea green eyes and mischievous grin.

"Good evening," Joshua called, bounding down the steps to greet them. "I'm glad you could come on such short notice. Meet my parents, Jeremiah and Patricia, and my baby sister Malinda."

"Oh, Joshua," his sister groaned. "I'm hardly a baby."

The family trait was strong in Malinda as well. Her curly black hair framed an oval face that had been blessed with creamy magnolia skin, while a light powdering of freckles across her nose gave her a charming and youthful appearance.

"Welcome to Sea Grove," Jeremiah

announced, after the introductions had been made. "Please, come inside."

As Joshua pushed his father's chair, Lynna took the opportunity to take a closer look at his parents. If not for a few wrinkles and grey hair, Jeremiah could have easily been mistaken for Joshua's brother.

His mother Patricia was an elegant lady with snowy white hair braided and pinned atop her head, and the same creamy smooth complexion as her daughter. "We are so glad you could join us this evening." Her smile was welcoming as she took the ladies' wraps and handed them to the downstairs maid. "Malinda, please show our guests to the parlor."

Malinda hooked her arm through Lynna's as though they had been confidants all their lives, and theirs was an immediate friendship. Malinda had no desire to become friends with the uppity Suzanne, who was her complete opposite. "Joshua has told me so much about you over the years, Lynna. I do hope we can find time to get better acquainted before you return to Georgia."

"I would be delighted." Why would Joshua speak to his sister about her, for years? "I'm afraid you have Suzanne and I confused. She has known your brother for some time, whereas I only met him a… few days ago." She refused to meet Malinda's eyes as she told the lie. "I'm certain it was her, and not me, your brother spoke of."

"Perhaps," Malinda whispered with a sly wink, which infuriated Suzanne as she strained to eavesdrop on their every word. Luckily, she missed the important ones.

Malinda opened the massive double doors, with a beautiful fanlight spanning the entire width. When Lynna entered the spacious foyer, she paused to admire the stunning interior.

On both sides of the hallway stood twin staircases, with finely carved mahogany banisters and handrails inlaid with brass. In the center of the house, the floor to the second story ceiling was open, airy, and cool.

"The house is magnificent," she breathed.

"What?" Malinda questioned. "Oh, the house, thank you." It was obvious that she was accustomed to this reaction from first time visitors.

The parlor was no less attractive. The walls were light blue with dark blue trim. Two rosewood sofas upholstered in regal blue faced each other in front of a marble fireplace. On the mantle, stood miniature statues carved from ivory, jade, bone and crystal. Displayed prominently over the mantle was a gilt and wood bull's eye mirror, and hanging on either side of it were beautifully done oil portraits of Joshua's mother, with each of her children.

Lynna took a seat in one of the overstuffed wingchairs, and was once again caught completely off guard by Joshua's bold behavior when he moved behind her to rest his hand possessively on the back of her chair. She glanced anxiously toward Daniel, but if he took offense he concealed it well. Not so Suzanne. Her body went rigid as she planted a shoulder against the wall, and her cold eyes never once lost their keen focus on Joshua's hand.

While the men discussed the price of cotton and politics, the ladies chatted about the weather and fashion, Suzanne's favorite topic, although she chose to remain curiously silent.

It would have been a pleasant conversation had Joshua's hand not rested so near. Lynna was noticeably ill at ease with his close proximity, going as rigid as Suzanne when his hand drifted down to finger a golden curl.

Joshua's hand itched, almost ached, to travel down to the swells of her creamy bosom displayed so enticingly from his vantage point. Again, he had been on the verge of throwing caution to the wind and smoothing a finger across her delicate skin. When the part he coveted was unceremoniously snatched from view, as Lynna moved forward to perch on the edge of her chair.

She wondered how this man's slightest touch could scorch her skin, when Daniel's most passionate kiss failed to stir the slightest response. She took time to ponder this question at length, but could find no answer to the burning question. She was greatly relieved when the maid announced that dinner was served, and since she had been grossly manhandled for what seemed like the last hour, she turned to present Joshua with a withering glare.

He chuckled, and ignored her little display of temper as he pushed his father's chair into the dining room.

She came to the conclusion that the fates were against her when she found herself seated next to the insolent rogue at dinner, but why blame the fates? This was Joshua's home, of course he would have a hand in the seating arrangements.

During the course of the meal, everyone sipped sweet tea and enjoyed lively banter with the person seated next to them, with the exception of

Lynna. As usual, with Joshua so near, her appetite deserted her.

While the others were involved in witty repartee as they nibbled on hot butter biscuits, Joshua bent to whisper in her ear, "Is something amiss with your food, or could there be something about me that ruins your appetite?"

She arched a delicate brow his way.

"I fear that if you and I were together for any great length of time, you would simply waste away." His gaze fell to her moist lips. "What a terrible loss that would be."

Lynna felt heat radiating from her cheeks, when in barely more than a whisper, she grated, "Sir, you should learn to conduct yourself in a more gentlemanly fashion. You don't know me well enough to make such brash remarks."

"Lynna, my pet, there is little about you that I don't know, intimately." His eyes sparkled as he passed her a covered basket of steaming buttermilk biscuits. "Biscuit?"

With a definite tilt of her pert nose, she took a biscuit and buttered it before dropping it to her plate. She was unsure if her queasy stomach could handle food at the moment, so she took a sip of tea and almost choked when Joshua's thigh brushed against hers.

"Allow me." He patted her back, which was more along the lines of a caress. "Did your tea go down the wrong way?"

Lynna longed to slap the smirk from his smug face. How dare he make such brazen advances and treat her like nothing more than a common lady of the evening.

Would this night ever end?

She bestowed upon him an icy glare that would have put any other man in his place, but not so Joshua, who had the audacity to wink.

The entire length of her body trembled with rage as she turned furious eyes on him. "I will not sit still for your abuse a second longer. If you so much as consider touching me again, you will feel the blade of my butter knife beneath your skin."

It was a harmless threat and Lynna knew it, but she hoped it would be enough to scare him. It didn't. When she held the butter knife in her hand for added conviction, it fell to her plate with a clatter as he threw back his head and laughed uproariously. The insolent rogue wiped a tear from his eye and continued with his meal.

Malinda giggled. "Pay him no mind, Lynna. He has forever been a tease, especially when a woman intrigues him."

Suzanne, who was again listening to their conversation, hated Lynna enough to scratch her eyes out. Joshua had never once teased her.

After a scrumptious dessert of hot apple pie with vanilla ice cream, they took their coffee and brandy to the parlor, where Suzanne refused to suffer through another second of watching Joshua lust after Lynna. With exaggerated weakness, she mewled, "Father, I have developed a simply monstrous headache, and I must ask that we return to Samuel's earlier than planned."

Silas expressed his immediate concern for his daughter's welfare while speaking to Patricia. "While it has been a most enjoyable evening, and we sincerely regret having to leave early, under the circumstances I hope you will understand."

"Of course we do," Patricia assured him, as she turned to take Suzanne's hands. "I hope you feel better soon, dear."

"Thank you," Suzanne simpered. "I'm sure I will feel much better tomorrow." *Or whenever Lynna decides to go back to where she came from.*

"If you're ever in Georgia, feel free to stop by Magnolia House for a visit," Silas issued the invitation to Jeremiah and Patricia. "You are always welcome."

"That's very kind of you, and we just might take you up on your offer," Jeremiah replied. "However, our son does the majority of traveling in the family."

Silas repeated the invitation to Joshua. "You are more than welcome to visit, anytime."

"Thank you, sir. I feel certain that I can find time for a visit soon." As his eyes strayed toward Lynna, everyone in the room felt certain that his visit would be in the not too distant future.

Outside in the dark night, Joshua assisted the ladies into their carriage. With his hands on Lynna's waist, he couldn't resist the impulse to allow his hands to linger.

In truth, Lynna's body turned to a mass of quivering flesh and her heart threatened to fly out of her chest, but he must never know how his touch affected her.

"What was that?" Mary questioned, as a slapping sound rang out in the still night air.

"Damn mosquitoes." Joshua chuckled, rubbing his stinging jaw. To be so petite, the little lady packed a wallop. "They're out for blood tonight." Even though it was too dark to see, Joshua could imagine Lynna's enchanting face beaming triumphantly in the still night.

He was absolutely correct. She leaned back in her seat with a satisfied smile, and felt entirely vindicated.

Upon their return to Cedar Hill, they were met with a messenger from Magnolia House. Jake Almond, the overseer, had taken ill and they must return at once. Their bags were packed that night, to be ready to set out on their journey home at first light.

Chapter 17

The group of weary travelers arrived home late, and exhausted. Lynna crawled under the covers shortly after she walked in the front door, feeling extremely happy to be home. She had just dozed off, when she was jerked awake by a loud voice, and one she recognized immediately. Her uncle was home, and as usual he was sloppy drunk.

"I told you, Tobias, I don't have any money," she heard her aunt Judith cry. "Please lower your voice before you wake Lynna."

"You always keep money hid around here somewhere, you lying bitch," Tobias slurred.

"Even if I did, I wouldn't give it to you to waste on rot gut whiskey."

"I will eventually find it, so save us both the trouble and tell me where you hid it."

"Don't you understand that we need that money to live, Tobias?"

Lynna heard a dull thud, and knew her aunt had been struck. She leapt from the bed and ran to the kitchen with lightning speed, to find Tobias holding Judith against the wall with his hands around her throat as he squeezed the life from her.

"Let her go!" Lynna screamed, grabbing him by the hair and pulling and kicking until he released her.

Judith collapsed to the floor with a sickly white pallor, and before Lynna could even attempt to defend herself, Tobias unleashed the full force of his fury on her.

In an attempt to dodge the blow that she knew was coming, she unwittingly backed into the table and was cornered. Tobias stood before her with a sinister grin, making sure she had time to fear what was coming before his fist smashed under her right eye with a painful crunch. The last thing she remembered, before the floor jumped up to greet her, was the look of absolute horror on her aunt's bloodless face, but at least she was alive.

When Lynna came to, with a pulsating headache that hammered in her temples, Judith was holding her head in her lap and sobbing pitifully. Her tears fell in earnest when Lynna at last opened bruised and swollen eyes.

"Is he gone?" Lynna gingerly felt around her puffy face to see if any bones were broken.

"He found my reticule and took what few coins we had. I pray he rots in hell for the pain he has caused you."

"My pain? What about your pain?" she cried, as she struggled to sit up, and winced at the throbbing pain the effort caused. "How badly did he hurt you?"

"He only shoved me against the wall and choked me, nothing out of the ordinary. It's you that I'm worried about." Judith tilted Lynna's face to the light for a better look. "You have a dreadful bruise, darling."

"I'll remain inside until it fades, nothing new there. We have so much work to do, I wouldn't be spending much time outside anyway, but look on the bright side. We won't have to worry about him returning for at least a fortnight."

Judith couldn't hide her overwhelming shame. "Please, forgive me for allowing this to happen to you, darling. I should have protected you. If your father knew…"

"Aunt Judith, you mustn't blame yourself, when neither of us could have stopped him. You can't reason with Tobias when he's drunk, and my father would never hold you accountable for someone else's sins."

That was a lie and they both recognized it as such. Nathan Rhodes would indeed fault his sister if he knew of her husband's vicious abuse toward his daughter, and heaven help Tobias Mathison if he ever found out.

Judith swiped at a tear as it streaked down her wet cheek. "Maybe he will take his ill-gotten gains and never come back."

Sadly, it was a known fact that Tobias would return the minute his stolen funds were exhausted.

Lynna didn't feel up to going through the motions of getting dressed the following morning, not when her body ached with each movement, and why bother? She wouldn't be showing her face outside the house for days.

So she spent the day in bed, wondering why her father hadn't sent funds, as promised. There was simply no excuse for his failure to do so. He was fabulously wealthy. Surely, he could spare a few coins to make life easier for his sister and only child.

Lynna forced her mind from the pain that thinking about her father caused, and slipped on a lavender and green checkered dress. She ambled barefoot into the kitchen, grinning sheepishly when her aunt gasped at her black and blue face.

"I look a fright, don't I?" She covered her face with her hands in hopes of hiding her disgusting appearance.

Before Judith was forced to tell a lie, a knock sounded at the open kitchen door. Luckily, Lynna's back was to the door as she silently pleaded with her aunt to send whoever it was away. Every ounce of blood drained from her face when she heard her aunt say, "Good morning, Captain Jordan. It's wonderful to see you again. When did you arrive?"

"Good morning, ladies." Joshua's voice floated through the open doorway. "I arrived last night, shortly before midnight."

"What brings you out and about so early on this fine morning?"

"Silas invited me to ride into town with him. At breakfast, he mentioned he was coming to see if you ladies needed supplies from the general store, so I volunteered to come in his stead."

"How very kind of you. As a matter of fact, we do need a few provisions. "Please come…" The loud clanging of a pot hitting the floor stopped Judith short. She had almost invited him in. "Please, have a seat on the… porch. I will be right back with my list."

Lynna stood motionless as she waited to hear the porch swing creak, a signal that he had sat down. It didn't come, which meant he was standing at the door.

Had her aunt suddenly gone mad? Why hadn't she sent him away posthaste, when nothing from town could be so important? Besides, did she forget Tobias had stolen all their coins last night, and she had never once known Judith to purchase on credit.

"Good morning, Lynna," came the sexy southern drawl that never failed to send her blood racing.

When she opened her mouth, no words were forthcoming.

"Why are you behaving like a spoiled child, Lynna?" When she didn't answer, he strode uninvited into the kitchen, pausing behind her for only a second before turning her around to face him.

He halted abruptly as the shock registered on his face and he struggled to gather his wits about him. "Who did this, Lynna?"

She attempted to shrug off his concern. "Clumsy me, I ran into a door. I should have brought a candle outside with me last night when I went to sit on the porch."

Where was her aunt, and why was she dawdling at a time like this?

Joshua's brow creased as he perused her face closely. "Are you sure? That's a nasty bruise. You had to be walking at full speed to hit the door hard enough to leave a bruise that large and discolored."

She shrugged. "Of course, I'm sure."

Joshua was far from convinced as he angled her face to get a better look. "I fail to see how colliding with a door could cause the entire side of your face to turn a deep shade of black and purple, and your eye to be almost swollen shut."

"It looks much worse than it actually is." Of all times for him to show up, when she must look like one of the voodoo zombies the servants were always whispering about.

"Try walking with your eyes open in the future," he whispered, intoxicated by the lilac fragrance of her hair. "It works amazingly well. I do it all the time."

Lynna opened her mouth for a sharp retort that died in her throat when Judith entered the kitchen. "On second thought, we don't need anything from town, but thank you for asking, Joshua."

"My pleasure, ma'am." He pasted on a fake smile, even though his cheerful mood had deserted him on first sight of Lynna's battered face. Something was off kilter here, and he intended to find out exactly what it was.

When Lynna finally heard the sound of his boots echoing down the porch steps, she sat at the kitchen table and massaged her temples, truly bereft. "Why did he have to show up this morning? Look at my face." She buried her head in her hands. "He thinks I go around walking into doors."

"You are still beautiful in Captain Jordan's eyes," Judith assured her. "It was obvious to one and all the night you met, that he was quite taken with you. I'll wager that you have never met a man quite like him before."

Believe me, Aunt Judith, I have.

"I won't deny it," her aunt called from her bedroom. "I think your Captain Jordan is quite exceptional, and there are few to equal him."

"My Captain Jordan?" Lynna cried, thoroughly astonished by her aunt's choice of words.

Judith peered around the doorframe. "Would you rather I say Suzanne's Captain Jordan?"

Although the day was frightfully hot, her question sent a chill down Lynna's spine that caused her to shiver.

Few women, young or old, could long stay immune to Joshua's masculine charms, and Jasmine was no exception. Joshua had totally charmed the cook during his brief stay at Magnolia House. She was lifting a heavy pot of vegetable soup from the stove when he entered her kitchen. "Here, let me take that. Don't you have a strong young man to help with the heavy lifting, Jasmine?"

Her plump body shook with mirth. "Mist' Joshua, you sho' is sumphin'. I lifts dis heah pot evah day of my life. Why, I 'spec' I could lift bout much as any man on dis heah plan'ation. Now you jus' sit down rite chere an' have some of my blackberry cobbler wit' frash cream."

"I'm sure you could, Jasmine, but my point is that you shouldn't have to."

Never one to be accused of being gullible, Jasmine motioned for him to sit. "Whut is you in heah tryin' ta sweet talk ole Jasmine fo', Mist' Joshua?"

"Why, Jasmine, I'm sorely disappointed in you. I thought we were friends."

"We sho' 'nuff is, but you done got sumphin' troublin' you, so you mite jus' as well spit it out."

Joshua took a bite of cobbler that had him wishing it could be wrapped and sold at the general store, and asked with all seriousness, "Have you seen Lynna's face today?"

"Whut 'bout her face?" Jasmine was immediately on alert, and fearing the worst as the cup of milk she was pouring overflowed the rim.

Joshua observed her reaction closely. "Her face is badly bruised. She claims to have run into a door."

"Run into a do' my big black behind." Jasmine's

body shook with anger. "Dat chile gwine run out of 'scuses one of dese days."

Joshua was instantly on his feet, grabbing her by the shoulders and forcing her to meet his eyes. "Are you saying that isn't what happened, Jasmine?"

Jasmine was thoughtful for a long time before speaking. "I won't der, so *I* cain say fo' sho' whut done happen."

"But you have an opinion," he said, urging her to continue.

"If you done seed as many bruises on dat chile as I have." She stopped suddenly, wondering if she should be voicing her opinion against a white man. "I done said too much a'ready."

Joshua wanted to shake the older woman and force her to tell him everything she knew, but there were easier ways. "I suppose it's just as she said. Lynna does impress me as being the clumsy sort."

"Whut you mean, clumsy?" Jasmine was not having it. She turned on him with her hands on her hips and her dark eye blazing. Joshua knew his gambit had worked beautifully. "Dat chile ain't run into no do'. Dat man done hit dat baby agin."

"What man?" The depth of rage Joshua felt in that moment was surprising, even to him. Knowing someone had struck Lynna, with enough force to leave her horribly bruised, caused his blood to boil. "Who was it, Jasmine?"

Jasmine knew she had been duped, but that was no longer the issue. Why should she go on protecting that po' white trash Tobias Mathison, when next time it might be too late to help Lynna? Next time, he might kill both her and Judith. "Her own uncle, Tobias Mat'son, he da one whut beats her. He come home lookin' fo' dey money in a flyin' rage, an' always find a reason to hit my sweet girl."

Hot tears coursed down Jasmine's plump cheeks. "How I knows is dat po' chile done broke down one day an' tol' me so herself. She said she had ta talk to somebody, so I jus' held her while she talk' an' cried, axkin' me why her own uncle hate her so much. Querstions I ain't got no answer fo'. Den, when she finish, she made me give my word dat I keep it to myself, an' here I done tol' you. Forgive me, Lawd!" she cried, stretching her arms to the ceiling and beseeching the heavens.

Feeling somewhat better after her come to Jesus moment, she dried her eyes and blew her nose. "I cain keep it to myself no mo', Mist' Joshua. Dat man gwine kill dat chile one day."

"Where is Tobias now, Jasmine?" Joshua couldn't be still, and paced the room like a caged animal. "I promise he will never get another chance to hurt her, if you tell me where to find him."

"He ain't heah," she sniffled. "Dey ain't be knowin' where he gwine, or when he comin' back."

"I will find him, Jasmine, you have my word." He strode determinedly out the door, without another thought for the mouthwatering pie.

Jasmine knew in her heart that Tobias Mathison was surely about to pay for his multitude of sins, and it was about time. As for her precious Lynna, she mumbled, "Whut don't kill will fatten."

Joshua made inquiries as to Tobias Mathison's whereabouts at the local taverns. He learned from a barkeep that Tobias had come into town the night before, purchased a bottle of whiskey, and went upstairs with one of the barmaids who was known for leaving a man with empty pockets. Joshua was halfway up the stairs as he imagined the thrill of his hands tightening around Tobias's neck, when a loud voice stopped him.

"He ain't here now," the burly barkeep called. "He rode out before sunup."

Joshua slammed his fist into the wall, making the barkeep jump. "Can you tell me which direction he traveled?"

"Naw, he slipped out without even paying what he owed for the room, the thieving low life." The barkeep swished a rag across the bar. "I should have learnt the lying beggar by now. Still, I can't figure him out. One day his pockets are overflowing with coin, and a few days later he can't afford a cup of ale."

Joshua swore under his breath as he left the smoky tavern, "You got away this time, but I will see you pay for your sins if it's the last thing I do on this earth."

✿ Chapter 18 ✿

Lynna remained indoors for the next four days, only venturing outside to stroll through her garden late in the evening when the big house was quiet.

When Daniel stopped by each morning, her aunt reported that she was feeling under the weather and resting in bed.

When the head housekeeper and cook at Magnolia House arrived with Lynna's favorite sugar cookies, Jasmine, being Jasmine, completely ignored Judith's excuses and went straightaway to Lynna's room. She found her sitting in a chair by the window, stitching lace on the bodice of a new ballgown for Suzanne.

"Good morning, Jasmine." Lynna averted her face, horribly ashamed for Jasmine to see that her uncle had once again used it as a punching bag.

"It ain't seem like sech a good mawnin' ta me, wit you in bed all swole up like you is," she muttered angrily. "Why you ain't gone out in dem woods an' got a big stick, an' next time he come at you lay it upside his thick skull, I ain't be knowin'."

Lynna attempted a laugh that failed miserably. "I may heed your advice and do just that, Jasmine."

Judith entered with a fresh pot of coffee. "Please sit down, Jasmine, and we'll sample these cookies that smell simply delicious." She glanced at Lynna, whose cheeks burned with shame and humiliation. "Since Lynna has been confined to this room for days, with only me for company, we're grateful you stopped by."

"This will be my last day of confinement." Lynna took Judith's hand in an attempt to ease her guilt. "The discoloration has almost faded, and look on the bright side, at least we completed Suzanne's ballgown."

"If dat gal was ta take up sewin' an' spend as much time at it as she do primpin' an' paradin' in front of dat mirror, it would put you two out of binness."

"Truer words were never spoken," Judith agreed, causing all three women to grin.

The laughter left Jasmine's eyes as she turned to Lynna with all seriousness. "Y'all needs to tell somebody 'bout Tobias fo' it too late. Dem bruises be gittin' sturdily worser each time he come home. He mean binness now, Lynna, an' fo' some reason he seem ta be takin' mos' of his anger out on you."

The following evening, a rider arrived with an urgent missive from a neighboring plantation owned by Thomas Morehead. A fire had swept through the main house and several cabins. Thomas had perished, and several of his workers had been severely burned. The rider was unsure of how many lives had been lost.

Silas and Daniel took every available man and rushed to the plantation, with Mary and Judith accompanying them to care for the injured.

With her aunt caring for the burn victims at the Morehead plantation, Lynna entered their quiet cottage alone that night. She was overcome by a strong sense of foreboding the second she closed the door behind her.

Something wasn't right.

As she entered the kitchen, her apprehension proved correct. Her uncle sat at the table slouched in a drunken stupor, with an empty whiskey bottle in his hand. She smelled him, a combination of liquor and unwashed body, long before she saw him.

Tobias glanced up with angry, bloodshot eyes. His hand shook as he pointed to the cold stove. "Why ain't you got supper cooking, you lazy good for nothing wench? I been keeping you up for the last three years, and you can't even keep a pot boiling on the stove? Where's my wife?"

"There was a fire. Aunt Judith is at the Morehead plantation helping nurse the injured."

"Well, do something besides spread your legs for Daniel Fletcher and fix me something to eat," he snarled with disgust, showing a mess of rotten teeth.

While the desire to turn tail and run was strong in Lynna, she desperately fought it. It would give him too much satisfaction to watch her cower in fear.

When she failed to respond quickly enough to his demands, Tobias leapt from his chair and sent it crashing to the floor. "Don't just stand there when I tell you to do something, girl, get busy and fix my damn supper."

"Fix your own damn supper," Lynna gritted. She was fed up with his constant demands and abuse. She was beyond disgusted with everything about the drunkard in fact. If he ate tonight, it would be food prepared by his own hand.

For having the impudence to disobey his direct order, Tobias slapped her so hard she stumbled backward and landed hard on her bottom, but this time her aunt wasn't home, and Lynna didn't have to worry about protecting her. She glanced around for a weapon, and spied a sewing basket with a large pair of sharp scissors on the table. Not thinking clearly, she made the grievous error of eyeing the weapon covetously.

Tobias saw where her eyes lingered, and wheezed with harsh laughter before sweeping the basket to the floor and scattering its contents to the other side of the room. "When did you grow a backbone, you little tramp?"

She had to find another weapon, and quick. His empty whiskey bottle was on the table between them, but she refused to look at it. She had no intention of making the same mistake twice. She stood slowly and painfully to her feet. "I have no coin, so you might as well leave."

Tobias licked his lips in a sickening manner as his gaze feasted on her heaving breasts. "I ain't leaving here without some recompense for my journey."

That was all the impetus Lynna needed. She lunged for the bottle to grab it before he could, and swung it toward his head. Whiskey dribbled down her arm as he dodged the bottle.

He threw back his head and laughed manically as he advanced around the table with a wide grin on his pockmarked face. She held up her hands to shield her face as his fist connected with her jaw with such force that she saw stars and nothing more.

Lynna came to in a haze of blinding pain, lying perfectly still and listening for any sign that he was still in the house. When all was quiet, with no creaking floors or the sound of Tobias digging through drawers in search of coins, she stood slowly and grabbed for the wall as the room spun around her. When the vertigo began to ease, she carefully walked to her room and paused before the mirror.

Scalding tears filled her eyes as she leaned in for a close up view of her colorful bruises and grotesquely swollen face. The same face that had stared back at her too many times in the past. If the truth be told, the bruises from his previous attack had only begun to fade.

Hot tears streaked a path down her puffy cheek as she gave vent to her misery. She was so alone, so frightened, and so miserable, with neither the will nor strength to continue fighting. She wanted to go home to France, where she was pampered and spoiled, and no one would dare lift a hand to her in anger. Home, where Gertrude would be waiting with open arms. Sadly, that was out of the question, since her own father had abandoned her.

She dried her sniffles and remembered her promise to help Jasmine cook blackberry jam the following morning, but she couldn't go to the big house looking like this. No more than she could endure another week of forced confinement.

With the hope of banishing her misery to the back of her mind, if only momentarily, she prepared a hot bath and slipped into the soothing oasis. For the time being, at least, her worries melted away, and she sighed blissfully as the heat penetrated her aching bones.

After soaking in the tub until the water was cold,

she dried off and slipped into a sleeveless pink nightgown that was cut low and gathered under her breast. It was too hot for anything else.

While the cotton was soft and cool against her tender skin as it enveloped her abused body, it did nothing for the sorry state of her mind. She felt herself being swallowed by a bottomless despair as she brushed her hair until it fell in rippling waves over her shoulders.

By the time she went to bed, feeling miserable and defeated, she had convinced herself that the only way to put an end to a wretched existence where Tobias came and went as he pleased, was to wed Daniel Fletcher. She would never be lonely again. Daniel loved her, and as he had told her so many times in the past, she would grow to love him, given time.

If she married Daniel, she could move her aunt into the big house, where Tobias could never torment either of them again. The Fletchers would hire another seamstress, leaving her aunt Judith to enjoy her golden years in peace. It was the perfect solution.

Lynna closed her eyes, not blissfully happy at the notion, but satisfied that she had arrived at a decision that would be beneficial for all concerned.

At some point during the night, she was startled from a deep sleep by a noise that came from *inside* the house. Fear gnawed at her gut as a cool breeze fluttered the curtains, and she prayed it was the sound that had awakened her.

Had her uncle really left, or was he hiding, and waiting for her to fall asleep? She stuck one foot out of the cover as she prepared to run. When she reached for the kitchen knife she had placed on the bedside table, she heard a flint strike, and candlelight illuminated the room.

Joshua.

She inhaled sharply to find him standing over her, holding a candle with a look of stark horror.

What was he doing here?

"I had a feeling that you needed me. Tell me who did this." His voice was cold as ice, and filled with venom. "That's all I ask of you, Lynna. Please, just tell me who did this to you."

She couldn't tell him the truth, no matter how much pain her uncle had caused her. She knew Joshua would search heaven and hell until he found her uncle, and end his deplorable life. For this, she would be grateful beyond measure, as she felt nothing but hatred for her uncle. What she couldn't risk, was watching Joshua rot in a filthy jail cell for avenging her.

"Lynna," he spoke softly, too softly. "Please tell me."

"I can't," she cried brokenly. "Please, don't ask me."

Joshua almost confessed that he knew her uncle was her abuser, only stopping short when he realized the humiliation it would cause her. He vowed to find the deviant, and take great pleasure in watching his life's blood drain away. If he departed immediately, perhaps he could find Tobias before he left the taverns.

While he had but one objective in mind, his stern resolve immediately deserted him upon hearing her softly whisper his name.

"Don't leave me alone, Joshua," she pleaded. "I

beg you to just hold me."

When he witnessed the tears on her bruised and swollen cheeks, he placed the candle on the bedside table and gently drew her into his arms. She shrank from the pain his gentle touch caused as he brushed away her tears, yet she never complained.

His heart went out to the beautiful girl who had withstood so much abuse, blaming himself for a portion of her pain. He was overwhelmed by the love and tenderness he felt for her, and lay down beside her, gently nudging her head to rest on his chest.

Lynna sighed blissfully, and nestled deeper into the security of his strong arms where she felt safe and protected. No harm could befall her as long as these arms held her close. If she married Daniel tomorrow, at least she would have this night to remember.

Joshua knew what would happen if he stayed, but he wondered if she was fully aware of the consequences of her actions. "Are you asking me to stay, Lynna?"

"Yes, Joshua." As she raised her head to meet his eyes, she had to wonder if she would survive another attack from Tobias. Jasmine was right, his attacks were escalating. "I can't be alone tonight."

Joshua needed no more encouragement as he gathered her close. "You are safe now, my love. No one will hurt you ever again, I swear."

She buried her head against his broad chest and sobbed until his whispered words soothed the chaos in her mind. When she lifted her face, their lips met in a kiss that left her breathless.

As her pain and humiliation were slowly pushed to the shadows, she permitted her mind to fill with the nearness of him, the smell, and feel of him.

Joshua wrapped his arms around her as he pressed her against his hard body, giving her one last chance to change her mind. "Are you certain this is what you want, Lynna?" He didn't want her to have regrets, or throw his actions in his face come morning.

She slipped her hands around his neck and pulled his lips down to hers, leaving no doubt in his mind of what she desired. "Love me, Joshua."

"You don't know how I have longed to hear you say those words. " His tongue explored every cranny of her mouth, lighting fires in her stomach that warmed her entire body. He had waited so long to feel her supple flesh against his, and had suffered through frequent dreams of his hands and lips roaming over her delectable curves until he physically ached. Still, she was a virgin, and he must go easy and not frighten her. With a strength of will that he didn't know he possessed, he forced himself to proceed slowly.

As he slipped the thin nightgown over her head, the sight of her full, satiny breasts were almost his undoing. His eyes closed blissfully as she leaned her head back, unaware of the world going on around them, aware only of each other and the intense desire they shared.

He gently kneaded her breasts as he watched the play of emotions, the doubt that registered briefly, then the wonderment on her angelic face. He banked his own desire, wanting her first time to be perfect.

Lynna watched, barely able to breathe as his mouth sprinkled light kisses on the tender underside of her breast, down over her flat stomach, and over the sloping curve of her hip. The sweet torture was almost unbearable, when at last his lips kissed their way back to a rigid nipple.

His touch caused the fire in her stomach to shift to a throbbing ache that demanded release as his tongue danced hot circles around the tender nub. Her body went limp as the creamy skin on her neck flushed, and she gave vent to her rising lust.

Joshua raised up on his elbow, and at the sight of so much raw passion surging through her, he knew he could deny himself no longer. He allowed his eyes to travel over her slowly, getting his fill of her curvaceous beauty before lowering his mouth to hers.

Low moans of pleasure slipped from Lynna's throat as he trailed hot kisses over her skin. She arched her back as his lips brought a return of the ecstasy she remembered so well, and ignited the all-consuming fire that had simmered since the night on the *Windjammer*.

Their eyes met, and Joshua gave her a knowing smile as she reached for him, desperate to feel him inside her. He lowered his body, careful not to put his entire weight on her slender frame. Then his lips found hers, and she opened her body and soul to receive him.

He entered her slowly, savoring her sleek moist warmth until he met with her maidenhead. He gazed down into her trusting eyes, waiting for final proof that she believed him.

"I will never doubt you again," she whispered.

He wanted her more than he had ever wanted any woman in his life, but she was making him forget his purpose, which was revenge on Tobias Mathison.

He was quick to decide that he could place it on hold for a few hours, while he took this enchanted creature's mind off her troubles. He placed his hands underneath her and cupped Lynna's buttocks, pressing his full manhood into her silky warmth as she cried out in pain.

Her cries quickly subsided as she raised her hips to meet his, thrust for thrust, more urgent still, until her body once again found the sweet release it so coveted. As her muscles convulsed around him, Joshua knew he had succeeded in making her forget, for now.

"You are in my blood, Lynna, and I will never get my fill of you. I want you with me now and forever."

Happiness swelled within her at his words. He wanted her with him, forever?

That could only mean one thing.

Joshua held her cradled against his chest as moonlight filtered through the open window, casting a golden hue over their glistening bodies. Lynna sighed contentedly, nestling closer to the man who rekindled the simmering fire. She felt no shame or remorse, only love.

Love?

The realization struck her like a bolt of lightning from the heavens. She loved him. He was the man she had been waiting for all along. He was a part of her, and had been for the past three years.

"Come back to Charleston with me," he breathed against her heated flesh, as his lips caressed her bare shoulder. "I won't leave you here to be assaulted by a madman."

Without thinking, she said, "He won't return tonight."

"Who won't return? Tell me, Lynna, please."

"I can't." She turned away in shame. "Please, don't ask me."

Why she felt the need to protect the low life scum was beyond Joshua's scope of understanding, but he would not pressure her, not after what she had been through. She had her reasons for keeping secrets, so he had no choice but to wait until she was ready to reveal them.

He lifted a wisp of golden hair to twirl around his finger, and rubbed the curl against his cheek as he breathed in the fragrance of lilacs. He fancied that he could look right through the clear blue mirrors of her eyes and see into her very soul, to discover her every emotion. Along with her small perfect nose and inviting lips, her features formed a face that was destined to forever haunt him.

Joshua rolled to his back and pulled her atop him. "Sleep now, my love."

She did as she was told, and drifted into a contented sleep as her fingers entwined in his raven locks.

He watched her as she slept, lightly touching the darkening purple bruise that was so vivid against her delicate skin. A murderous fury assailed him as he imagined the great joy he would derive from returning each and every blow the devious monster had inflicted on her.

When Joshua at last closed his eyes, it was not the peaceful sleep of the one he held so close, instead it was a fitful sleep. He was squandering time. He

should be on the road searching for Tobias, yet the
desire to be with Lynna was stronger. Her drew her
ever closer as he breathed a contented sigh, and slept.

Dawn was fast approaching when the lovers
awakened in each other's arms. Joshua was
understandably wary, wondering if the morning sun
would bring about a shift in her feelings. His worries
were for naught, since Lynna felt secure in the
knowledge that they would soon be betrothed, and
she had never been happier.

Watching him watch her for several minutes, she
moistened her lips, threw one leg over his hip, and
climbed provocatively atop him. Joshua held his
breath as her tempting mouth lowered to his,
realizing the little minx was enjoying her newly
minted power over him. She was a fast learner,
having changed from a hesitant young girl to a
woman in full bloom overnight, and very much
aware of her needs.

Joshua had felt a slight aversion to forward
women in the past, not so with Lynna. He would
gladly lay passive, if possible, while she took
complete control. He wanted everything she had to
give, and then some.

After a long lingering kiss, while rubbing the
tips of her breasts against his chest until he thought
he might go mad with desire, she moved to her side
and pulled him to face her. A teasing smile curved
her lips as she draped her right leg over his hip and
pressed her soft flesh against his. A white hot fire
ignited low in his stomach when she reached a cool
hand to guide him into her dewy body. He entered
her slowly, hearing her moan softly as he buried deep

inside her.

Lynna's hips moved in the age-old rhythm of love, carrying Joshua almost to the brink. Still, he wanted more. He eased her onto her back and rolled atop her to penetrate more fully, as she moved to meet his every thrust. There was no time for words as their bodies joined, carrying them to a magical place of enchanted bliss.

Chapter 19

After a brief nap, Lynna snuggled against Joshua and draped her leg over his hip.

"Do you never get enough?" he inquired insolently.

"Do I hear complaints?" she inquired just as insolently, leaning over to suck his bottom lip into her mouth and cause a rush of blood to his groin.

"Never, my love. While I am ready and most definitely willing, in order to remain able, my body may soon require sustenance." Joshua chuckled, and lifted her to sit exactly where he wanted her.

Lynna was quite content with the seating arrangement.

She was in the kitchen washing breakfast dishes when they heard a carriage approach. "It's my aunt Judith," she cried. "Quickly, Joshua, go out the back door before she catches us."

He placed a soft kiss on her lips that only left her wanting more, and was closing the door behind him when Judith called out a greeting.

"Lynna, I'm home, darling. It was so horrible at the Morehead plantation, you would not believe… oh, dear God!" Judith's hands flew to her mouth in horror. "When was he here?"

How did she know?

"Oh, you poor dear," her aunt cried. "Let me look at your face."

Heavenly days, her aunt was referring to Tobias, when she had all but forgotten the incident. "It isn't as bad as it looks. It should heal quickly."

"When was Tobias here, Lynna?" Judith's features crumbled as she reached for a handkerchief. "My poor, sweet girl."

"He was here to greet me last night when I came home." She was ready to change the subject, not at all concerned with her uncle's visit at the moment. "How are things at the Morehead plantation this morning?"

"Somewhat better now, but they lost five slaves, and two are badly burned. Miss Fannie, the most knowledgeable healer in these parts, is tending them. We can only pray that she's able to pull them through, but even if they survive, they have a long road to recovery ahead of them."

"We will certainly lift them in prayer. Now, sit down and talk to me while I cook your breakfast."

"Thank you, darling. That would be lovely, but first, tell me why you are so cheerful?" Judith sniffled. "What happened to cheer you up after Tobias…"

"Nothing… happened," Lynna leaned over the steaming pot and stirred the grits in earnest, to hide her blazing face. "His visit wasn't as bad this time, I guess, because I have never slept better." If only she could share her newfound happiness with her aunt, but she would wait until Joshua actually proposed, so they could join in the celebration together. "After breakfast, I plan to work in my flower garden, since the weeds have taken over lately. Then, I'll come inside, and we can begin work on Suzanne's new gown."

Judith dried her eyes and was quietly observing her niece, when she realized that *something* was different about her.

Lynna hummed gaily as she cooked bacon in a cast iron frying pan, without a care in the world. "If anyone from the big house should see me, I will simply say that I fell off the porch. No one will doubt my words, as everyone on the plantation knows I am eternally clumsy."

Judith was dumbfounded by her niece's carefree banter. Usually, after one of Tobias's visits, she would linger in a state of depression for days. Now, here she stood, almost euphoric. Something out of the ordinary had happened during her absence, of that she was certain.

After clearing the table and washing dishes, Lynna gathered her gloves and garden tools, kissed her aunt's cheek, and strolled to the garden, still humming. She kept her face hidden under the wide brim of a straw hat.

When she finished carefully weeding and hoeing the dirt around her flowers, she picked one ruby red rose and started toward the house, when a deep sultry voice stopped her dead in her tracks.

"Good morning again, my love."

Lynna's heart skipped a full beat, and she had to restrain herself from rushing headlong into his arms. "Good morning, Joshua," she greeted, and scolded herself for secretly wishing her aunt had remained at the Morehead plantation a few more hours.

"I must say, you look exceptionally lovely this morning." His eyes perused her from head to toe. "I trust your night was satisfactory?"

"I look hideous and you well know it." She

turned away, realizing how repugnant her face must look in the bright morning light. "To answer your question, I have no complaints, sir."

He bestowed upon her a seductive wink that turned her insides to mush. "It would have indeed been a first if you had." When he smiled, his eyes twinkled and a dimple formed in his cheek.

"You, sir, are outrageously conceited," While Lynna attempted to sound convincing, she failed miserably when she tried to keep a straight face.

"Admitted." He took the rose from her fingers and brought it to his lips, wishing it were some part of her anatomy instead. "Shall we take a walk by the river?"

The slamming of the door caused them both to glance up, leaving Joshua with an irritated frown, until he noticed Judith approaching with a tray.

"Joshua, I didn't realize you were here." *Was it Joshua?* Judith watched as the besotted man's lips caressed Lynna's rose. "Come join us for a glass of lemonade. I fear it will be another scorcher today." She placed the tray on the porch rail and returned to the house. "I'll just get another glass."

"Any chance of your aunt being called away again tonight?" Joshua muttered.

"Joshua," Lynna chastised him. "You, sir, are far too convinced of your charm and good..." she stopped herself short.

"Go ahead and say it." He grinned his self-assured grin. "My dashing good looks. I've been told that once or twice by members of the opposite sex."

She was about to bring him down a peg or two, when her aunt returned. Instead, she removed her gloves and sipped lemonade as Joshua's heated gaze caused a knot to steadily tighten in the pit of her stomach.

"How have you been, Joshua?" Judith queried.

"Never better," his answer was directed to Judith, while his smile was solely for Lynna's benefit. "As of this moment, Judith, I am the happiest man alive."

"Will you be staying with us for a few days?" Judith hoped that if she kept him talking, she might succeed in gaining his attention.

The grin, as well as his carefree demeanor, fled as his eyes met Lynna's. She had succeeded in making him forget his purpose, again, for he wanted to be alone with her when he broke the news of his departure. A rider had delivered a message from one of the detectives he hired to find Tobias. The despot had supposedly rented a room in a small town just outside Charleston. "I'm afraid I must leave today."

Lynna was speechless as the glass she was holding slipped from her hand. She watch silently as the dry earth greedily absorbed every drop of liquid. Of course, he would eventually return to Sea Grove, but why today, when they had just found each other again.

As she bent to pick up the broken glass, her hands brushed Joshua's in his attempt to assist her. They had only parted a few short hours ago, yet she pined for his touch.

When their eyes met, their hunger for each other was clearly evident, and Judith had her answer. She could not be happier.

Of course, she realized she shouldn't be happy about the fact that her niece was no longer chaste. Nathan had placed his trust in her, and he would be hell bent on someone's destruction to discover that his daughter was no longer an ingénue.

Still, if she was being honest with herself, that was of little consequence now. Her brother had not been a father to Lynna in years. What mattered was Lynna's happiness, and the only way to achieve it was by putting her pain in the past where it belonged and enjoying the life she had been born to live.

"How clumsy of me," Lynna whispered, hoping she sounded convincing. "My hands perspired in the gloves, and the glass slipped."

Judith took the broken pieces. "I'll just take this inside before someone gets cut."

Lynna waited until her aunt was safely in the house. "When are you leaving?" She couldn't bring herself to look at him as her eyes stared unseeing into the copse of trees behind the cottage. The thought of the lonely days and nights to come settled around her like a heavy blanket, suffocating her.

Joshua took her soft hand in his and brought it to his lips. "Within the hour, I fear. I couldn't leave without seeing you, but remember, this will be a short separation. We will be together again soon at Beth and Samuel's Harvest Ball." He turned her hand over and held her palm to his cheek. "This will be our last separation, Lynna."

It wasn't fair.

She shouldn't have to give him up so soon.

Wait.

Their last separation? What exactly did he mean by that?

That was the question on Suzanne's mind as well. What *did* Joshua mean? She felt rage bubbling in her breast the likes of which she had never known, as she hid beneath the tendrils of a weeping willow tree and heard every disgusting word.

Lynna was about to ask Joshua to clarify his statement, when Suzanne came waltzing toward them. She primly held up the lacy white hem of an elegant gown that would have been more appropriate for a lavish Ball.

She glanced only briefly at Lynna, and cried, "For heavens sakes, sugah, whatever happened to you? Why, you look like your poor face was trampled by father's old Brahma bull."

"I ran into a door." Lynna busied herself with pulling nonexistent weeds, in an attempt to hide her bruises.

"I see." Suzanne pursed her lips, and nodded. "Well, you *have* forever been exceedingly clumsy. Oh, Joshua, darling, there you are." She hurried to his side, and leaned in to brush nonexistent lint from his sleeve. "I have hardly had a moment alone with you, and now I hear you are leaving us today. Why, I must be losing my charm." When no one bothered to argue the fact, she continued, "Alas, there will be sufficient time for us to get reacquainted during our journey."

This piqued Lynna's curiosity, causing her to turn and face Suzanne, bruises and all. "What journey?"

"Why, my journey with Joshua, of course." Suzanne cast a contemptuous gaze at Lynna as she forced a fake smile. She wiped a light sheen of perspiration from her forehead, terrified the blazing sun might create a freckle on her alabaster cheeks.

She hated the sun. "Father has granted permission for me to return to Charleston with Joshua."

"He did what?" Joshua's tone was menacing as he glanced from Suzanne's jubilant face, to Lynna's miserable countenance.

"For me to accompany you to Charleston, silly. You wouldn't mind dropping me off at Cedar Hill, would you?" One hand went to rest on Joshua's chest. "Why, Father would be simply devastated if you refused, after he has extended so much hospitality to you. The remainder of the family will be following later to attend the Harvest Ball, but as I explained to father, Beth certainly could use my help with that spoiled little Bethany Breanne at such a busy time."

Joshua turned to take Lynna in his arms and assure her that she had no cause to worry, when Silas ambled around the corner of the big house. Suzanne grabbed Joshua's hand and simpered, "Anyway, since I am always willing to help my family in any way I can, I graciously volunteered to go early and help with the preparations. Surely you don't mind having little ole me as company on the long ride." She tucked her arm securely in his as she deftly maneuvered him away from Lynna.

Lynna's heart plummeted as Suzanne snatched the red rose from Joshua's hand and spun it around her fingers, before viciously snapping the stem and tucking it behind her ear. "Oh, thank you, darling. A little color is just what this outfit needed."

Suzanne tugged on Joshua's arm to steer him toward her father. "Father wishes to have a word with you before we depart, so let's not keep him waiting, and please," she leaned toward him to whisper, "just agree with him when he prattles on and on about the dangers of us sharing a carriage for that length of time, and how it is of the utmost importance that my virtue remain intact."

Joshua could only glare at her as he clenched his fists tightly by his sides, refusing to create a scene in front of Silas.

As the carriage rolled away in a swirling cloud of dust, Lynna couldn't bear to witness Joshua's departure, or Suzanne's gloating victory. Instead, she went home and pondered several worst case scenarios. It really boiled down to whether or not she trusted Joshua on the long trip home. Of course, she trusted him, but she didn't trust Suzanne not one whit.

Still, she must accept the fact that it was completely out of her control, and put her faith in Joshua to withstand the many seductions Suzanne would use to lure him in during every hot and dusty mile of the trip.

She was sitting in a rocking chair on the front porch when Jasmine climbed the steps. She carried a steaming bowl of Lynna's favorite food, blackberry cobbler, and a spoon.

"Miz Suzanne sho' nuff is taken wit' Mist' Joshua, ain't she?" Jasmine was determined to hide her shock and not comment on Lynna's colorful new bruises.

"She certainly does seem to be."

"He sho' ain't taken wit' her doe. Actin' like po' white trash an' runnin' aftah dat man. Why Miz Mary let dat chile go, when Mist' Joshua sho' ain't wantin' ta take her, is plum confusin' me."

"You know Suzanne always gets her way, Jasmine. Silas makes the decisions at Sea Grove, and they are always in favor of Suzanne." Lynna sighed wistfully. "I expect to hear any day now that she will be moving to Charleston permanently."

"Ole Jasmine ain't miss much whut goes on round heah, an' I's heah ta tell you dat Miz Suzanne ain't gwine be da one whut move ta Char'ston wit Mist' Joshua."

Lynna knew Jasmine spoke one truth. She didn't miss many of the happenings around Magnolia House. What little she did miss was soon filled in by one of her daughters. Rose, Suzanne's chambermaid, was often presented with the opportunity to listen to her mistress's most private conversations. While Iris, the downstairs maid, reported the most infinitesimal details that may have slipped past the other two sets of ears. Lynna knew better than to dispute a word Jasmine said.

"Whatever do you mean, Jasmine? Who do you suppose is moving to Charleston with him?"

"You is." Jasmine chuckled.

Lynna was struck dumb. Had Joshua revealed his innermost secrets to Jasmine? She had to know. "Why, Jasmine, I fear you are dreadfully mistaken. If anyone relocates to Charleston to reside with Joshua, it will in all likelihood be Suzanne."

"I ain't wrong." The old servant was adamant. "I can't love dat chile no mo' if'n she drapped out my own body, but she ain't da one whut Mist' Joshua done set his cap on." Jasmine couldn't keep a secret, no need in trying. "He done much as tol' me so."

Lynna dropped a spoonful of cobbler and turned

to face her. "He told you what, Jasmine?"

"Well, he ain't come rite out an tol' me, but silent rivah's run deep. His querstions done tol me all I need to know."

"What questions?" Lynna wanted to know every syllable that passed between them.

"I cain recollect jus' when it was, he jus' come in my kitchen one day axkin' did I see yo face, an axkin' a bunch of querstions."

"You didn't tell him about Tobias, did you?" She couldn't bear the shame if Joshua were to discover that her own uncle loathed her so. She would never be able to face him again. "Please, tell me you didn't, Jasmine."

Jasmine was at once contrite as she witnessed the shame on Lynna's face. She would never hurt her by admitting her own breach of trust. "No chile, I ain't tol' him dat de man he searchin' fo' is Tobias." She turned her head away, unable to look Lynna in the eyes after her dishonesty. She had never lied to her before, and didn't like doing it one bit.

"Thank you." As Jasmine stood to leave, Lynna gave her a warm hug. "I knew I could trust you."

Jasmine walked to the big house consumed with guilt. At the doorway to the kitchen, she turned and felt a rush of sympathy when she noticed Lynna still sitting on the porch, staring off into space. The poor girl would be stuck inside for days, again. She wondered if Joshua had found that lowlife Tobias Mathison, and gazed toward the heavens to issue a fervent prayer that he had.

Chapter 20

Suzanne stood in the shadows of the conjure woman's cabin, peering through the window as the woman of indiscriminate age, anywhere from sixty to ninety, sat by a roaring fire. She knew old Amari presided over ceremonial meetings, and ritual dances.

She had also heard from the housemaids that Cedar Hill's conjure woman earned a considerable amount by selling charms, amulets, and magical powders that were guaranteed to cure ailments, grant desires, and destroy one's foes. That was her greatest desire, to destroy Lynna.

Suzanne's arms were loaded with food, blankets, and clothes, as payment for Amari's help in removing Lynna from her life. The servants had already warned her that Amari refused to accept money. The conjure woman claimed that passing money from one hand to the next was the easiest way to lay a curse on someone.

Suzanne knocked on the door, and after hearing the woman call a greeting, she entered the cabin and was confronted by the strong smell of sage.

Amari accepted the supplies with a nod, and motioned for Suzanne to take the seat opposite her. "What can I do for you, Miss Suzanne?"

Suzanne was left shocked as she glared at her in surprise. Why, her cultured speech was that of one of the more refined citizens of Charleston. "Your speech. Where did you learn to speak like you do?"

Amari chuckled softly to herself, accustomed to this reaction from strangers. "I was raised in New Orleans. My mother was a quadroon ladies maid, and I was raised in the big house at her skirt." Dancing flames reflected the firelight in the conjure woman's eyes. "When the Misses passed, her only son sold us to plantations in different states and I never saw her again."

"Forgive me." Suzanne couldn't suppress a giggle. "I assure you that I'm not laughing at your horrible circumstances, but at the fact that I would imagine her son lived to rue the day he separated you."

Amari peered at Suzanne from underneath her lashes. "He did not live to rue another day."

Suzanne shivered, as Amari closed her eyes and relaxed in her seat. Judging from her facial expressions, she seemed to be reliving some particularly intense moments from her past. In a determined effort to not dwell on the fate of the son, Suzanne moved on to her needs. "I came here seeking your help in a matter of dire importance."

The old woman folded her hands in her lap and sat, patiently waiting. "I'm listening."

"I need you to make someone suffer." Suzanne couldn't help but grin at the thought of causing Lynna excruciating pain. "Can you do that?"

"It depends on who it is." Amari threw something in the fire that caused it to roar and burn so brightly for a few seconds that it almost singed Suzanne's eyebrows. "How badly do you want her to suffer?"

Suzanne scooted her chair back a few inches,

in case the conjure woman felt the need to showcase her skills again. "Lynna Mathison, and I need her to suffer unimaginable agony."

"Lynna Mathison?" The shock on Amari's face was hard to conceal. "Joshua's new love?"

"Hardly," Suzanne practically snarled. "What makes you think she is his new love?"

Amari peered into the fire for several minutes, deep in thought. "I know many things about many people, Miss Suzanne. As such, I know that now is not the time to bring this woman to her knees."

"What do you mean now is not the time," Suzanne argued. "I need it to happen now."

Amari met her eyes. "We do not always get what we want."

Suzanne pursed her lips and smirked. *I usually do.* "I suppose I can wait a few weeks, but when the time is right, what can you make happen to the little strumpet?"

"Whatever you wish to happen," Amari inched her chair closer to the roaring blaze. "Whatever your cold heart desires."

Chapter 21

Although it seemed like an eternity, at long last the day arrived for their departure to Cedar Hill, to attend Samuel and Beth's annual Harvest Ball. The morning dawned cool and overcast, and promised a more comfortable journey than before.

Lynna jumped out of bed at the crack of dawn and ran straightway to her aunt's room. "We must hurry, Aunt Judith, and get dressed before the carriage leaves without us."

"You are certainly anxious to get to Charleston. Why, I had no idea you missed Suzanne so much," Judith teased, knowing full well Suzanne was the last person her niece had a desire to see.

Within the hour, Lynna, Judith, Mary, and Rose were settled in the carriage for the long ride to Charleston. Lynna was scarcely able to sit still, leaving Mary puzzled, and Judith and Rose smiling. They knew the reason for her excitement. Lynna would soon be with the man she loved, and the waiting was agony.

The ride was uneventful, and they arrived at Cedar Hill late, extremely relieved to finally reach their destination and remove themselves from the dusty confines of the carriage. Lynna fell into bed exhausted, and wishing she could sleep undisturbed for a week.

When she awakened the following morning, the guests had already begun to arrive.

The lawn was scattered with brightly colored gowns of every color, with matching sunbonnets and elaborate twirling parasols. She searched among the handsomely garbed men for Joshua, yet he was nowhere to be found. Good. She had time for a leisurely bath before preparing to greet her love, and the new day.

She felt refreshed after soaking in a tub of lavender scented water, and realized she was the happiest she had been in… well, she couldn't ever remember being this happy. She stretched lazily in front of the mirror and closed her eyes dreamily. She would soon be with the man of her dreams.

Would he ask her today?

Her hands trembled so that she could hardly accomplish the task of dressing. She combed her hair until it shone, and entwined green ribbons to stream down her back. The ribbon matched her dress of lime green watered silk, cut with a square neck and short puffed sleeves.

She went to the balcony to peer across a well-manicured lawn that bustled with activity, as couples strolled arm in arm and children romped with delight. The delicious aroma of cooked pork and poultry drifted to her from below, causing her mouth to water.

She turned from the gay vista spread out on the lawn, so excited she could barely contain her emotions. This was the moment she had been waiting for. She picked up her skirts and hastened down the stairs before she could lose her wavering nerve. What she saw waiting patiently at the foot of the stairs caused her heart to lurch.

Joshua stood with one foot propped on the bottom step. If possible, he was even more handsome than she remembered, in grey trousers and a white ruffled linen shirt. She took each step carefully, willing her feet to move as she watched his grin become wider with each step she made toward him.

"I've been waiting for you to make an appearance, my love." He reached for her hand and brought it to his lips. Had there been fewer eyes and gossiping tongues, he would have brought his lips to hers as well. "You can't imagine how much I have missed you."

They gazed hungrily into each other's eyes, until Lynna at last found her voice. "I thought this day would never arrive."

He placed her hand in the bend of his elbow and grinned that devilish grin. "We will join the others for the noon meal, then I would have a private word with you."

Did she dare hope?

He escorted her to the lawn, where they found long tables set up under the shade of fragrant magnolia trees, and filled with a veritable feast.

"Joshua Jordan, shame on you for keeping Lynna all to yourself," Malinda teased. "I haven't had a chance to speak two words to her since she arrived."

"You two go ahead and critique the fashion choice of every female in the county, while I return to the tables for a second helping."

"I'll have you know we do not gossip," Malinda insisted.

Joshua winked. "Then, I beg you to excuse such

an egregious error on my part, dear sister."

While Lynna listened to the ladies chatter about fashion, childbirth, and what a blessing it was to have a wet nurse, the men discussed their politics and cotton.

She didn't have another chance to speak to Joshua alone, before she and the other young ladies were ushered to their rooms to rest for the Ball. Since she wasn't the least bit tired, and was much too excited to sleep, she sat on the edge of the bed twiddling her thumbs and puzzling over Suzanne's unusual absence from the morning festivities. It was very unlike her to miss being the focus of attention at a social function.

Lynna had questioned Mary earlier, and was told Suzanne had a stomach malady and had decided to spend the day in bed so as to be well rested for the Ball.

Judith shook Lynna awake. "Wake up, sleepyhead. It's time to dress for the Ball."

Lynna rubbed her eyes, having finally drifted off to a dream filled sleep. She slowly became aware of her aunt standing over her and grinning from ear to ear.

"I simply cannot keep this secret a second longer, darling. I have been positively dying to give it to you." Judith beamed with excitement as she offered Lynna a large box. "Open it."

Lynna sat up sleepily and lifted the lid on the box, coming fully awake. "Oh, Aunt Judith," she cried, as she lifted ruffle after ruffle of silky material from the wrapping and held the bodice to her chest. It was the most exquisite ballgown her eyes had ever beheld. "It is… it is… I have no words to describe it," she marveled, as she fingered the expensive silk. "Where did you get the fabric? How could we afford it? Oh, Aunt Judith, you shouldn't spend your hard earned money on me."

Judith grinned. "Wouldn't you agree that it is my money to spend as I please?"

"Well, of course, it is, but when did you find the time? You were so busy with Suzanne's gowns." Tears of love and immense gratitude glistened in Lynna's eyes.

Judith had promised Joshua not to tell Lynna he purchased the material when he and Silas rode into town, during his visit to Magnolia House. He had also delivered a bolt of green silk for Judith, who slipped it in their cottage undetected.

Now, she had to admit that Lynna's gown was her best work to date, far surpassing any of Suzanne's. "I stitched it in between Suzanne's gowns, when you weren't looking. The gown has love sewn into every stitch, darling."

"Oh, Aunt Judith, you are simply too wonderful for words, and I love you so much." Lynna hugged her fiercely. The gown was creamy yellow silk, off the shoulder, with frilly ruffles sewn into the hooped skirt. Yellow satin formed a bow around the tiny waist. "You will never know how much this means to me, today, of all days." She glanced up with a beaming smile, giving her aunt the slightest hint of what the night promised.

Many sighs and whispers were heard as Lynna descended the curving stairs, looking the part of a regal queen arriving at her court. Joshua didn't need to look, for he knew only Lynna could draw such a chorus of murmured responses. He sauntered toward the stairs and glanced up, stopping dead in his tracks as he was once again mesmerized by her dazzling beauty.

When he purchased the material for her gown, he imagined her slim figure sheathed in yellow silk, but his imagination had failed to do her justice. She was breathtaking. "I always know when you enter a room, and as always you are ravishing."

"Thank you, sir." She took his hand and allowed him to lead her to the dance floor. "You cut quite a dashing figure yourself."

His whispered words caressed her ear, "Would you care to dance, my love?"

"Only with you."

Joshua proved to be an excellent dancer as they danced a lively reel. When the music slowed for the attendees to catch their breath, he took her in his arms and breathed deeply of her lilac fragrance. The heat radiating from his body warmed her so that she wished desperately to be alone with him; to leave her sumptuous gown discarded on the floor, and once again feel nothing other than his strong arms encircling her.

"You make every female jealous, and leave men awestruck by your beauty." He gazed into her sultry azure eyes, glazed with her longing for him. "Let's step outside, Lynna. There is something I would ask you."

Lynna's knees went weak and her pulse quickened.

This was it.

Joshua had taken her elbow to steer her toward

the open side doors, when he noticed Daniel bounding towards them.

"Joshua, my father would like a private word with you," he called in an uncommonly crisp tone, successfully stopping them before they could make their exit.

"Can it wait, Daniel?" Joshua still had his course set for the balcony doors. "I have been attempting to have a word with this fair lady all day, yet we seem to be constantly interrupted."

"No, Joshua. I'm sorry, but it cannot wait." Daniel's words were solemn, although his eyes danced with excitement. "My father insists."

"Very well. Please excuse me, Lynna." He held her hand to the very last second, then gave her a sly wink and a promise. "I will return shortly, my love. Keep a spot on your dance card open for me."

As she watched him go, Malinda came rushing to her side. "While the men are cloistered in the parlor, let's try the rum punch, Lynna."

While she followed Malinda to the punch bowl and accepted a cup of the tasty beverage, and nibbled on a fresh from the oven oatmeal cookie, she was unable to control her racing thoughts for a second longer. She whispered behind her fan, "Malinda, please, you mustn't speak of this to another living soul, but I'm almost positive your brother is going to ask me to be his wife."

Malinda gasped, nodded her head once, and opened her mouth to speak. Apparently, thinking better of it, she grabbed Lynna's hand and proceeded across the crowded ballroom.

She knew!

Malinda knew Joshua was going to propose

tonight. Was his entire family aware of her upcoming engagement as well?

Malinda led her to the verandah where Mary, Judith, and Patricia were discussing their next quilting bee.

"What is taking the men so long?" Lynna wondered aloud. She wished for Joshua to hurry with his discussion of politics, secession, war, or whatever they were debating at the moment, so she could twirl around the dance floor in his arms.

"Where on earth is Suzanne?" Mary posed the question. "Has my daughter even ventured downstairs yet, or is she still in her room primping?"

"I hope Suzanne is feeling better," Patricia offered sympathetically.

"There she is." Malinda frowned, noticing the smug smile on Suzanne's face and not liking it one whit.

Suzanne exited the parlor, of all places, in an extremely low cut, pink satin ball gown, with diamonds dripping from her ears, neck, and both wrists. What Malinda found most disconcerting was the fact that she wore a triumphant smirk on her face, and she was practically gloating.

Joshua followed close behind with a look of stark rage. He sent Lynna a forlorn look of defeat and misery that almost sent her to her knees when Suzanne clutched his arm possessively, and they followed behind her father.

Samuel and Daniel brought up the rear of the procession, with Samuel pushing Jeremiah's chair. What could it mean? Why was Suzanne so jubilant that she almost floated across the room?

Once Suzanne and the men had made it through

the throng to the bandstand, Silas immediately made his way to the band and motioned for them to stop playing. He climbed the steps to the stage and cleared his throat. "Ladies and gentleman, I'm glad you could be here tonight to share in our joy. I have an announcement to make."

He drew everyone's rapt attention, and spoke loud enough for even the ones in the back of the room to hear. "Tonight, I would like to announce the engagement, and approaching marriage, of my daughter Suzanne Nicolette Fletcher to Captain Joshua Jordan."

Loud whoops and whistles arose from the crowd as the band struck up a merry tune. Several of the guests glanced toward Lynna with a bewildered expression, as she had so recently been in Joshua's arms on the dance floor as they gazed hungrily into each other's eyes.

Applause and shouts of congratulations echoed from well-wishers.

"You finally fell in love, didn't you, Joshua?"

"It's about time you settled down and raised a family."

"After all these years, a little lady finally came along who was impossible to resist."

"I knew someone would eventually tame the rogue."

"My God, Joshua," Lynna heard Malinda whisper in a state of shocked disbelief. "What have you done?"

Lynna leaned against the wall as her heart pounded in her chest. Surely, there must be some mistake, but there wasn't. She knew this to be true after only one glance at Suzanne's haughty expression.

Judith rushed to take Lynna in her arms, as Malinda went to her mother's side. When Lynna witnessed a stunned Patricia leaning against her daughter for support, she lifted her skirts and raced up the stairs, praying with each step for the ground to open up and swallow her.

She had been such a fool.

When Joshua could extricate himself from the crowd, and Suzanne's clutches without making a scene, he silently crept up the stairs. His hands trembled as he knocked softly and opened the door to Lynna's room, to find her wrapped in her aunt's arms weeping pitifully. The sound tore at his heart, and made him hate his new fiancé with renewed vigor.

While he yearned to hold Lynna, console her, and assure her that it was all a horrible misunderstanding, he couldn't. It was not a misunderstanding. It was a mistake of his own doing, and one that he would be forced to pay penance for the remainder of his insufferable life. He had only added to her pain, when she had known nothing but abuse and suffering at the hands of men since the day she left France. "Lynna?"

She was so overcome by feelings of hurt and betrayal, she didn't realize Joshua had entered the room. She glanced up, then quickly buried her head in her aunt's shoulder, unable to look him in the eyes and allow him to witness her misery. He must never know the agony his treachery had caused her.

She would hate Joshua until the day she drew her final breath for leading her to believe that he loved her, and wanted to marry her. It was obvious now that he had only been toying with her affections, while making wedding plans with Suzanne behind her back. She had never felt, or looked, more like a consummate fool. "Please, Joshua. I just want to be left alone."

"Judith, would you mind if I have a private word with Lynna?" His eyes beseeched Judith to be understanding. "There are some things I must explain."

Judith was far from understanding any of this. "Can you not leave her alone, Captain Jordan, as she requested? Have you not caused her enough pain?" Judith felt the urge to strip the expensive silk from Lynna's back and throw it in his handsome face.

"Please, Judith, I beg you. I must try to explain the madness that has transpired tonight. I owe Lynna that much."

Judith left the room, but not before giving him a look that told him what she, being a lady, could not.

Joshua didn't know where to begin. Everything had changed in a split second. Everything, except his love for Lynna, which was stronger than ever. Had his father not been in the parlor, expecting his son to accept his responsibility and do what was right, he might have refused the demands of Silas and his sons entirely. Yet, he would never embarrass his father, a man who had raised his son to be honorable in all matters, even if it hurt.

Still, he had to hold Lynna one last time, before losing her forever. When he walked across the room in an attempt to do just that, she pulled away from his touch as though she had been scalded. "Don't dare touch me," she cried. The enormity of her pain was clear in her trembling voice.

"Please, listen to me, Lynna. Don't for one second believe that I have the slightest desire to marry Suzanne Fletcher, when I am being forced into it against my will."

"Forced by your greed. You chose Suzanne over me because I live in a small cottage behind her huge plantation house, and my aunt and I work for our wages. Have you perhaps forgotten who my father is, Joshua?"

Her words were like a slap in the face, making him understand some of what she must be feeling. Without thinking, his hands bit into her shoulders. "Is that what you think? That I chose to marry Suzanne for her money? Why, you little fool." He laughed harshly. "I'm not after her money. You should know that I have more than enough of my own, and yes, I recall who your father is. If it was money I was after, don't you think I would have jumped at the chance to marry you three years ago?"

"Then why, Joshua?"

He went to stand at the open balcony door, glaring at the bench under the tree where he had sat that morning and been so perfectly content with his lot in life. Now his life had been plunged into the very depths of hell.

"She is carrying my child," he finally admitted. "I don't have a choice."

"Are you certain?" Lynna cried, grasping for any sliver of hope. "Perhaps her monthly curse is only... late, as mine was."

"Her father assures me that it is so, Lynna." His tone was final.

Suzanne was carrying Joshua's child.

How could he allow this to happen, knowing full well the consequences of his dalliance with the insatiable vixen? Lynna wondered if he had any idea of what a dismal future lay ahead of him, being bound to a woman like Suzanne. She came to the conclusion that they deserved each other, leaving her to bear the brunt of the suffering for their indiscretions.

It was too much. She couldn't bear to be in his presence another second. "Please, leave me alone, Joshua." Her tormented sobs brought Judith rushing into the room.

Joshua stopped short when he realized there was nothing more to say. No way to ease Lynna's pain, or his guilt for causing it.

With a gut wrenching sigh of defeat, he left the woman he loved, to join in a celebration with the woman he loathed. True, Lynna was miserable, but no more so than he would be with Suzanne tied like a ball and chain around his neck.

He exited the room in search of whiskey, quick to realize that a bottle of spirits would most likely be his closest companion in the years to come.

Chapter 22

Sometime after the celebration had ended, Lynna's tears finally slowed as she lay beside her aunt. "Thank you for understanding that I must go away, Aunt Judith."

"Of course I understand, darling. There is no reason for you to return to Magnolia House for the…" Judith had almost said wedding. "Your Aunt Gypsie will be thrilled that you finally decided to visit her in Charleston."

Theirs would be a tearful farewell, but Lynna was well versed in the art of losing someone she loved. She wanted nothing more than to go home with Aunt Judith to their little cottage and close out the world around them, sequestered from any and all outsiders, but that would be impossible. Magnolia House would be a beehive of activity as plans were drawn for Suzanne's upcoming nuptials, and lavish reception to follow.

Aunt Judith would be working around the clock on a trousseau for the bride to be. Deirdre Chisholm would sew the actual wedding gown, she was sure. Only the best for the daughter of Silas Fletcher, and the bride to be of Captain Joshua Jordan. Mary would be merrily flittering about as she made preparations for the society wedding.

Lynna prayed never to see Suzanne's smirking face again. She recalled the glowing look of triumph Suzanne had worn as she slithered into her room, after all the guests had departed. "Will you marry my brother now?" She asked so sweetly Lynna was surprised sugar didn't drip from her lips.

Lynna continued with her packing, hoping to hide her tear stained face. "I won't be marrying anyone."

"Well, why ever not, sugah?" Suzanne cried, twisting the knife in Lynna's heart a little deeper. "We could have a double wedding. Wouldn't that be a splendid affair?"

Lynna forgot her tears and spun around, wanting only to hurt her. To make her feel a small portion of the heartrending agony that ripped through her very soul. Before she had a chance, Suzanne's next words stopped her cold.

"Lynna, darling, I know how you must feel. But honestly, you really must forget any misguided illusions you had toward my betrothed. You see, I know all about that silly night the two of you shared in Judith's cottage, and you must realize that an occasional romp with a smitten female means nothing to a man like Joshua. He has, or had, them on a regular basis. I'm sure he will be quite content with what he has in his own bed now."

Suzanne clasped her arms around her waist and spun around the room gaily, strictly for Lynna's benefit. "He told me about your little tryst, and I was gracious enough to forgive him."

"Forgive him? For what?" Joshua would never betray her confidence. *Would he?* "What are you going on about, Suzanne?"

"You don't have to deny it, Lynna, and you shouldn't feel ashamed when it was beyond your control. I, of all people, know what a desirable man my husband to be is. Why do you think I'm marrying him?" She breathed a put upon sigh. "At any rate, the poor man told me how he went to deliver a message from your aunt after the Morehead fire, and you cried so pathetically, and begged him to stay."

Suzanne watched Lynna closely for a reaction to her lie, yet she kept her emotions well hidden. "I was furious when he first confessed this to me, but he does apologize so... lustily. He assured me that you meant nothing to him, and he was only offering to comfort you after your trying ordeal, when things got carried away. So, I forgave him." Lynna must never know she had stood outside the open window that night and heard every word.

"My ordeal?" Lynna whispered.

"With your uncle, you poor thing." Suzanne had a bright twinkle in her eye. "To have an uncle who beats you like a dog. Why, I simply cannot imagine anything quite so heinous."

A vision of Joshua and Suzanne laughing at her, him recounting to Suzanne how she had asked, no begged him to stay, sent a fresh wave of agony coursing through her. Dear God, she had been so stupid.

Then, suddenly, she was able to smile through her tears, as she envisioned the two of them growing old together.

Just before midnight, Lynna was a lone figure on the quiet streets of Charleston. Her carriage had busted a wheel on the outskirts of town, making it impossible for them to continue. Rather than waiting until morning, she had taken one of the horses and continued to her aunt's house alone, against the stern wishes of the driver.

She saw the tower of Saint Michael's Episcopal Church looming up ahead stately and proud, watching over the sleeping port city, and noticed a bright ring around the moon. What were the superstitions Jasmine had warned her of, concerning a ring around the moon? She wished she had listened more closely.

Suddenly, the horse slowed, and pricked up his ears, alert. Lynna gradually became aware of a tinkling noise, as if from gently ringing bells. That was odd. She searched for the origin of the sound and didn't see anything unusual, as the moon chose that moment to hide behind the clouds.

With increasing alarm, she became aware of a steady rumbling noise that seemed to come from beneath the ground. This, combined with the ringing sound, was almost deafening.

Church bells.

All through the city church bells began to ring in an erratic cacophony. The horse was terrified and reared, throwing Lynna to the ground in a painful heap upon the suddenly shifting earth. In a blind panic, she ran down the street until she came to the welcoming doors of Saint Michael's.

Across the sleeping city, eyes widened and fear took root in the soul of every citizen as chimneys crumbled and rained brick into the streets. As the thundering noise grew louder, families ran from their homes.

Inside the saintly structure of St. Michael's, the bells chimed without the rope being pulled. Not the usual enchanting melody, but a horrible uncontrolled noise that vibrated through the saintly structure.

Lynna fell to her knees and prayed harder than she ever had before, begging God to be merciful rather than just, and allow her a quick death. She was certain this was her punishment for giving herself to Joshua without the sanction of the church.

Joshua.

If only she could be held in the safety of his strong embrace once more before she died.

That would never happen, for her life would soon be over. As if to add credence to her thoughts, the earth suddenly heaved upward. The force tossed holy statues from their pedestals behind the altar, and caused them to crash to the floor only inches from where she lay crouched under a pew. The trembling became extremely violent, causing the beautiful stained glass windows to shatter and fall around her.

She knew nothing of the destruction that was destroying the city and claiming many lives outside the church. Her mind was filled with the ringing of bells, and the horrible rumbling noise. She remained in her crouched position, too terrified to move, until the trembling earth stood still and the maddening clanging stopped.

When all was quiet, she crawled out from under the pew, unsure of which way to turn. The church was filled with thick smoke, making it difficult to breathe. In a frantic search for fresh air, she made her way through the rubble, across overturned pews and crumbling statues. She tripped and fell every other step, cutting her hands and knees on broken glass and other debris littering the aisle. Still, she kept moving steadily forward toward the dim light that filtered through the open door, terrified of what she might find when she reached it.

While the full moon was bright, the smoke and dust created a thick fog that would hide most of the destruction from view, until the stark morning light would illuminate it.

Her horse was nowhere to be found, and she could only pray that her driver had survived the chaos. She must hurry and reach her aunt's house, and send someone back for him.

She noticed a crowd beginning to gather in the streets, a crowd that had been roughly yanked from their beds.

Lynna was lucky to be in the business district when the earthquake struck the city of Charleston. Had she been in the residential section, she would have heard the awful screams as bodies of men, women, and children were pulled from the wreckage.

As she moved carefully through the crowded streets, fires burned out of control all around her, with burning embers carried high into the sky on a breeze that blew in from the river. Men, women, and children formed a human conveyor belt that carried water to put out numerous fires. Her first impulse was to join them, but first she must see to the safety of her aunt.

She broke into a run as sharp talons of fear dug into her sides and urged her forward. She ran until her parched throat and aching sides forced her to slow down. Finally, she noticed a candle flickering in a downstairs window.

To Lynna, it resembled a beacon guiding a ship in a violent storm. She followed the light, and breathed a heartfelt sigh of relief to find the house miraculously intact, and her aunt standing on the front stoop with welcoming arms.

Many of the picturesque homes and stately mansions of Charleston were destroyed during the earthquake, but by far, the worst tragedy was the loss of life. Many people were killed in their sleep, while others were trapped under the rubble, knowing there would be no chance for a rescue until morning. Some died before the rescuers could dig them out, while many of the severely burned and injured prayed for the relief that only death could bring.

Over the destruction of the city, the tower of Saint Michael's could be seen as a reminder to the people of Charleston. They had survived fires, hurricanes, and tornadoes in the past, and even though the earthquake had proven to be a formidable foe, the Holy City would come back stronger than ever.

Lynna's Aunt Gypsie didn't have the fortitude to remain, and watch the long process of rebuilding her city. Miraculously, her shotgun house had sustained only minor external damage, yet no matter which room in the house she happened to be in when she looked out a window, her eyes fell upon destruction.

Her once beautiful city, where her beloved husband had been born, raised, and buried, now more closely resembled a battlefield. A battle Charleston had lost.

The downtown area still smoked from the raging fires that swept the city, leaving ashes where a thriving business district had once been. Gypsie had lost two of her dearest friends to the earthquake, and the pain was almost unbearable.

Lynna returned from a walk around the smoking city to find her aunt staring dismally out the window, a pathetic sight.

"Aunt Gypsie, are you ill?" The disheveled woman was a poor caricature of the effervescent aunt she remembered.

It was a long time before Gypsie could trust herself to answer. "While I may be fine physically, emotionally I am a wreck." She took a deep breath and let it out slowly "After careful consideration, I have decided to visit my sister Bertie and her husband Cliff, in Jamaica."

Now where would she go?

Lynna swiped a tear from her cheek as she realized she couldn't return to Magnolia House, the only home she had known for the last three years. Perhaps she could borrow the needed funds from Samuel, and return to France.

"I think that is a splendid idea, Aunt Gypsie. You will feel much better once you are away from the destruction."

"Oh, I certainly don't intend to go alone. I mean for you to accompany me, Lynna. I couldn't possibly travel by myself, and after the awful tale of betrayal you confessed to me last night, you have no reason to remain here either." Gypsie gazed upon the smoking remains of her ruined city. "We will send a message to Judith and sail on the first ship out. Neither of us shall return until our beloved Charleston has risen from the ashes, like the phoenix that she is."

Chapter 23

Suzanne and Daniel perspired in rocking chairs on the verandah at Magnolia House, amidst the searing heat of an Indian summer. Suzanne's ever present servant child fanned unenthusiastically by her side, stopping often to swat at a pesky insect and cause Suzanne to cast an evil eye her way.

Daniel's eyes were lowered, ashamed for having gone along with his sister's calculating scheme to coerce Joshua into marriage, especially since the ploy had been such a spectacular failure.

True, Suzanne had finagled a proposal from Joshua, but Lynna was an ocean away. Daniel had accepted the fact that he was partially responsible for dooming Joshua to a lifetime of misery, for naught, and hung his head guiltily. "Have you gotten yourself with child yet, dear sister?" he sneered, as his tone conveyed his true feelings for his sibling. "The wedding is tomorrow, you know."

"I know when my own wedding is, Daniel Fletcher," she snapped. "While I'm not carrying Joshua's offspring, yet, I should have no difficulty resolving that minor issue after tomorrow."

Suzanne was almost overwhelmed with the notion of spending the rest of her life in Joshua's arms. "After my wedding tomorrow, it shouldn't be difficult at all."

The wedding was a simple affair. Suzanne had begged and pleaded for a grand event, complete with an orchestra, dancing, and hundreds of guests. Yet, for once, Silas had put his foot down and gone against his daughter's wishes. Even her mother had agreed that due to her condition, the ceremony would not be an elaborate one.

So, few people saw her in the virginal white, silk organza wedding gown that boasted a ten-foot train, and had been painstakingly stitched by Deirdre Chisholm's own hands. The gown was magnificent, and had set Silas back a small fortune, but his daughter's happiness was all that mattered.

While Suzanne and her parents were convinced that a more beautiful bride had never walked down an aisle, her bridegroom saw nothing to brag about. Even though he made the requisite responses during the vows, his mind was lost in thoughts of another.

After the ceremony, with his wife's arm entwined securely through his, Joshua drank to toast after toast of whichever spirit was available, already feeling suffocated by her cloying nearness. He relaxed somewhat as the chilled liquid warmed his insides, and allowed him to recall happier times. Still, no matter how much he imbibed, he couldn't drown out the vision of Lynna's tear stained visage.

When at last Silas claimed his daughter for a dance, Joshua took the opportunity to slip away unnoticed. He had to get away from the crowd, the music, the heat, and his wife.

Wife.

How the hell did he allow himself to get tangled up with Suzanne Fletcher, of all people? Make that Suzanne Jordan, officially. He even detested the name.

As he turned the corner of the house, his eyes fell on Lynna and Judith's cottage. Would she ever return? Should he be made to pay for the remainder of his wretched life for his foolish mistakes? Did he really have a choice?

Not one that he could find, when the only other option was for his child to be reared by Suzanne's hands alone. He would not wish such a fate on his worst enemy, let alone his own flesh and blood. While he might be made to suffer a lifetime of misery, his son or daughter would not.

Long before the festivities had ended, Joshua stumbled upstairs to their room with the help of his wife. Their room. He could hardly abide the notion of being in the same house with the shrew.

As Suzanne undressed her intoxicated husband, she allowed her hands to wander slowly over his body, caressing him slowly and thoroughly until they drew the desired response. She kicked her expensive wedding gown into a crumpled heap in the corner, ignoring the sheer peignoir that had been placed at the foot of her bed, and stretched out beside him. She pressed her slim body against his as she slid her practiced hands over his muscular frame until they reached his manhood, and took it firmly in hand.

Joshua gasped, pulling her close as their lips met in a rough kiss that caused her lower region to pulse. Passionate moans erupted as his lips slid down her neck to suckle her small breast.

She smiled deliciously and breathed a contented sigh as his hand slid over her hip, then up her curving waist. As of this moment, she had everything she could ever want in this life. No man had the power to make her body ache for his touch the way Joshua did, and he was her husband, now and forever.

Even in a drunken state, Joshua realized that something was amiss with this situation. He stopped short, yanking his hand away as awful memories of his wedding day swam through his booze soaked mind. He opened his eyes and was quick to realize the female in his bed was not Lynna. In the dark, and officially drunk, it was easy to tell the vast differences in their curves. "Suzanne?" he slurred.

As the events of the day came rushing back, he was at once repulsed by her touch. He may have been forced to marry her, but he damn well did not have to share her bed. He rolled over and closed his eyes, as his steady breathing confirmed to Suzanne that he had fallen asleep on their wedding night, without consummating their vows.

Being quite sure of her charm and appeal, Suzanne came to the erroneous conclusion that his rejection was to be blamed on the large quantity of wine and rum consumed during their reception. She was confident that was it. After all, what man could fall asleep with her naked body pressed against him?

She would allow him to shirk his duty tonight, but no more. She couldn't afford to waste precious time. He had to plant his seed in her before everyone, including Joshua, learned of her deceit.

When Joshua was sure his new bride was asleep, he crept silently from the house and into the barn for his rendezvous with the provocative servant girl Juanita, Malinda's maid. Perhaps a few hours with her would help him dismiss from mind his current plight.

How had he gotten himself into this sorry state of affairs anyway? This was a question that reiterated over and over in his scrambled brain as he waited for the voluptuous Juanita to appear. He was married to a woman he despised, while the woman he loved was God only knows where.

He had beseeched Judith shortly after the wedding, pleading with her to give him Lynna's whereabouts. Her eyes were as cold as shimmering stones in a glacial pool as she glared at him with unmasked fury, and happily informed him that if Lynna had wanted him to know her destination, she would have certainly told him herself.

Not one soul on the plantation could be persuaded to tell him Lynna's whereabouts. Suzanne, Daniel, Silas, and Mary pretended not to know her location. Even the suddenly frigid Jasmine couldn't be tricked into revealing her secret hiding place.

He had ridden to Charleston in hopes that her Aunt Gypsie might offer the slightest hint as to where she might have gone. Although her house remained standing amid the smoking rubble of the city, it was locked up tight as a drum, and Gypsie was nowhere to be found.

Joshua resigned himself to the fact that Lynna didn't wish to be found, not by him anyway. He couldn't blame her for hating him, hell, he hated himself.

He grinned for the first time all day as Juanita stretched out in the hay beside him. If anyone could make him forget his troubles for a few hours, she could.

Sometime later, with both of them spent, Juanita whispered against his ear, "Dey's sumphin I needs ta tell you."

"What's that?" He nuzzled her ear as he took her full breast in his hand.

Juanita loved Joshua, and was always thinking of ways to make him happy. She knew her secret would do the trick, and for a few hours she would be his absolute favorite person. "Rose done tol' me dat Miz Suzanne ain't knock' up fo' real."

Joshua chuckled, raising up on his elbow to face her. "How would Rose know this?"

Juanita crossed her arms over her chest and pursed her full lips, perturbed that Joshua would even consider doubting her word. "Cuz she wash' her clothes, an' she done be seein' proof dat she still be havin' her curse. Dat's how."

Alarm bells rang in Joshua's head. Could Juanita's words be true? Was Suzanne really that devious?

Of course, she was.

The conniving bitch had been lying all along, and he had been stupid enough to fall for her deception without question.

Oh, but she would pay dearly for breaking the heart of the woman he loved more than life itself.

After several days of wedded bliss, Suzanne still hadn't coerced Joshua into making love to her. He adamantly refused to touch her, rarely even joining her in the marital bed.

Still, she was forever attempting to lure him into her arms with skimpy negligees and bottles of whiskey, confident that his resistance was weakening.

They left for Sea Grove a week after the wedding, where Joshua went straightway to the housekeeper and insisted rather loudly that he and his bride have separate rooms. He totally ignored the questioning glances of servants and family.

Suzanne had been furious, beyond furious, with loud bouts of crying, pouting, and shouting at the top of her lungs.

Patricia, who had never heard such carryings on in all her born days, rushed to calm the distraught girl. She was woefully unsuccessful in her efforts, and after only a few minutes of her furious screeches, Patricia eagerly fled the room.

Suzanne would have been positively irate to know the servants were fair rolling with mirth behind her uppity back, due to the fact that Joshua refused to share the bed with his eternally sniveling wife.

Malinda was still put out with the entire situation and refused to welcome her new sister into the family fold, pulling Joshua aside. "You told me not to worry, that you would never allow yourself to be trapped by Suzanne's feminine wiles. Instead, you succumb to her, dare I say... meager charm, and end up committing yourself, and our entire family, to a lifetime of misery."

"I could not agree more, Malinda." Joshua winked as he made his way up the stairs in search of the voluptuous Juanita, who could always be counted on to lift his spirts. "Admittedly, I have been nothing short of a fool, dear sister. However, rest assured that I will not allow the misery I brought upon this family to last."

"Joshua, whatever do you mean?"

At the top of the stairs he turned and put a finger to his lips. When he was just outside Suzanne's door, he shouted for the very agreeable Juanita to bring hot water to his room for a bath.

This set about an episode of foul language that had every member of the household covering their ears, and praying that Joshua would swiftly return his new bride back to Georgia.

Late that night, Suzanne slipped into Joshua's room and stood beside his bed, slowly and seductively removing her clothes. "Joshua darling, what is it about me that you find so unappealing? Is my body so repugnant that you cannot bear to touch me?"

He continued to snore.

"How can you lay with another woman when your own wife is waiting with open arms?" Stark naked, she held out her hands. "I am your lawfully wedded wife, darling, please make love to me."

Joshua was totally void of any emotion as he declared unequivocally, "I will not risk jeopardizing the life of my child. When the child is safely delivered then, and only then, will I execute my marital duties."

"Duties?" she snarled. "You never considered it a duty before."

He didn't attempt to stifle a yawn as he turned over, ignoring her outstretched arms.

"How in the hell am I supposed to deliver a child when you refuse to touch me?" With a shriek of barely concealed rage she fled the room, slamming the door hard enough to send picture frames leaping from the walls.

Time was fast running out, and she was getting desperate. Family and friends would soon question why she wasn't showing.

Several times she had caught Joshua fixated on her flat stomach, and didn't miss the glimmer in his eyes and the smile that played across his lips when he thought of his little brat. The sheer horror. Even though the mere thought of ruining her slim figure appalled her, she had no other choice.

In a state of total desperation, she realized that Joshua might not desire her, but plenty of other men did. She may never know who fathered her child and, to be honest, she really didn't care. Her only concern was conceiving one before it was too late. Besides, it would serve Joshua right to raise another man's offspring after his cruel and neglectful treatment of her.

So, it happened that by the end of their first month as man and wife, Suzanne had frequently been with William, the new stable boy, and Sawyer, the son of a neighboring plantation owner. She found Sawyer to be too unskilled, and William too slow for her taste. However, under her careful tutelage, William was able to pick up a little speed and actually satisfy her.

Five weeks after her wedding, she was distraught to once again find undeniable proof that she didn't carry Joshua's, or anyone else's, child. What if there was a female problem, and she was unable to conceive? How would she excuse such deceit?

If she hadn't been so convinced of becoming

with child shortly after their marriage, she could have feigned a miscarriage, although Joshua would have probably had the marriage annulled. How was she to know he had ice water flowing through his veins instead of blood?

Joshua was now sure beyond any doubt that Suzanne was not carrying a child. She had paraded around in front of him naked enough while trying to entice him into her bed, giving him a birds eye view of her concave stomach.

In the days that followed, Joshua kept a careful vigil, and observed Suzanne's every move. He was watching when the deceitful bitch slipped silently out of the house in the early morning hours to greet William, and the two of them entered the barn from the rear.

Joshua wore a broad grin as he entered the barn with eager anticipation, guided to their hiding place by Suzanne's passionate moans.

He crept to the edge of the dimly lit stall and towered over the thrashing couple. He actually felt sorry for the man as Suzanne dug her long nails into his back, leaving bloody trails in his flesh as she sought to devour the poor man.

"Well, now, what have we here?" Joshua drawled, lighting a cheroot. "It would appear that I have ignored my duties as a husband for too long, and my darling wife was forced to turn elsewhere to satisfy her voracious needs."

Suzanne roughly shoved William away as she grabbed her gown and tried to cover herself. "Oh, thank God you came when you did, Joshua," she cried. "He threatened to kill me if I refused to submit to his lust."

"Heaven forbid, my darling wife, are you saying the moans I heard were cries of fear?" Joshua eyes danced merrily as he enjoyed her groveling immensely.

"Oh Joshua, I was so terrified." She clutched her gown to her breasts and reached out to him. "Thank you for saving me."

"Don't touch me, Suzanne, and please do not think me dimwitted. Your touch sickens me."

He watched her cringe from the pure malice in his voice. "I watched you from the time you left the house until now, and you certainly were not forced against your will. In fact, you were enjoying yourself so much I regretted having to disturb you."

"You bastard," she sneered, sensing that her ruse was up. "I know what you hope to accomplish with your hateful words, but believe me, our marriage will never be annulled. Lynna will have you only over my dead body."

"That can be easily arranged, I assure you," he replied ominously. "You are woefully mistaken on one point, Suzanne. You see, you will grant me an annulment, for I have witnesses who will attest that you coupled with them during our marriage. Our Marriage. Hah!"

He laughed, harshly. "What a farce, but not to worry, for it is almost over." His eyes were shivers of green ice. "You will grant me an annulment, or I will drag your family's good name through the mud and create a scandal the likes of which Georgia has never seen."

He turned to William, who cowered against the

wall. "William, will you swear in a court of law that you fornicated with my new bride?"

"Yes sir, Mister Jordan. I be rite happy to," he replied without pause. "We forn'cated more times than I can count, in fact." He was getting off lightly if that was all he had to confess to. He didn't even glance at Suzanne as he made a hasty retreat from the barn. He had expected Mister Jordan to kill him when he caught him with his new bride. Instead, much to his surprise, the man actually seemed genuinely pleased to find them going at it. Damn, but rich people was a peculiar lot.

"Get packed, Suzanne. You will be returning to your parent's home first thing in the morning. If you agree to the annulment, we can put this entire fiasco behind us and move on with our lives. If not, your parents will be appalled to learn of your lies and multiple indiscretions."

"Joshua, you can't mean this," Suzanne cried. *She couldn't let him go.* "You could love me if you would only give yourself the chance. William meant nothing to me. It was a mistake I will regret for the rest of my life."

"What about Sawyer?" Joshua chuckled. "Was he a mistake as well?"

Suzanne's startled gasp echoed throughout the otherwise quiet barn. "How did you…?"

"It doesn't matter. What matters is that I don't care to love you." His tone was final as he looked her dead in the eyes before turning and walking out of the barn, and out of her life. "It gives me great pleasure to inform you that Lynna is the only woman I will *ever* love."

Chapter 24
Jamaica
Three Months Later

The magnificent waterfall cascading down the mountain reminded Lynna of a giant staircase rising majestically into the sky. The sight left her breathless. If ever there was a paradise, it was Jamaica.

Almost without thinking, she removed her dress and plunged into the cool inviting water, knowing she had found her place of peace and tranquility in this new land. Many times since coming to Jamaica, she had climbed the slippery slope to the top of the waterfall and been tempted to dive. So far, she had chickened out when she stood at the top of the precipice and gazed into the clear blue pool below.

She left the water, shaking her head as her eyes wandered over the tanned legs on display below her chemise. The Jamaican sun had turned her skin a rich golden brown. Would she ever be magnolia blossom white again? If not, and if she ever returned home, she would be shunned by polite society. Although the residents of Jamaica seemed to have no problem with skin that had been tanned to a golden hue.

Besides, she had no desire to return to Magnolia House and watch Suzanne parade around, flaunting her impending motherhood in Lynna's face at every opportunity. Her only regret was that Aunt Judith couldn't be here to enjoy the splendor of this lush tropical paradise with her.

"Hello."

Lynna whipped around to see who the voice belonged to. Finding no one else in the clearing, she scrambled to grab her dress and clutch it to her breast as she quickly rushed into the shadows of the forest.

"Hello," a little girl repeated, from her perch on the lowest branch of a tall tree.

"Oh… um… hello." Lynna exhaled a deep sigh of relief to find an adorable child with long golden locks and deep brown eyes watching her closely. "I didn't realize anyone else was here."

The child giggled secretively as she leapt from the branch of the tree. "You never do."

Lynna felt an immediate sense of panic. Who else had been watching her? "Have you been here before, when I was swimming?"

"Lots of times." The child sat down at the edge of the pool and gazed at her reflection in the water. "I told Father and told him there was a beautiful mermaid who lives in the pool at the waterfall." She removed her shoes to dangle her dainty little feet in the cool water. "He never believes me."

Lynna peered anxiously into the forest, and issued a silent prayer that the child's father wouldn't pop out of the trees and catch her in her shimmy.

The darling little girl looked Lynna over from head to toe, with a baffled expression. "I finally convinced him to accompany me today. Then, just as we were about to leave, there was a problem at the distillery and he couldn't come. He never fails to get called away whenever we plan a fun day together."

"Thank goodness for that." Lynna shivered

involuntarily at the thought. "I mean, not that he was called away when the two of you were hoping to spend the day together. I was referring to today, in particular. It would have proven most embarrassing if he had accompanied you today, and caught me frolicking in the pool."

"You are a mermaid, aren't you?" the child asked with all seriousness, leaning over to give Lynna's feet a closer inspection, and appearing extremely crestfallen to find feet instead of a tail. "My mother used to read me stories about mermaids, so I know they are beautiful creatures who live in the water and have fancy tails. Where is your tail?"

Lynna's hand went to cover her mouth, not wanting the very observant child to think she was ridiculing her. "Thank you very much for the compliment, but no, I fear I am not a mermaid. See? I have legs and feet just like you. Now, come sit with me and tell me your name. I am new to the island and know few of its residents."

The child peered at her curiously, evidently deciding that she liked the beautiful woman even though she didn't possess a mermaid tail. "My name is Crystal. My father named me for the crystal clear water in this very pool," she announced proudly, before her angelic face clouded with sadness. "Mother and I came here to swim often, before she died."

"I'm so sorry, Crystal. I know how you must miss her." In hopes of changing the subject, and brightening the child's mood, she asked, "Where do you live? It must be close by."

"At Eden." The child playfully kicked her feet, splashing them both.

"What a fitting name. Is your home very far?"

"Father won't allow me to go far from home, and I'm eight years old." Her bottom lip jutted out in a pout. "Can you credit that he still treats me like a child? He's such an old fussbudget."

"I'm sure your father worries because he loves you so much. If you were my daughter, I wouldn't allow you stray too far from home either. Now, you were telling me about Eden."

"It's on the other side of the cane field." Crystal jumped to her feet with her eyes twinkling merrily. "Will you come home with me, so my father will know I didn't create you in my vivid imagination?" she pleaded. "Please?"

"Why, I couldn't, especially with your father being so busy. You said yourself there was a problem this morning at the distillery. We wouldn't want to interfere with his work."

"Oh, he's always busy. Please," she pleaded. "Pretty please."

How could she refuse such a darling face, especially when she was eager to make friends in her new home. "Very well. Let me get dressed, but I can only stay a short while, since it's almost lunchtime."

Crystal giggled. "We'll stop to eat a stinking toe on the way home."

Lynna couldn't have heard the child correctly. Did she just invite her to consume a stinking toe? "Excuse me?" Then again, she had heard Jamaicans had rather bizarre appetites.

"I said a stinking toe, or 'tinkin toe' as some Jamaicans call it, because the seed pods look like big fat toes and have the scent of smelly feet. It's delicious, however, and the pulp is very sweet.

Father says it's good medicine for relieving headaches, and rheumatism."

A short while later, Lynna munched on the fruit as she climbed back into the cart. "A stinking toe tastes much better than it smells. Once you get past the odor of stinky feet, the powdery fruit tastes like vanilla flavored milk, mixed with a hint of cheese, not bad."

She wiped sweat from her brow as the little cart traveled down the narrow road that snaked through the sugarcane fields.

Sugarcane stalks rose ten feet in the air to block even the slightest breeze from reaching them, yet the narrow path allowed the blazing sun to beat relentlessly upon their heads. Lynna clung to the side of the little cart for dear life as it bounced over ruts, pulled by a frisky donkey. When they cleared the twin fields of towering cane stalks, the magnificent plantation Eden was visible in the distance.

Crystal took her on a guided tour of the plantation, and described in surprising detail the many buildings they passed. First were the coolie houses, row after row of cabins surrounded by umbrella trees to provide shade from the tropical sun. Lynna knew that sugarcane, often described as a rich man's crop, was labor intensive, and had a relatively small window for harvesting.

Next, were the workshops for the blacksmiths, carpenters, and coopers, alongside the overseer's cottage, the office, and the bookkeeper's cottage. Crystal brought the donkey to a halt in front of the white pillared plantation house.

"There you are, little lady. You almost missed

lunch," a voice called from the verandah.

Lynna turned to find a rather handsome man, with a wide grin brightening his features at the sight of the lady with his daughter.

Crystal jumped from the cart and into his waiting arms. "Father, this is the mermaid I was telling you about. Isn't she beautiful? You were right though; she isn't really a mermaid, as she doesn't even have a tail. Alas, she is just like us."

"Cheer up, my darling." Her father laughed. "Perhaps she is an enchanted mermaid, with the ability to take human form at will. Still, I would have to agree with your assumption, as she does possess an exceptional beauty to be a mere mortal."

The child's eyes twinkled as she considered this new and interesting theory.

"She is an inquisitive child with a vivid imagination. Please, accept my apologies." The child's father extended his hand and introduced himself. "I am Michael Devereux, and the little minx is my daughter."

"Lynna Mathison, and I assure you there is nothing to apologize for. Your daughter is adorable, and quite an accomplished little tour guide." His hands on her waist were firm as they lifted her from the cart.

"Will you join us for lunch?" Michael asked, catching her completely off guard. "We don't receive much company out here, and we would be delighted to have you."

"I really couldn't intrude," she insisted.

"Please?" Crystal pleaded. "Have lunch with us."

Although her aunts would surely think her

having lunch with total strangers inappropriate, why not? She was hoping to make friends on the island, and here was her first opportunity. "I would be delighted to join you for lunch, but I feel as though I am imposing on your generosity."

"Nonsense." Michael winked. "How often does one have an honest to goodness mermaid to lunch?"

"Oh, sir, I fear you are a terrible jokester." Lynna grinned. "How will I know when to take you seriously?"

"You will know."

Chapter 25

Michael lifted his giggling daughter to his shoulders and carried her inside, before sending her off to wash for lunch.

"Your home is lovely, Mr. Devereux," Lynna admired the richly appointed furnishings, and the wide-open, airy expanse of the house. "How long have you lived here?"

"Please, call me Michael, and while it is indeed lovely, I cannot claim ownership. I only oversee the plantation during the owner's absence." There was a harshness in his tone Lynna hadn't detected earlier.

"I see." She immediately realized she had hit upon a touchy subject, and made a mental note not to mention it again.

"It was an understandable mistake. You see, I was the overseer for several years before the original owner passed away. He had no living kin to leave the estate to, so it was auctioned off to the highest bidder."

"Where is the new owner?" she wondered aloud, seeing that Michael and Crystal seemed at home in the big house.

"He isn't the new owner. Eden has been his for the past several years. In answer to your question, he travels a great deal, coming here only occasionally to check on his investment.

"He must trust you implicitly."

"I have never given him reason not to," Michael

stated simply, leading the way to the dining room and seating her at the table.

"What are we having for lunch?" Crystal held up her hands to verify their cleanliness.

"A traditional Jamaican delicacy, cow's feet soup."

Lynna shuddered, thinking the island's inhabitants certainly considered toes and feet to be appetizing fare. Surely, he was only teasing her again.

He was.

After a pleasant lunch of shrimp in coconut cream sauce, and molasses cake for dessert, they sought out the shade of the verandah in an effort to ward off the afternoon heat. Lynna couldn't help but be amazed as she surveyed the vast workings of a sugar plantation. "I had no idea there was so much work involved in making the spoonful of sugar I add to my coffee each morning."

"You are not alone, few people realize how labor intensive the making of sugar really is." Michael walked to the edge of the porch to gaze across the towering cane fields. "Would you like to see the cane works? They should prove fascinating as well."

She caught the note of pride in his voice when he spoke of the mill. "I would love to see it, just not today. My aunts will be worried if I don't return soon. You have work to do, and I am hindering you from getting it done. Could I see it another day?"

"Certainly, whenever you wish. I cannot think of a more enjoyable way to pass an afternoon."

Lynna felt a blush stain her cheeks as she stood to smooth the wrinkles from her skirt. "Now, if I may borrow your daughter, I'm afraid I don't quite know my way around the area yet." She quickly discovered that to be an impossible request, as Crystal was sleeping soundly on the cushioned porch swing.

"I'll be happy to take you home." Michael chuckled, calling for the cart to be brought back around.

"Absolutely not. I couldn't possibly take you away from your work. Why, I've taken too much of your time already."

"Believe me, this place will not fall apart if I take a few hours off. Besides, anyone who witnesses your beauty will certainly not begrudge me the time I spend with you."

"You, sir, are an outrageous flatterer."

The ride home was pleasant. They stopped often, with Michael pointing out sights she might otherwise have missed. When he turned his head to gaze upon the acres and acres of sugar cane, Lynna took the opportunity to study him more closely. He was of average height and build, a few inches taller than her, with sandy brown hair. He was handsome in a boyish way, and his brown eyes sparkled when he laughed.

"How am I supposed to take you home, when I don't even know where you live? Don't that beat all. I forgot to ask." He thumped the heel of his hand to his forehead. "Perhaps you *are* an enchanted mermaid with the power to cast a spell, making a man forget all but you."

"Perhaps I am," she smiled slyly and arched a brow, surprised by the realization that she was actually flirting with a stranger.

Michael threw back his head and laughed heartily. "My daughter and I are going to enjoy having you around. Enchanted or not, you brighten the day." They stopped at a crossroads, and he asked, "What brings you to Jamaica?"

She would never reveal Joshua's callous treatment of her, instead she gave the most recent set of tragic events. "Has news reached Jamaica of the devastating earthquake that struck Charleston?"

"No, I hadn't heard the news." Michael placed his calloused hand on hers. "What a terrible tragedy."

"My aunt was quite distraught, and insisted that we leave the city until Charleston can be rebuilt. That's why we came here to visit her sister." Lynna closed her eyes against a horrible memory of the devastated city. "Jamaica is doing a wonderful job of soothing our troubled souls."

"While I feel terrible about the earthquake, I'm happy that you and your aunt chose our island to help you heal."

"I couldn't ask for a more beautiful place to visit, or to meet nicer people than you and your charming daughter."

"Thank you kindly, my beautiful mermaid." He reached to push a lock of stray hair behind her ear, surprising Lynna with his boldness. "Now, let's get you out of this unforgiving sun, shall we? Which way?"

"Left... or... right, maybe. I'm not sure." She was truly perplexed. "I'm visiting my aunt and uncle at Springfield, perhaps you know of it?"

"Springfield?" Michael turned to her with a look of surprise. "I can't believe Cliff and Bertie failed to mention they had such a lovely niece. I'll make a point to call on them more often."

Springfield was a quaint little house. Lynna's first impression upon seeing it, was that it reminded her of a gingerbread cottage. Her Uncle Cliff was short and bald with a perpetual smile on his face. Aunt Bertie towered a foot over him, with her long grey hair braided and pinned atop her head. The two constantly joked and teased each other, yet when their eyes met, it was something akin to worship that visitors saw.

Bertie, Cliff, and Gypsie came down the steps when the little cart rolled up to the door. "Hello Michael, I see you found our errant niece and brought her home," Cliff teased, shaking Michael's hand. "We were about to form a search party."

"I was not lost, Uncle Cliff." Lynna laughed. "However, Michael was kind enough to drive me home."

"Why you must be famished, child." Bertie hurried down the steps. "It's almost supper time and you missed lunch. Come in the house while I prepare plates for both of you."

"Don't bother, Aunt Bertie. I had lunch with Michael and his charming daughter Crystal."

"Oh, did you now?" Bertie was obviously pleased with the idea of a prospective romance, especially one that could keep Lynna on the island permanently. "Then it's only fair that you stay to supper with us, Michael."

"I wish I could, Bertie," Michael was already climbing into the cart. "I still have a few hours of work left before the sun goes down. Will the invitation hold until tomorrow evening?"

"It certainly will, and bring Crystal," Bertie reminded him. "It has been too long in between visits."

"She's been pestering me to bring her over to see all of you." As the cart pulled away, Michael called over his shoulder, "She will be delighted."

"What a fine young man," Gypsie remarked, as they watched Michael's cart disappear down the dirt road in a cloud of dust.

"That he is." Bertie placed her arm around Lynna's waist to usher her into the house. "A more charming man is not to be found, and such a sweet little daughter, poor thing. A child without a mother is such a pity."

"A hard worker too," Cliff added. "Still, he's a bit of a puzzle. It has been how many years since his wife passed away? Almost three, I think, and he has shown absolutely no interest in women since, that I can tell."

"Perhaps the girl of his dreams hasn't come along, yet." Gypsie remarked, feigning innocence. "A girl would be fortunate to find herself with Michael Devereux for a husband, wouldn't she, Lynna?"

"A woman would be fortunate indeed, Aunt Gypsie," she answered dutifully, accepting the fact that both aunts had matchmaking on their minds. She intended to *make* herself not be opposed to the idea.

Supper the following evening was a gay affair, with traditional Jamaican cuisine and lively conversation. Lynna found that she enjoyed Michael's company immensely, and they were never at a loss for a topic to discuss. He had the group rolling with laughter when he recounted the mermaid story.

Crystal rarely left Lynna's side, sitting beside her at supper and curling up on the sofa next to her when they adjourned to the parlor for coffee. "Lynna is going to step on you if you don't stay out of her shadow," her father joked.

"Oh, don't tease her, Michael. If she gets underfoot I will simply change my legs into a mermaid's tail, so I won't cause her harm."

Crystal was immediately alert. "Can you really do that?"

"Of course, not." Lynna grinned as she leaned over to tickle the child's midsection.

When Crystal settled down, she wiped tears from her eyes and blurted, "Will you be my mother, Lynna?"

Michael rolled his eyes toward the heavens before lifting his daughter from the sofa and heading to the door. "Thank you for inviting us to supper. It was delicious, as always." Lynna noticed the look of longing in his eyes as he mouthed the words, "I'm sorry."

"Nonsense." She quipped, using his earlier explanation. "She is but an imaginative child."

Michael hesitated on the porch. "Would you like to see the cane works tomorrow?"

"I would love to," she answered, to the delight of both aunts. "I have been looking forward to it."

"Come by for lunch, and afterwards I'll give you the grand tour."

"I'll see you at noon," she just had time to reply, before Crystal rushed back into the room to give her a bear hug and a resounding smack on the lips.

The following afternoon, after a delicious lunch,

Lynna was amazed by the mill works. There was a boiling house, a curing house, and a still house. At the mill, Michael explained the process of extracting sugar from the cane and how it was separated into golden sugar crystals and molasses. He went on to explain that the majority of his molasses were used in the making of Jamaica's famed rum.

All the facts seemed to jumble together in Lynna's mind. "It seems terribly complicated."

"I suppose it would to a newcomer, while its second nature to me." Again, his voice took on a sharp edge. "I would wager the man who owns Eden doesn't know half as much about cane as I do. Yet, that is neither here nor there, as his pockets are considerably deeper than mine."

So, it came to be that in the weeks that followed, Lynna was a frequent visitor at Eden. During the day, while Michael was busy at the distillery, she and Crystal often rode in the little cart to the cooling oasis of the waterfall. If they weren't playing in the cascading water, they could be found searching for small fish in the tidal pools at the ocean's edge, building sandcastles, or laughing gaily as they frolicked through a field of wildflowers.

Lynna couldn't love the child more if she were her very own daughter.

When the sun began to sink low on the horizon, Lynna and Michael took rides in the cart, or relaxed on the verandah to enjoy breathtaking sunsets.

❦ *Chapter 26* ❦

Two months from the day they met, Lynna became Mrs. Michael Devereux in a simple ceremony held on a cliff overlooking the ocean. She was breathtakingly beautiful in a white, off the shoulder gown, stitched by her own hands. She cried tears of joy, and tears of regret that Aunt Judith wasn't there.

Uncle Cliff gave her away in her father's absence, and Crystal was her only attendant, scattering rose petals from a hand woven basket.

After the ceremony, Aunt Bertie insisted that Crystal visit with them for a few days while Lynna and Michael enjoyed a brief honeymoon.

Lynna was as fidgety as a schoolgirl as she slipped a lacy peignoir over her head. Would Michael stir the same feelings of ecstasy as Joshua?

Thus far, Michael hadn't seemed overly romantic. He had never even tried to kiss her. It was obvious that he wasn't the man of passion Joshua was. He was more shy and reserved, but she was comparing Michael to Joshua, and that wasn't fair.

Few men could compare to Captain Jordan.

Michael was kind, gentle, caring, and devoted to his daughter. He would make a wonderful father to their children, and Jamaica was a marvelous place to raise them. Passion would come in due time, hopefully, tonight. She desperately longed for someone to love, and be loved in return.

She went to the balcony, and inhaled the sweet smell of approaching rain as jagged heat lightning flashed, and dark clouds heavy with rain drifted over the mountains. A gust of wind molded her negligee to her body as fat drops of rain began to fall. Brief thunderstorms were an evening occurrence in Jamaica.

An hour later, she paced the room and wondered at her husband's delay. What could be keeping him on their wedding night? Surely there wasn't a problem at the distillery, or he wasn't in his office surrounded by paperwork, having completely forgotten his bride waited in their bed.

On bare feet, she hurried downstairs, and what she saw caused her heart to ache with an all too familiar pain. She shuddered as one thought circled over and over in her mind.

Had she been cursed to live a life of misery?

She was at once beset by a flurry of emotions. She was offended, hurt, and angry all at the same time, to find him asleep, and snoring on the sofa with an empty rum bottle close by.

Was he drunk? He couldn't be. She had never even seen him tipsy. Still, his intoxicated state was proof that he had little interest in consummating their wedding vows.

Lynna had never felt more completely dejected as she climbed the stairs to her empty room. After much tossing, turning, and heartfelt tears, she finally drifted into a restless sleep in the early morning hours.

"Good morning." Michael smiled across the table during a breakfast of hominy corn porridge, country ham, and thick cane syrup poured over flapjacks. "You slept well, I trust."

"I slept alone," Lynna mused, sipping coffee and trying to keep the irritation out of her voice as she stabbed at a thick slice of ham. She must look a fright with her eyes red and puffy from a night of crying.

"Oh, that." Michael waved a hand in the air, dismissing her words. "I imbibed too much of my own rum."

"Apparently."

Michael was growing annoyed with her accusing tone. "Most women find that obligation more of a chore than a pleasure, do they not?"

"This wife wouldn't," she answered honestly. "I look forward to being your wife in every sense of the word, Michael, and having your children. I certainly wouldn't consider making love to you a chore. If I felt that way, I wouldn't have married you to begin with."

Suddenly, looking mad enough to spit, Michael stormed out of the house without a word, leaving his breakfast untouched. Lynna could only stare after him, utterly confused by both his erratic behavior and the bizarre circumstances of her life. What had she said to set him off?

In the weeks that followed, other than the disturbing lack of intimacy from her husband, Lynna's days on the island were filled with joy. She and Crystal spent many carefree hours at the waterfall, or down by the beach splashing in the waves, chasing fiddler crabs, or finding seashells to take home and deposit in a glass vase. Her days were wonderful, while her nights were nothing short of torture.

Six weeks after their wedding, her husband still hadn't made love to her, or even attempted to for that matter. His nights were spent in a drunken stupor on the sofa, and a hurried peck on the cheek was the most romantic gesture he offered before rushing off to the mill. As embarrassing as it was for Lynna to admit, she accepted the fact that her husband had no desire to bed her.

Was he repulsed by her? Did he already regret his hasty proposal, and even hastier marriage? Was he in the habit of getting intoxicated every night, to drown the sorrow he felt over being tied to her for a lifetime?

Just before drifting into an exhausted sleep, Lynna decided to have a heart to heart discussion with her husband the following morning, and ask if he would be agreeable to having their farce of a marriage annulled. She would cut her losses, and find a way to return to home to France, and her father.

Surely *someone* who could love her.

Chapter 27

Michael was asleep on the sofa, just after midnight when the owner of Eden tied his horse to the hitching post. He entered the quiet house to find his overseer still fully dressed, passed out cold, drooling on the embroidered sofa pillow, and snoring like a lumberjack. A strange and unusual sight indeed.

The docks were abuzz with rumors of Michael's recent nuptials to a young lady of exceptional beauty. Why then wasn't he enjoying the fruits of his marriage?

"Michael?" The stunned man shook his overseer vigorously in an attempt to wake him from a drunken stupor. "Michael, wake up."

Michael opened one blurry eye and squinted when he saw two faces leaning over him. "Evenin', boss."

"A good evening it is, Michael." Still, his boss was deeply disturbed by the sight of his overseer, who was semi-conscious at best. "For some of us, at least." He hadn't known Michael to imbibe so heavily in years, not since the night his wife died of a sudden illness. Then, it was to be expected, but now? Surely his recent marriage hadn't brought about such stress. "I hear a celebration is in order. You finally tied the knot after all these years, did you?"

"Yes *sher*, I did," Michael slurred the words, and

barely opened his eyes before passing out again.

Determined to get to the bottom of this charade, his boss shook him. "Michael, why are you turning to a bottle instead of your new bride? You haven't forgotten what to do behind closed doors, after so long a dry spell, have you?"

Michael partially opened one eye, then closed it. "You can't forget something you never acquired knowledge of in the first place, now can you?" In his state of extreme drunkenness, Michael was admitting more than he ever had before.

"What do you mean you never acquired the knowledge? Do you perhaps require a few pointers on the subject? It really isn't that difficult unless she's of the unattractive sort then, admittedly, it can sometimes be a bit of a challenge to remain... attentive. If such were the case, I might understand why you chose to drown your sorrows in a bottle. Yet, scuttlebutt has it that she is anything but an ugly duckling."

Michael sighed. "She is the most beautiful woman I ever laid my eyes on, boss."

"Then pardon me for sounding dimwitted, but your words make little sense to me."

"I can't make love to nobody. Do those words make sense to you?" He sat up too fast, and held his spinning head in his trembling hands as he blurted out his sorrowful tale. "When I was just a boy, I entered the barn one morning to feed and water the horses, that was my chore. I had been tending them for years. On this particular morning, for reasons I still can't figure out, I startled Pa's favorite stallion Samson and he commenced to kicking."

Michael paused, scrubbing his hands over his

face. "I often wonder how different my life would be if I had just made a noise that morning, and let Samson know I was entering his stall." He laughed harshly. "At any rate, old Samson took deadly aim and kicked me right square in my privates. They been useless ever since."

"I'm sorry to hear that, Michael." Some men would consider it a fate worse than death. "The little lady must be sympathetic to your unfortunate condition to wed you, knowing you cannot father her children."

"She doesn't know, and she never will," Michael admitted, hanging his head. "She's probably upstairs now, imagining that I soon will join her and make passionate love to her for the remainder of the night." He laughed bitterly. "I pray she doesn't hold her breath."

"Let me see if I am understanding you correctly. You married a woman under the false pretense that you could make love to her, and give her children?"

Michael nodded drunkenly. "I reckon that's about the gist of it."

"Then you are not Crystal's father?"

"Her mother was already carrying her when we married, so I claimed the child as my own."

"In my humble opinion, you have done your new bride a dire disservice, Michael. Then, by not being honest with her, you hurt her further by leaving her alone each night, which I would imagine leads her to believe you simply don't desire her."

"I don't desire her, since I've never known the insatiable lust that drives so many men to distraction." Michael held his throbbing head in his hands as he eyed the empty whiskey bottle. "I married her to give Crystal a mother."

"While I understand your love for the child, surely you will admit that's its a feeble excuse for a marriage. You owe her the truth."

"I don't owe her a damn thing," Michael snarled. "She has a beautiful home, an attentive husband during daylight hours, and a child who adores her. That's all any woman wants."

"No, Michael, it isn't." The man shook his head sadly. "Most women are born with a motherly instinct to nurture a child at their breast."

"I'm going back to sleep now. We can continue this discussion in the morning if you feel the need, but I believe everything has been said." Thus said, he passed out, and was snoring in seconds.

His boss climbed the stairs, shaking his head with pity for Michael's bride. She was waiting for a husband who would never come to her. First thing tomorrow morning, he would have a discussion with the little lady, and find out for himself if she was content with her current arrangement. While it might not be any of his concern, he couldn't tolerate the notion of the poor girl lying in bed, in his house, prostrate with grief at having to bear the brunt of her husband's cruel deception.

At the top of the stairs, he paused just outside her door. He really shouldn't get involved. This was between Michael and his wife, and he should wait until morning to have this discussion. Still, as owner of the plantation, he felt the need to right any wrongs being committed under his roof.

Michael said she was the most beautiful woman he had ever seen, while the men on the dock swore she had descended on a stairway straight from heaven. These comments were intriguing to say the least. One little peek couldn't hurt. The poor girl had probably cried herself to sleep hours ago.

He quietly opening the door, to find the woman in question reclined on the bed in a sheer nightgown, peaceful in slumber. He moved closer to the bed, to see her more clearly by the moonlight filtering through the open balcony doors.

"Michael was correct," he whispered. "You are beautiful indeed."

The deep voice penetrated Lynna's sleep drugged mind, causing her to awaken with a start. With the belief that her husband had finally decided to join her in their marriage bed, she smiled seductively. "I was beginning to worry that you did not desire your new bride."

His lips found hers in a kiss filled with longing, and months of pent up passion. Lynna smiled as he swiftly removed her nightgown and his clothes. She sighed deep in her throat as he crushed her naked body against his broad chest. All thoughts of the many lonely nights she had spent in this bed crying herself to sleep, were at once forgotten.

Thank God, she wouldn't have to pretend to enjoy making love to her husband. His touch thrilled her, and made her body squirm with anticipation.

She turned on her side to press her soft, feminine curves against his. She draped her leg over his hip, behaving like a woman starved, for she was.

He placed his hand on her hip and gently pushed her to her back, nudging her knees apart with his thigh, and entered her. Neither of them could hold out for more than a few strokes, and clung to each other desperately as their bodies pulsed with glorious release.

After several minutes had passed, and their breathing returned to a normal rhythm, he rolled to the side and raised up on his elbow to bury his face in her hair. "You don't know how long I have dreamed of this moment, my love."

His voice immediately froze her ebbing passion. She knew that voice.

Joshua.

"Turn me loose and get out of my room at once," she cried, lashing out at him with her tiny fists.

"Not likely, my dearest. It took me too long to find you."

"Get out." She was enraged that he would leave Suzanne's bed and think to slither into hers. "I am a married woman, and if you don't leave this room at once I will scream for my husband."

"As you wish, but neither your husband or anyone else at Eden will come to your rescue, so save your breath." He was angered both by her rejection, and by hearing her refer to another man as her husband. "By the way, your dear husband is passed out cold on the sofa."

He knew her husband didn't desire her, and he chose to callously throw it in her face. Lynna wanted to claw his eyes out of their sockets for the pain he had caused her. "Do you want everyone in this house to know what a vile and disgusting cretin you are?"

"I care not what others think."

She opened her mouth to scream, when he clamped his hand over her mouth and whispered in a voice that was deadly serious, "I am going to make love to you, again, Lynna. I have thought of nothing else, and what just transpired between us was far too hasty for my liking."

Lynna glared at him as her mind worked furiously. She couldn't depend on her husband to save her, he would be useless in his inebriated state, and her strength was no match for Joshua's. Still, there had to be a way to stop him, but why was he in Jamaica? In this house? How did he find her?

"After what we just shared, you cannot deny that you still desire me, Lynna." He placed a finger on her lips upon seeing her open her mouth to dispute his words. "You can't lie to me."

"I am a married woman now, Joshua." She snatched his finger away. "What gives you the right to take what belongs to another man?

"You belong to me, and don't you dare say otherwise. You have since that first night on my ship."

"Joshua?" She stopped, losing the will to fight. What was the point of trying to make him listen anyway? "Just get it over with, satisfy your lust and leave."

"Satisfy my lust, indeed." He smiled wickedly. He would enjoy making her beg.

As his kisses left a hot trail down Lynna's neck, she knew she was fighting a losing battle.

He kneeled beside the bed and leisurely kissed his way up her leg, feeling her tremble as he neared her tightly clenched thighs. She relaxed somewhat when his mouth moved down the opposite leg, only to draw in her breath sharply when his tongue flicked the tender spot beneath her ankle. She steeled herself against his sensuous onslaught, praying it would be over soon.

She clenched her teeth and remained perfectly

still, willing her body not to respond as he left a burning trail over her stomach. One traitorous moan escaped when his mouth traveled to her neck, without touching her throbbing breasts. She willed her hands not to pull his head back to the rigid peaks.

Please let me be strong enough to withstand this torture, and not give in to him.

"Tell me you want me, Lynna," he whispered.

"Never," she breathed. "I want only to be left alone."

His tongue went to her ear, nibbling the tender lobe as his warm breath served to further weaken her resistance. She refused to admit defeat, even as she silently cursed her betraying body. His soft lips outlined her own, causing them to part and allow his tongue to dart through her smooth teeth and bring the desired response. "Tell me you want me, Lynna."

She cooled instantly. "I want no part of you."

He blew warm breath on the rosy peaks of her full breasts as she bit her lip to keep from crying out his name. He continued to explore her body for what seemed like hours of sweet torture as her insides churned with need. When his soft mouth at last closed over her hardened nipple, and his teeth tugged ever so gently, the will to fight deserted her.

"Oh, Joshua," she moaned. "I cannot stand another moment of this torment."

"Tell me you want me," he whispered.

"Yes," she cried. "I want you." Her body was on fire, every nerve alive to his touch. She arched against him as her hand guided him into her eager body. Then her hands were on his buttocks, pressing, as their passion climbed higher and higher until her insides shattered, leaving her in a state of euphoric bliss.

Joshua rolled to his side as a silent tear slid down her cheek. How could she behave so wantonly in his arms when she was wed to another? If only Joshua was her husband, she would be the happiest woman alive. Yet, he was married, as was she, and the realization made her burst into heartbreaking sobs.

Her tears were too much for Joshua. "What's wrong, my love?"

"How can you ask me that?" Why wasn't he as distraught over this situation as she was? "Do you have no feelings?"

"I fear that my feelings are too strong." He brushed her tears away and caressed the line of her jaw. "I love you, Lynna."

How she had longed to hear him say those words, but they came too late. She couldn't allow herself to fall under his spell tonight, then have her heart ripped out of her chest again tomorrow. This night of passion would have to last them for an eternity. "Did Suzanne present you with a son or daughter?"

"There was no child," he answered testily.

"What do you mean there was no child?" She sat up with a puzzled frown. "Did Suzanne miscarry?"

"There was never a child to miscarry." Joshua leaned against the headboard and struck a match to a cheroot. "Suzanne fabricated the lie to coerce me into marriage. In the weeks that followed, when she realized her husband was loathe to touch her, she turned to a few others.

Suzanne had lied about carrying his child?

"I can't believe Suzanne would stoop so low, or be so devious."

"Your eyes do not deceive you, Lynna."

"You saw her?" she gasped.

"I caught her with the stable boy. Although she cried rape, I had been following her for days." His voice was cold, and unforgiving. "I gave her an ultimatum. She could either grant me an annulment, or I would guarantee her a scandal the likes of which her family would never crawl out from under."

He was free from his vows to Suzanne, and he loved her, but she was no longer a free woman. Her tears flowed in earnest as she pondered this wicked turn of fate.

"Dry your eyes and come here, darling." He cradled her head on his chest as he stroked her hair. "Do you love me?"

"Joshua, I..."

"Answer me, Lynna. I must know the truth."

"Then, yes, I love you. I have always loved you. I would never marry Michael had I known of Suzanne's lies and treachery, but now it's too late."

"It's never too late." Joshua hugged her so hard she thought her ribs might crack. "We love each other, and that's all that matters."

They slept wrapped in each other's arms, afraid to let go. Afraid the other might disappear with the harsh light of morning.

Sometime in the early morning hours, Joshua's voice penetrated the fog of her deep and satisfied sleep. "I will wait for you to come to me tonight.

"You, sir, will have an awfully long wait." She snuggled deeper under the cover and returned to her dream world, not sure whether his rumbling laughter had been real or imagined.

When she awakened, the cook reported that Michael had taken an overnight trip into town. Lynna found Joshua and Crystal on the verandah, chatting as if they had known each other for years. "Good morning, Lynna," Crystal chirped.

"Good morning, sweet girl." Lynna smiled, leaning over to drop a kiss on her forehead. "Joshua, I see you have met my adorable stepdaughter."

"Uncle Joshua already knew me." Crystal laughed merrily. "He didn't just meet me."

"I see." Lynna frowned. "So, you have visited Eden before, Captain Jordan?"

"Uncle Joshua doesn't visit," Crystal giggled, finding Lynna's questions hilarious. "He owns Eden."

"You own Eden?" Lynna was so caught off guard by the child's statement she almost dropped her coffee cup. "But… but… how can that be?"

Joshua beamed as his eyes swept the entire length of her. "I purchased the plantation several years ago at auction. Michael was already the overseer, so he continued under my employ. Him and, eventually, this little cherub."

Joshua was the owner Michael had so often railed against?

"What did you bring me, Uncle Joshua?" Crystal wheedled, as her eyes danced with excitement.

"As a matter of fact, there is a box on my bed that I bought for… someone." He placed a finger on his chin, pretending to ponder. "Who did I bring it for? Let me see, if I think hard enough perhaps it will come to me."

"It was me." Crystal squealed with delight and

took off running. "You brought it for me." The door slammed behind her.

"You never mentioned that you owned property in Jamaica." Lynna stood beside the rail as the elated child footfalls echoed up the stairs.

"You never asked. There are still a few things about me you have yet to discover, my love."

Less than five minutes later, Joshua was too busy playing with Crystal to finish their discussion. The child immediately plopped down on his lap, opened a box filled with a paper doll and numerous paper dresses, and consulted Joshua's opinion on which frock the doll should be attired in for the noontime meal.

After her doll had modeled the last dress, she turned to Joshua and asked, "Uncle Joshua, will you come to the beach with Lynna and me today? Pretty please?"

"I can think of nothing I would enjoy better than spending a day at the beach with my two favorite girls." He laughed as he lifted her over his shoulders. "Let's go ask Sadie to pack a lunch and be on our way."

Chapter 28

The day on the beach with Joshua far surpassed any other day Lynna had spent in this lush tropical paradise. Joshua rolled up his breeches and waded in the water with Crystal, taking her hands to jump incoming waves.

The threesome walked for miles on the beach, and found several perfect spiral shells for Lynna to add to her collection jar.

They picnicked on fried chicken and corn on the cob under the shade of a silk cotton tree. While Lynna and Joshua gazed with longing into each other's eyes and fought to keep their hands to themselves, Crystal frolicked in the surf.

Watching Joshua and Crystal together caused Lynna to marvel at what a wonderful father he would be. If only he could father her children. What a glorious life that would be.

That evening Joshua's words, "I will wait for you to come to me tonight," drummed furiously in Lynna's ears. She had laughed at him then, but what a fool she had been. Her body craved his sweet touch, and the pleasure that he alone could give her.

She was unable to sleep, and still wide awake when she heard his door close, and she waited. He had left to tour the distillery shortly after their return from the beach.

She waited with bated breath until there was no

more movement in his room. She imagined his muscular body stretched out on the bed with a lazy grin tugging at the corners of his mouth, and his sea green eyes shining. So sure she would come to him, certain that no woman could resist his masculine charm.

Lynna relaxed as a delicious languor settled over her, erasing from mind all unpleasant thoughts and leaving only Joshua. When she closed her eyes, his smiling eyes beckoned her.

Michael was due home tomorrow, so tonight would be their last night together. Would she deny herself one last night in the arms of the only man she would ever love?

No.

She would not.

She slipped into a thin cotton robe and tied the sash at her waist with suddenly nervous hands. She decided against what she was about to do three times, before finally finding the courage to open her door and ease into the dimly lit corridor.

Her hands trembled as she turned the knob and pushed open the door to his room. He was on the bed, just as she had imagined. His even breathing assured her that he was asleep and she still had time to change her mind. In all honesty, she was feeling rather piqued that he had lost no sleep worrying over whether or not she would come.

She bent to touch his hair, even as she longed to caress his sleeping features, but she quickly came to her senses and jerked away. What had come over her? This was utter foolishness.

Not only was she married, but she was in another man's bedroom, desperately wanting him to make love to her. She rushed through the open balcony doors, hoping the evening breeze would cool her heated skin and clear her befuddled mind.

The air was sweet as the crisp trade winds blew down from the mountain to fan her hair out behind her, molding the thin robe to her body.

"I have been waiting for you, my love," he whispered against her hair.

"I... needed to... talk to you," she lied, suddenly ashamed of her wanton behavior.

"You don't want talk, Lynna, we both want the same thing." He slipped his hands around her waist and nuzzled her neck. "Let me love you."

Their lips met in a tender kiss as he lifted her and carried her to the bed. "Yes, Joshua."

What followed was the stuff that sweet dreams are made of.

Just as they were sitting down to breakfast, the first mate on the *Windjammer* came rushing into the dining room. "I think we got troubles, captain," his voice was ragged, out of breath.

"What is the cause of your obvious distress, my good man?" Joshua was immediately concerned for the safety of his crew.

"There may not be trouble, but a ship just dropped anchor in the harbor flying the Jolly Roger." His eyes were wide with alarm. "The ship's got everybody running to their houses and boarding up their doors and windows."

"Have my horse saddled and I will join you on the ship."

Joshua needed time alone with Lynna, before he must leave her. He drew her into his arms for one last meaningful kiss. "Remember this, my love. When I return, we will continue where we left off. You and Crystal stay inside today."

"Will there be trouble, Joshua?"

"It is most likely nothing more than a show of force. Pirates have a reputation to uphold. There are too many armed ships in the harbor for them to openly attack us."

Michael returned not long after Joshua left, as tense and nervous as a caged animal. He stormed through the door without even pausing to greet his new bride. "Where's the boss?"

"I assume you are speaking of Captain Jordan. If so, one of his men came with an urgent message that he should return to his ship." Lynna assumed his agitation was caused by the appearance of the pirate vessel.

Michael threw his hands into the air. "Well, what was the damn message?"

"It would seem that a pirate ship has anchored in the harbor. Captain Jordan's first mate was worried there might be trouble."

Why was he shouting at her, and why was he suddenly so concerned with Joshua's whereabouts?

His attitude changed abruptly, in a split second, to that of a kind and caring husband. "Would you like to ride into town with me, Lynna?"

"You just returned from town, Michael. Why do you wish to go again so soon?"

"With all the talk of pirates, I completely forgot about the list of supplies Sadie asked me to purchase." He glanced at her askance. "Surely, my darling wife will not refuse me the pleasure of her company."

"Of course not, Michael." Even though she had no desire to accompany him, Lynna saw no way around it. "I'll just get my wrap."

"Bring Crystal with you." He waved his hand, dismissing her. "She will enjoy the outing as well."

The day was terribly hot, with the occupants of the buggy perspiring profusely as Michael stopped the conveyance on a hill overlooking the harbor. "How does a cool drink of lemonade sound for my two favorite ladies?"

We can't be your two favorite ladies, too, papa." Crystal giggled. "Uncle Joshua said we were his two favorite ladies."

"Did he now?" Michael sent Lynna a look of pure contempt as he reached across his daughter to caress the line of her jaw. "Well then, I guess Uncle Joshua and I will just have to share the beautiful mermaid."

Lynna fought to control her emotions as she gazed across the harbor in search of the *Windjammer*.

Michael knew.

"Drink up, girls," His grin was one of pure malice, that sent alarms bells clanging through Lynna's head as he handed them each a cup of lemonade. "It's going to be a bumpy ride."

❧ *Chapter 29* ❧

The pain in Lynna's head was steady, throbbing with each beat of her heart. She wished the bed would stop its constant swaying, for she was beginning to feel nauseous. She became slowly aware of her surroundings when she noticed sunlight filtering through a small round hole in the wall.

A porthole.

She was on a ship, but how could that be, when she had no knowledge of coming onboard? How did Joshua manage to bring her on the *Windjammer* without her knowledge? She forced her eyes open and glanced around the filthy, sparsely appointed cabin. She definitely was not on the *Windjammer*.

Had she been abducted?

Had the kidnappers found her after all these years? Of course, it had to be the villains from France. She hadn't dwelled on that horror for years, erroneously assuming they had been unable to locate her and given up the search. Alas, they had discovered her hiding place, and were now holding her for ransom.

She choked back a sob as the thought crossed her mind that at least her kidnapping would gain her father's attention.

Suddenly, all the horror stories she had heard of women being abducted by pirates came back to haunt her. She lay on a hard smelly bunk infested with bugs, and squinted at the too bright sunlight shining through the open porthole.

She prayed that no harm had come to Michael and Crystal, and they had somehow managed to escape this nightmare.

She ran to the door and found it locked. "Open this door!" she yelled at the top of her lungs. "I demand to see the captain!" When no answer was forthcoming, she fell down on the bunk and cried tears of abject misery.

Hours later, with her throat raw from screaming, Lynna heard keys rattle against the door. She jumped out of the way as it was thrown open to bang against the wall.

"While I'm not the Captain, I can probably answer any questions you might have."

"Michael?" A strong sense of foreboding seeped through every pore in her body as her husband sauntered. "Why am I on this vile ship? Where is Crystal?"

He strode casually into the cabin and held up his hand to quiet her. "Let me start by answering the most obvious question. How you arrived here?" He sat on the bunk and brushed away a cockroach that boldly crawled across the filthy spread. "I thought it best to drug you."

"You drugged me? Why? Where are you taking me?" The fact that she had been drugged, and taken against her will was of little consequence now. What mattered was finding a way off this wretched ship.

"We are relocating to another island," he replied calmly, walking across the cabin to gaze out the porthole. "This latest turn of events necessitated our hasty departure from Jamaica."

"Michael, I insist that you return me to Jamaica at once. You have no right to hold me against my will."

"Oh, but I do." His eyes were forged of steel as he turned to glare at her. "You forget that you are my wife, and as such you must go wherever I deem fit to take you."

"Why are you doing this, Michael? Why are you leaving your home?"

"My home?" he spat venomously. "It would have been, if that old fool Morrison hadn't died before I could convince him to make me sole beneficiary of Eden. I knew he had no living kin to claim the plantation, and no son could have treated that feeble old man better than I did. I deserved Eden." He slammed his fist on the table. "If I'd just had a little more time with him."

His face was a stone mask of hatred. "After his death, the plantation was sold to Captain Joshua Jordan of Charleston. I wanted to kill him the day he came riding up on his black stallion to announce that he was the new owner of Eden." Michael's hand rested on the hilt of his cutlass. "After years of plotting, and thanks solely to you, I conceived of the perfect plan to exact my revenge."

"Which is?" She would discover his plan, and find a way to warn Joshua, but how? The ship was probably well out to sea by now.

Michael left the room momentarily, and returned with a metal box. He placed it on the table, and opened it to reveal more gold doubloons than she had ever seen, an amount of coins one might expect to find on a pirate ship.

Pirate ship?

Suddenly, it dawned on her. She was on the pirate vessel they had seen in the harbor. Did that make her husband a buccaneer? "Michael, where did you get these coins?"

"By rights, the treasure is mine," he seethed, coming to shake her roughly by the shoulders. "I'm the one who worked and sweated this money out of the land, while the mighty Captain Jordan navigated the high seas without a care in the world. Why should he live large on plantation profits, when he never turned over a hand to earn it?" A triumphant smile curved his lips. "He has a surprise awaiting him the next time he opens his safe."

"Michael, he trusted you." Lynna could hardly fathom this startling shift in her husband. How could his personality change so drastically, almost overnight?

"That was his first mistake." He laughed as he placed the heavy box on her lap. "We can start a new life with the treasure in that box, Lynna."

"I will have no part of such deception," she cried, rising to her feet and causing the gold coins to scatter noisily across the floor. "Please, Michael, I beg you to take me home."

"Unfortunately, your wants are of little concern to me, my *lady*." He sneered the last word as he bent to retrieve the coins. "You will need to accustom yourself to a vastly different way of life, as the island we will call home is rather primitive compared to Jamaica. There are no magnificent plantations, or doting servants."

"Whose ship are we on, Michael?"

"We sail on the ship of my brother, Sean

Devereux." He watched her face closely for a reaction, but Lynna's face registered only relief that the captain of the ship was related to her husband, even if he was a detestable pirate. "Do you not recognize the name?"

"The name means nothing to me. Sean Devereux," she repeated the name. "I have never…" her voice trailed off as her face took on a deathly white pallor when she recognized the name.

Sean Devereux was Michael's brother?

A man rumored to be the most ruthless cutthroat of the band of pirates currently roaming the Caribbean. They were well known and feared for attacking helpless vessels, looting coastal towns, plundering, and murdering innocent victims.

"Why did you bring me here, Michael? You have made it abundantly clear that I mean nothing to you. You never even cared enough to consummate our wedding vows."

His answer was final, cutting through her like a knife. "I wed you only to give Crystal a mother, but since the life of a pirate is no life for a child, I had one of the men take her to Cliff and Bertie. They will care for her as their own, so you need not concern yourself for her welfare."

He eyed her contemptuously. "As for why I took you, the answer is simple. Captain Joshua Jordan. Since he has been fed anything his heart desired with a silver spoon, it gives me great joy to take what he desires most, above all else."

"What is that, Michael?" Lynna held her breath, dreading his answer.

"Why you, my darling wife." He grinned. "He desires you above all else." He walked out the door and slammed it behind him, and she heard the keys rattle as he locked it.

Had Michael discovered Joshua in her bed? If so, it was no wonder he despised her. She had no doubt that he would make it his personal mission to keep her and Joshua apart, forever. He would also make certain that the remainder of her life was unbearably miserable for having cuckolded him.

Lynna threw herself on the soiled bunk as scalding tears soaked the filthy mattress.

Chapter 30

Her eyes were red and swollen when Michael returned later in the afternoon. "What is this?" She eyed the bowl he placed before her suspiciously.

"It is called salmagundi." Michael's anger toward her seemed to have abated, for the time being. His voice was almost gentle. "Try it."

Lynna shoved the bowl away, refusing to eat anything prepared on a foul pirate ship, no matter that she was starving. "What's in it?"

"A little bit of everything. Fish, chicken, pork, beef, and pigeon is roasted and cut into chunks. Then you add cabbage, pickled herring, mangoes, onions, grapes and anything else you can find. Pour in a little wine, add salt and pepper, and voila." He laughed heartily at her shocked expression of distaste. "Don't make such a face. It really is very tasty. Just try it, Lynna. You might like it."

"I'm not hungry," she lied, although she had to admit the stew smelled awfully tempting.

"Take my advice, and eat while you can. Once we're out to sea and our fresh food supply has been exhausted, you will find the fare far from palatable. You can look forward to gruel, which is a mixture of wheat and water, or boiled and salted beef, with biscuits that are alive with maggots and weevils. You will regret passing up this fine meal."

Lynna turned her head in distaste. "I would find it impossible to eat any food prepared aboard this infested ship."

The cabin was alive with vermin. Cockroaches crawled the floor and walls around her, and the tiny bunk where she was supposed to sleep was covered with disgusting bugs. A large number of the pests were on her now. She clawed at her head where lice and God only knows what else were digging into her scalp. Her entire body was covered with itching red spots, where the insects had fed upon her tender flesh.

"I will leave the meal with you," Michael warned solemnly, before opening the door to leave. "Heed my advice and eat, Lynna. You will need your strength where we are going."

She jumped up to run after him, afraid to be left alone to fend for herself against an entire ship filled with degenerates. "Please, don't leave me alone, Michael."

"I'm afraid I must. Don't make the mistake of believing that because I am the Captain's brother, I don't have to pull my share of the weight. Actually, quite the opposite is true, as I am expected to do twice the work of any other man."

"Why, Michael?" She motioned toward the box. "You have more money than you could ever need. Don't join up with this vile band of cutthroats."

"While I have more money than I could ever need, for now, how long do you think I would live if the men onboard this ship found out? Our lives would mean nothing. Therefore, if you value your life, you will keep this bit of information to yourself until we reach port. No one must learn of the money, Lynna, not even my brother."

"When will we reach port?" She had to get off

this wretched ship and find a way to get word to Joshua.

"Not in the near future, I would suspect. Once Sean puts out to sea, he doesn't return until the hold is overflowing with riches."

"Where is his home?"

"Sean and I were raised in Trinidad with our grandmother, after the death of our parents. Since my brother wouldn't want her to know of his law breaking activities, he now calls Tortuga home."

Tortuga? The name brought to mind lurid tales of the pirate stronghold, unspeakable tales of horror. A place where the scum of the earth congregated to torture their helpless victims.

Michael grinned. "I can tell from your expression that you know what to expect when we arrive."

Lynna merely nodded, acknowledging that her future would not be a pleasant one, if indeed she had a future. Only one hope kept her from giving up completely.

Joshua.

He would rescue her. He had to. She wouldn't permit herself to think otherwise. Her only problem would be surviving until he found her.

Michael once again made to leave, when she grabbed his arm. "Would it be possible to have a bucket of water, and a sponge?" She slapped at a nasty cockroach making its way up her skirt, and watched as Michael swiped it off to crush beneath his boot.

"I will see what I can do," he answered, mumbling about the foolishness of women as he locked the door behind him.

Lynna moved to the porthole and breathed deeply of the fresh sea air. It was the only thing around her on this godforsaken ship that was clean. She glanced at the table and noticed a steady stream of ants and other creepy crawlies advancing on the stew, and greedily grabbed the bowl. If they were to be at sea as long as Michael suggested, she had better learn to eat what was offered, or starve.

Surprisingly, the concoction of meat, fruit, and vegetables was a meal to be savored, and she did. She was tipping the bowl to get the last spoonful when a timid knock sounded at the door.

"Who is it?"

"It be Rob, ma'am, de cook," someone answered in a low whisper. "Let me in."

She opened the door to find the biggest, blackest man she had ever seen smiling down at her. "I brung you dis heah watah an' sponge you done axk fo." He sat the bucket inside the door and stepped inside, closing it quietly behind him. "I put a cup of vinegar in dis bucket, cuz you ain't gits too far wit' jus' plain watah." She saw the fear register briefly on his face. "Please, ma'am, you cain say nothin' to de Cap'n bout it. Heah have me flog' if'n he foun' out."

"Thank you, Rob. You are most kind, and rest assured that the captain will not learn of your generosity from me, as I pray that I never have to meet him." As Rob opened the door to peer up and down the corridor, she whispered, "Thank you, again. I simply could not live with this pestilence."

Rob left the cabin with pity for the slip of the girl strong inside him. She would meet the captain, of that he was certain, probably before the day was over.

Lynna washed the bedclothes in the bucket of vinegar and water, and hung them on hooks to dry. She vigorously scrubbed every inch of the floor and walls, squashing hundreds of bugs in the process, until she was satisfied the cabin was as clean as she could possibly make it. Now for her.

She simply had to have another bucket of water to bathe and wash her hair. Perhaps she could find Rob and ask him.

She tried the door, amazed to find that Rob had left it unlocked. She peered into the corridor to the right and saw the hatchway leading to the deck. She definitely didn't want to go in that direction. She hurried out the door and turned left, only to run headlong into the arms of Captain Sean Devereux.

He was a strikingly handsome man, well turned out with his leather waistcoat, three-inch wide black belt with silver buckle, and cutlass strapped bandolier. He wore no bandana, and surprisingly, with appropriate attire, he would not have looked out of place in the parlor of some of Georgia's more refined homes.

"Well, shiver me timbers." He smiled as his eyes slid appreciatively over her slender form, lingering on the soft swell of bosom above the bodice of her gown. "So, you are the wife of my brother?"

"Yes, I am Michael's... wife," she stammered. "Now, if you will excuse me, I will return to my cabin." She rushed back inside and swiftly attempted to bolt the door, only to find it blocked by his booted foot.

"Not so fast, little one. I have a desire to become better acquainted with my new sister." The pirate shoved the door open with ease, and Lynna's noticed that his dark eyes were menacing as he licked his lips. "Much better acquainted."

She read the intent in his eyes as her gaze darted around the cabin in search of a weapon. None were to be found. The only objects in the room were a bunk, a table, and a chair, all too heavy to be lifted by her. "Don't come near me," she warned.

His bold laughter filled the room, sending chills to traipse along her skin even though the heat in the cabin was sweltering. "What, pray tell, will you do if I come near you, little one? Beat me to death with those tiny fists?" He paused to gaze out the porthole. "You have a long voyage ahead of you, dear sister, and you will need a man on the journey."

"Have you forgotten, sir, that I have a husband?" Did his brother know Michael refused to share her bed? That he refused to touch her?

"I did not forget that you have a husband." The pirate smirked. "If you will recall, I said you will need a man."

"Michael is a man." Lynna tried her utmost to sound convincing. "I might add that I find him most satisfactory in every way."

The pirate appeared to find her words amusing. "Then might I suggest that it takes very little to satisfy you." His ridicule of his brother was lost on her. "You will soon find that unlike my little brother, I have what it takes to please a woman."

She tried to run past him, but was halted by his steely voice. "Stay where you are."

She was too frightened to remain still, and bolted for the door. He jerked her around to face him, causing her to cry out as his fingers dug into the tender flesh of her arm. "I am not accustomed to having my orders disobeyed."

"And I am not accustomed to following orders," she replied defiantly.

"My brother should have taught you better manners." His fingers were like vises around her arms. "You see, you have no choice whatsoever in the matter, little one. This is my ship, and everyone onboard must either obey me, or suffer the consequences, which I assure you will not be pleasant."

"No punishment could be worse than being mauled by a disgusting pirate."

"We shall see." The pirate's eyes sparkled with desire. "If you prefer the cat-o-nine-tails to me, I will be happy to oblige."

She stood her ground, preferring the whip to his lust.

Sean hated the thought of marring her exquisite flesh. Flesh that would be most pleasing in the lonely weeks ahead. Little did Lynna know that Sean was a hard man, yet soft where beautiful women were concerned, and he could never remember seeing one more beautiful.

His hand trailed up her arm to lightly caress the swell of her breast, squeezing painfully when her fist crashed into his jaw with a force that stunned him. His huge hands moved to the slim column of her neck, closing around it to apply gentle pressure. "I could snap your neck with one twist, as I have done so many times in the past for far less crimes than you just committed."

A muscle in his jaw twitched angrily. "It might behoove you to consider who you are dealing with the next time you feel the urge to strike a man, for all men might not be as lenient, or swayed by your beauty, as I am. Nonetheless, you must be punished for your carelessness, but that can wait until after I have my fill of you."

He lowered his mouth to hers as his lips demanded a response she refused to give. "I can't imagine that deed being accomplished anytime in the foreseeable future. Now, allow me to demonstrate the pleasures to be found in the arms of a real man."

She needed to think fast, but her mind was still sluggish from the effects of the drugs. "I am your brother's wife, Captain Devereux. Do you feel no loyalty toward him?"

"The answer to your question is no. Believe me, at this moment my feelings do not run toward family." His eyes rested on her heaving bosom. "That's not entirely true, as I have rather pronounced feelings for the newest member of my family." He lifted her easily, and carried her flailing and screaming to the bunk as she clawed at his face and sunk her teeth into his shoulder.

She cowered, expecting to feel the blows from his fist, but none were forthcoming. Instead, he gazed down at her in deep thought.

What Sean wouldn't give to have this lovely creature come to him of her own volition. The hold of his ship was overflowing with bounty. Therefore, if he was of a mind, and he was, he could take her to his island and lock her in his bedroom until his lust for the captivating creature had been satisfied. By then, she would be his, and he would devote his entire life to pleasing her.

Even as he contemplated his possible devotion, she continued with her assault. She was enraged, pulling fistfuls of his hair and trying to dig her long nails into his skin.

Once on the bed, the strong smell of vinegar assaulted Sean, and a workable plan began to take shape in his mind. "Who gave you vinegar, dear sister?"

Lynna immediately stilled, taking the look of one completely innocent of all crimes. "I'm sure I... don't know what you are referring to. What vinegar?" The lie fell from her lips with ease, as she was suddenly more frightened for Rob than for herself.

"Answer me." He jerked her face around and forced her to meet his eyes. "I will know who onboard my ship so carelessly wastes supplies. Was it Rob?" He interpreted the fear in her terrified gaze. "He is the only man onboard who would be foolish enough to go against my orders and give in to the foolish whims of a woman." Sean had used her fear for Rob to his advantage, and the ploy was working beautifully. "He must be punished. He will receive twenty lashes for the theft."

"Twenty lashes?" Lynna temporarily forgot the danger she faced, and shoved Sean off to leap from the bunk. "Twenty lashes for a cup of vinegar? You cannot be serious."

"Alas, I see that your memory has not fled you after all, little one."

She scrambled through her pockets for the gold doubloon she found while cleaning under the bunk. "Here, I will pay for the vinegar I used. This should more than cover..."

"I will prove that I do not issue false threats," Sean roared theatrically, as he strode angrily out the door and slammed it behind him. "The man must be punished for his disobedience."

Lynna sat at the table and dropped her head in her hands, trying to reassure herself that the pirate captain would not execute his vicious threat. Of course, he wouldn't. No man could be so heartless.

She heard footsteps outside her door.

She cracked open the door to find a stoic Rob in the hallway, with a glowering Sean holding a sharp cutlass to his back.

Rob showed no emotion as he walked solemnly toward the deck. He knew exactly the excruciating fate that awaited. He was no novice at having his skin laid open by the cat-o-nine tails. Seeing Lynna, he stopped to smile encouragingly.

"Move," Sean ordered. "Or do you wish to be run through in front of a lady?"

"Please," Lynna cried, rushing forward and attempting to pull him, and his sword, away from Rob. "I implore you, sir, to cease this madness and not carry through with your vile threat."

Sean pretended not to hear her as he marched Rob toward the hatchway. Lynna realized that once the crew discovered what was about, they would halt their work to urge their captain on, eager for any diversion from the tedious monotony of daily life on a sailing ship. If she was to stop this vicious act of violence, it would have to be now.

"Wait," she cried, tugging on Sean's sleeve until he stopped prodding Rob with his sword and looked down at her. Appalled by what she must do, yet without hesitation, she timidly touched his bare chest where his shirt fell open. She stood on tiptoe and whispered close to his ear, even as the words choked her. "I will do... anything, if you do not flog this man."

Sean rubbed his jaw and pretended to ponder her request, when in truth he had hoped this would be her reaction to his threat against an innocent man.

"No, Ma'am," Rob stated adamantly, ignoring the cutlass at his back. "Don't do dat."

"Avast, you fool," Sean commanded, having no desire to whip a man without just cause. "Who do you think will be most apt to see the sun rise tomorrow morning? You, after twenty lashes from the cat-o-nine, or her after a night with me? Now shut your trap and return to the galley, before I change my mind."

With a sly grin curving his lips, Sean followed Lynna to her cabin. He was elated, while she felt numb all over.

Could she carry through with her promise? Where was her husband? Why didn't he stop this insanity? Silent tears coursed down her cheeks as she heard the door close, and nervously turned to face the pirate captain she had bartered her body to.

She wasn't ready. She had to stall him until she could devise a plan. "Tell me about your life, Captain Devereux. What makes a decent man turn to piracy?"

"I will be happy to discuss my life choices with you at a later date." The pirate grinned. "After I have made love to my heart's content. So trust that your stall tactics will not work. I held up my end of the bargain, now come to me as you promised."

There would be no turning back now. His eyes glazed with lust assured her of that.

Sean's hands were surprisingly gentle as he slowly unfastened her dress, stopping often to touch, caress, and stare in amazement as her exquisite loveliness was unveiled to him. He desired this stunning beauty with an urgency he hadn't felt in years, if ever.

"My husband will kill you for this," she whispered, as he cupped a breast in each hand and nuzzled her neck.

"That is a risk I am willing to take, little one." Sean knew that she was most likely a virgin, and one he would most thoroughly enjoy deflowering. He eased her down on the bunk and his lips had just found hers, when the unmistakable sound of a cannon blast striking the ship made Sean forget his purpose.

On his way out the door he turned to her. "Do not forget your promise to me, little one." Then, he raced from the cabin, leaving the door open in his haste.

Now was her chance. She was midway to the deck when Rob grabbed her arm and yanked her around to face him.

"Dis way, ma'am," he shouted, over the cries of injured men and the noise of shots being fired. The sharp smell of gunpowder, and the frightening sound of wood splintering filled the air around them. The smoke from cannons being fired choked her as she ran to the deck. "I must see who is attacking us. It could be my rescuers."

"Naw, Ma'am, I done seed dem, an' it jus' another pi'ate ship. Our onliest chance is to jump ovah de side and swim fo it." Without giving her a chance to refuse, Rob lifted her easily and tossed her over the rail, just before a cannon blast left the entire front portion of the smoking ship in splinters.

Lynna just had time to draw a deep breath as the murky water rushed up to meet her, filling her heavy skirts and dragging her under. As she sank to the bottom, she struggled to push away the heavy skirts that wrapped around her head, as her lungs began to ache, and demand that she breathe. Her chest was on fire.

For what seemed like an eternity, she struggled to the surface, only to be dragged under over and over until she could fight no longer. At the point of total exhaustion, when she was too tired to move her arms or legs and continue her quest for survival, she longed for death to release her from this insufferable agony.

Suddenly, Joshua's face appeared in the black water, and she swam toward him.

Chapter 31

Shivers of stabbing pain behind her eyelids caused Lynna to open her stinging eyes. She was immediately forced to lift a trembling hand against the blinding rays of a blazing morning sun. She squeezed her eyes shut, and painfully rolled onto her stomach, groaning as her parched and swollen face made contact with the scorching sand.

Every muscle in her body screamed with agony. Where was she? How did she get here? How long had she been here? Most importantly of all, why couldn't she remember the answers to these questions? Her mind was a complete blank.

She had no memory before opening her eyes to a brilliant sun that seared her skin.

The roar of crashing waves sounded extremely loud in her pounding ears, answering one question. She was on a beach. With tremendous effort, she lifted her head and peered into a vast nothingness.

Ahead of her was the endless ocean, and on both sides was sand as far as the eye could see. Gritty wet sand, that clung to her face and stung her eyes. She felt it grinding against her teeth like sandpaper.

When she brushed at the sand with her fingers, her gentle touch brought fiery pain to her sunburned skin, and scalding tears to eyes that were covered with a layer of salt. Her hands reflexively went to her hair in a failing effort to smooth the knotty mass of tangles there.

Sadly, with the combination of salt, seaweed, and whatever else had been deposited in her hair, she found it to be an impossible task. She closed her eyes and sobbed, allowing her body to vent her misery.

Feeling somewhat better after a good cry, she took a deep breath and pulled herself up. Her arms jerked violently as she rose on quivering hands and knees, and cried out at the pain the small effort caused, especially her upper arms and shoulders.

After several failed attempts, she was able to stand slowly and wonder if her knees would buckle as they threatened at any moment to do. As she turned from the beach, she noticed a forest, and the cool shade beckoned her. If only she could dig deep into her soul and find the strength to make it to the cool shade of the forest, she would never ask for anything more as long as she lived. "Please, God," she prayed, "just let me make it to the shade."

Even though she was sure each step would be her last, after what seemed like hours of lifting the dead weight of her legs over and over, she finally reached the edge of the forest and sank down into its shady haven. She closed her burning eyelids as exhaustion seeped from her pores, and she welcomed the soothing darkness that once again enveloped her.

"Wake up. Is you alive?" The voice seemed to come from far, far away, pulling her back from the blessed darkness. "Dis heah's Rob, kin you heah me?"

Lynna slowly opened her eyes to find an enormous black man kneeling before her. He seemed determined to shake her bones loose. The whites of his eyes were angry red and bloodshot, causing her to back against the trunk of a coconut tree in fear for her life.

"Why is you actin' like you sceared of me?" He asked, puzzled by her reaction. He reached out to gently brush sand from her face. "I ain't gwine hurt you."

Lynna noticed the look of genuine hurt in his eyes and for reasons unknown to her, her fear for the bear of a man gradually began to dissolve. From somewhere deep within her soul, she knew this gentle giant would cause her no harm.

"You knows I ain't gwine hurt you aftah whut you done fo' me." He hung his head in shame, recalling how she had bravely given herself to the pirate captain to save him from the lash.

"What I done for you? I don't even know who you are." Her words came out as a scratchy croak. "Where am I?"

"I cain answer dat, ma'am." Rob shook his head sorrowfully. "I come to down on de beach dis mawning'. I figured I was de onliest one whut made it ta sho' alive. So, I struck out through dem trees lookin' fo' food an' water." He pointed to the thriving jungle behind them.

"Water," she croaked, as she tenderly touched her dry and swollen lips. "Did you find water?"

"I sho' nuff did." His huge calloused hands pulled Lynna gently to her feet. "Can you walk, or do I needs to carry you."

"Thank you... but, no... I... can walk." She looked at him oddly. "Who are you?"

"Rob, ma'am. My name be Rob." For the first time, he noticed the distant look in her eyes. "You 'members me, from de ship."

"What ship?" Although Lynna scarcely got the words out, Rob didn't mistake the sincerity in her tone. It was then he realized that she had not survived the ordeal unscathed, as he had first hoped. He tried to make light of the situation and hide his concern. "Weah talk 'bout dat later. Fo' now le's git you some watah."

With his strong arms supporting her, Rob led her through the jungle to a small clearing with a sparkling pond. He heard her soft gasp and then she was gone, plunging headfirst into the cool water.

Lynna drank deeply of the salt free water. When she had her fill, she began rubbing the thick layer of salt, sand, and grime from her hair and skin. She closed her eyes and breathed a blissful sigh as the soothing water rinsed the grit and grime from her body.

Rob watched silently, thanking God for sparing her life. He had searched under the black water until his lungs threatened to burst. When he surfaced, he called to her over and over until he finally gave up hope of ever seeing her again. No one could stay under water that long and survive. Rob knew that only God's hand had carried her safely to shore.

"You stays rite chere til I gits back, ma'am. I'se gwine find you sumphin' to eat."

"Thank you. I will," she promised. "Rob, do you know my name?"

"I sho' don't, but since you got all dat yeller hair I's gwine call you Buttercup."

She floated dreamily in the water that was so cool on her sunburned skin. She glanced around and was left awestruck by the lush splendor of the tropical paradise, as beauty surrounded her on all sides. She relaxed, allowing the tension to seep from her taunt muscles, when her body went rigid as something… large bumped against her back.

Her gasp echoed through the still forest as she froze, too terrified to turn and see what manner of man or beast lurked behind her. Who knew what hideous creatures slithered beneath the depths of the inviting water? She tensed, galvanized for attack.

She held her breath, not daring to move a muscle for a full minute. When she realized that no harm had befallen her, she gathered her courage and slowly turned, only to giggle in a burst of merriment.

It was a water lily, or at least she assumed it was. Having never seen one with such huge dimensions, she couldn't be sure. At least six feet in diameter, the lily pad was strong and buoyant, with a brilliant color somewhere between lavender and pink. The flowers in the center were closed, and she would later learn that they opened only after the sun went down.

Feeling strangely adventurous, she climbed into the lily pad to see if it would support her weight, and surprisingly it did. She relaxed into the cushiony softness and dangled her feet over the side, as exhaustion from her trying ordeal settled over her.

Rob returned to find her asleep on the giant floating lily pad. "Buttercup," he called several times, to no avail. Her sleep was one of physical exhaustion.

While he debated over whether or not to let her sleep, he decided she needed food in her stomach. When he called her a few more times, and received the same response, he threw a rock in the water. He couldn't help but grin when she sat up sputtering and wiping streams of water from her face.

"What did you do that for?" she muttered, sounding put out.

"I call' and call', but you ain't wake up. Come eat dese nuts an' berries I done foun' fo' you."

Lynna forced herself to leave the comfort of her lily pad and sit beside him on a patch of springy moss, when a gnawing in her stomach made her realize how long it had been since she had eaten. She grabbed a handful of berries and stuffed the sweet juiciness in her mouth, then another, and another.

She found the berries to be much to her liking, the same with the pistachio like nuts. Yet, while the tasty fare stopped the growling in her stomach, it left her far from satisfied. She needed something to stick to her ribs, like meat and potatoes.

Rob noticed. "Aftah we finds us a place ta sleep tonite, I see whut kind of meat I kin roun' up fo' supper. I done seed plenty of rabbit' an' squirrel' on dis heah island, an' dat big ole sea is full of fish. We ain't gwine starve."

Lynna stood slowly to her feet, determined to pull her share of the weight. "Where do we begin?" She had no desire to sleep on the open ground tonight.

Rob's attention was focused on an overgrown path directly across from the pond. From the height of the grass, in comparison with the surrounding vegetation, he would guess the path had been well traveled. He forced his suddenly tense body to relax, lest he alarm the girl. They might not be as alone on this island as he had previously thought.

He wondered if the natives were friendly, and issued a silent prayer that they weren't the cannibals the pirate captain had often threatened him with. His insides tightened involuntarily at the thought of Lynna meeting such a horrible fate. He hid his fear, while vowing to protect her with his very life.

Since she seemed a little woozy, he took her hand as they followed the path for several hundred feet through the dense jungle. They came upon another shaded clearing of soft grass, surrounded on all sides by towering trees, scrubby plant life, and a wall of rock. Again, Rob noticed the undergrowth had been trampled in the clearing, and near the wall.

He wondered why there would be so much foot traffic at the base of a mountain, and parted a thick tangle of vines to discover the entrance to a cave.

He motioned for Lynna to stay back as he peered into the inky darkness. He was met with a pitch black interior. Still, judging by the path leading up to it, the cave had been well used in the not too distant past. He wasn't sure what it had been used for, but he intended to find out.

He walked around the clearing to gather dry leaves, twigs, and two flint rocks as Lynna reclined on a soft carpet of grass. The poor girl was still recovering from her gut wrenching ordeal at sea.

Rob rubbed flint rocks together over a pile of kindling until a spark ignited, he then fashioned a makeshift torch and headed back to the cave to investigate. "You waits heah while I takes a look inside."

"Surely, you jest. I'm not staying out here alone with... with..." Lynna peered into the jungle and moved even closer to Rob when she heard what sounded like a woman's piercing scream. "That."

"It jus' a bird, Buttercup. I spent time on a

plan'ation in Jamaica, so I knows dat sound. Ain't nothin' to be sceared of."

"Just the same," she insisted adamantly. "I am going with you."

"Come on den." Rob chuckled.

At the opening of the cave, they shoved spider webs and other debris aside, gasping in unison as the light from the torch illuminated the unbelievable interior.

"I can't believe it," Lynna whispered.

"We ain't de onliest ones on dis heah island, dat's fo' sho'." Rob's huge hands clenched into tight fists as his sides, ever alert to danger.

While he stood motionless, Lynna took the torch and walked around the spacious cave lighting torches that were attached to the wall.

Light spilled across the room to reveal a roughly hewn oak table with two sturdy chairs. If that wasn't mind boggling enough, a hand-carved cabinet stood in the corner, filled with an assortment of wooden plates, bowls, cups, spoons and forks chiseled from wood. What she found most pleasing was the bed. It was a crude four-poster, with a stuffed mattress and canvas spread, presumably made from the sail of a ship.

"It's… incredible," Lynna breathed, completely astonished. "Someone must have lived here for quite some time to carve all this furniture from the forest. She was quiet as she moved around the room, amazed by their good fortune. "My guess is that this cave has been empty for several months. I wonder what happened to the previous occupants, Rob?"

"I can't answer dat." He relaxed, convinced that neither natives nor cannibals were accustomed to the lifestyle exhibited in the cave. "I reckon weah be safe 'nuff in heah, fo' now."

"I reckon we will."

The cave was covered with cobwebs and dust, and from the numerous piles of animal droppings on the canvas spread, the table, and every other surface, a menagerie of small furry creatures called the cave home. Lynna immediately set about cleaning, hoping against hope that they could make it livable by nightfall.

On closer inspection of the much cherished bed, they found the moss filled mattress to be the home of a lively family of chattering squirrels. Rob chased the critters away and carried the mattress outside to fill with fresh moss, while Lynna lugged the canvas spread to the beach for a good washing. She spread the material across several pieces of driftwood to dry in the sun.

When they returned to the cave, they confronted the filthy interior as a team.

"Rob?" Lynna asked, unable to reach the ceiling. "Can you pull down those cobwebs for me?"

"Yassum," he answered dutifully.

Lynna turned serious blue eyes on her only companion in the world. "Just yes, Rob. On this island we are equals, with no color barrier between us. Who knows? We may be on this island for the remainder of our lives with only each other to lean on. I hope we can be friends."

"You is a mite' fine lady, Buttercup, dat's fo' sho'." He walked out of the cave with a beaming smile. "I'se gwine look fo' supper. It mite be a w'ile fo' I gits back."

"You might need this." In one corner of the cave

stood a various array of spears of all shapes and sizes, a wooden bow and arrow, and a collection of hand carved knives. Lynna picked a spear at random and tossed it to him.

A huge grin split Rob's face. "A man cain axk fo' a better place to be shipwreck', can he?"

✣ *Chapter 32* ✣

Rob was lost in thought as they sat at the table, after a satisfying meal of baked fish and oysters, cacoon stew, and fresh fruit. Lynna was proud of the meal she had prepared. Cacoon stew was made from a vine called cacoon, with pods that grew up to three feet in length. Rob taught her to boil the pods and make a stew that was surprisingly tasty.

After a fine meal, they went outside to sit around a firepit Rob had fashioned from stones. He stared into the fire and gave thanks to the good Lord for delivering them both to the safety. "I hope some of de others on dat ship was lucky as we was."

"What ship?" They were so busy making the cave habitable, there had been little time for discussion. "You said we were shipwrecked. Whose ship were we on?"

"I keeps forgittin'." Rob sighed wistfully. "You done forgot err'thang, so I mite as well start at de beginnin'."

As his unbelievable story unfolded, Lynna's astonishment grew by leaps and bounds. She found it difficult, if not impossible, to believe that she had given herself to a pirate captain to save this huge black man from being whipped. It was even harder to believe she was a married woman.

"What did you say my husband's name was?"

"Michael Debero," Rob answered patiently. "He be de brotha' of de pi'ate captain, Sean Debero."

"Then my name is Devereux, at least we know that much." Lynna stood to roam aimlessly around the clearing, in an attempt to make sense of what he was telling her. She picked a gorgeous yellow flower and tucked it behind her ear.

Why couldn't she remember?

"So, my husband Michael is the brother of this pirate captain? We were on our way to Tortuga when the ship was attacked, and sank." She stopped suddenly, as fear gripped her heart. "Does that mean my husband is dead?"

"I cain answer dat, Buttercup. He mite be alive, but I gots my doubts. De las' time I turn' 'round an' look, dat whole ship was gwine up in flames." Disbelief registered on Lynna's face as his words sunk in. "Whut I done tol' you is de truth. De ship was on fire, we jump' ovah de side, an' dat's alls I members 'til I come to down on dat beach."

Lynna shook her head dismally. "I wonder if the rest of my life was as adventurous?"

"I cain tell you nothin' 'bout yo life fo' I seed you on dat pi'ate ship. 'Cept dat you live' on a fine sugah plan'ation wit' Mist' Michael."

They went inside the cave, and Lynna lay down on the clean canvas spread as the events of a long and exhausting day caught up with her. 'What happened to me, Rob? Why can't I remember my life before the shipwreck?" Her eyes filled with tears that glistened in the waning light.

"I cain say. Sometime it be bes' ta forgit de pas'." Rob stared into his cup, seeing images he had hoped to forget. "I got into a fight a few year' ago, wit' a man whut was tryin' to mess wit' my sistah, an' I kilt him." With no desire to face the hangman's noose, he slipped away that night and made it to the harbor, and the notorious pirate ship.

He glanced up after spilling his guts to find Lynna fast asleep. He gently pulled the spread over her and went back to the table, thankful that she had fallen asleep before he finished his story. She would fear him if she knew he was a.

With Lynna asleep, Rob left the cave to bury the skeleton he'd found in the forest, presumably the occupant of the cave. He had no way of knowing what had killed the man, whether it was sickness, snakebite, or attack from beast or man. He would probably never know.

The following days were carefree and happy ones. Lynna tore apart her tattered dress and petticoats to fashion two thigh length sarongs that she tied at the shoulder. With her skin tanned to a rich golden brown, bare feet, and loose shining mane, Rob fancied her to be a golden goddess. While he had no doubt that she was the most beautiful woman he would see in this lifetime, he felt no desire other than to protect her.

Rob had worked at backbreaking labor since he was old enough to drag a cotton sack, pouring gallons of sweat into the land. Picking cotton had required him to use only his hands, not his mind, but life was different here.

Lynna valued his opinions, listening intently as he explained everything from shooting a bow and arrow, to opening a coconut. Having someone to trust in him, and come to him for advice, had made Rob a changed man, and the happiest he had ever been. He also had something that had been absent in his life, until now. Pride. Lynna had been the catalyst to bring about such change.

After many days of practicing under Rob's patient tutelage, she was soon able to spear fish and sometimes, if the animal would cooperate and remain still, small game. They often made a game of who could capture their meal first, with Rob frequently allowing her to win.

They dined on roasted clams, oysters, cacoon stew and their staple diet of fish and shrimp. This, combined with an abundance of fruits, nuts, and berries proved to be most satisfying.

"How long have we been here, Rob?" she asked one morning, as she cleared the table and placed dirty dishes in a handwoven basket to carry to the stream. She was content with her life on the island, choosing not to dwell on the uncertainties of the past.

He pointed to the wall where he scratched off the passing days with a seashell.

"Eighty nine days, that's almost three months. It doesn't seem like we've been on the island that long, does it?"

"No, ma'am." He turned suddenly somber. "I been tryin' to figure out a way to git you off dis heah island."

"You will do no such thing," Lynna cried. "I'm happy here with you, Rob, and I have no intention of leaving our island sanctuary."

"I'se happy here too, Buttercup. De happiest I done been my whole life, but I was thinkin' 'bout yo family. I reckon dey done worrit deyselves sick wonderin' is you is dead or alive."

"I don't even know if I have a family, Rob. I may not have anyone to return to." His words struck a soft

spot in her heart, as Lynna had caught herself
questioning that part of her past as well.

"Dat's whut I'se sayin', Buttercup. Ain't you
wantin' ta find out?"

"What I do or do not want is of little
consequence, Rob. I don't see a fine sailing vessel
floating in the harbor, waiting to carry us home.
There is no way off this island, so that settles it."

"We only seed dis one side of de island. We ain't
knowin' whut's on de otha' side." Rob was
thoughtful for a minute. "The man whut carve' dis
fine furniture an' fix up dis heah cave musta got on
dis island by ship. Dat ship mite be tied up on de
otha' side of dis island fo' all we knows. I's gwine
strike out in de mawnin' an' see whut I kin find."

"I will pack supplies for the trip. Food may not
be as plentiful on the other side of the island." Lynna
reached for a basket when Rob's huge calloused hand
covered hers.

"Naw, Buttercup. I kin make bettah time by
myself. I know you be safe in dis cave or I ain't leave
you heah alone."

"Alone?" Shivers of fear tingled along her spine
at his words. "I couldn't possibly stay here alone,
Rob. Why, these woods abound with wild beasts."

Rob chuckled. "How many wile beast' you done
seed 'boundin', Buttercup?"

"Well… none, but that's not to say they aren't
here."

"You know I ain't leave you heah alone if'n I
'spect you be in *any* danger, Buttercup."

"How long will you be gone?" She had dark
visions of the lonely days and nights ahead, in a
paradise that suddenly felt more like a prison.

"I ain't ritely sho'. I ain't got no way of knowin'
how big dis heah island is." Rob wished she wouldn't
look so lost and forlorn. He would be happy to take
her with him, but he knew how demanding it would
be to scale the mountain and get a bird's eye view of
the island. She would be safer in the cave.

The following morning, Lynna waved to Rob
until his receding shape was no longer visible, as hot
tears streamed unchecked down her sun-bronzed
cheeks.

He was her only friend in the world, and now
even he was forsaking her. God forbid Rob should
meet with an unforeseen accident and never return,
leaving her to spend the rest of her days on this island
alone. She would surely go mad.

Neither of them knew what mysteries lay
beyond their secluded hideaway. She often wondered
what happened to the previous dweller of the cave,
yet she had no clue as to his disappearance.

She dreaded the nights most. She had heard
hideous, blood curdling screams that woke her from
a sound sleep. When she called to wake Rob, as he
slept on a soft pallet of moss in the corner, he would
chuckle and explain which of the forests' many
creatures had made the peculiar sound.

She was still far from convinced that some
monstrous beast wasn't lurking just outside the cave,
waiting to rip her to shreds. That was only when the
strange noises filled the deep dark jungle at night.
When the morning sun cast its brilliant beam over the
tropical island, she felt no such fear. Until now,
realizing that tonight would be her first night on the
island without Rob nearby to protect her.

After Rob had been gone for a few days, and no man eating creatures had invaded her cave, the feelings of loneliness began to abate and Lynna took the opportunity to explore her lush island sanctuary.

The island reminded her of a sparkling jewel, floating in the clear blue waters of the Caribbean. On one side towered rugged green highlands, on the other stood an exotic rainforest brimming with lush flora and fauna. She found great joy in discovering the many delights the beautiful island had to offer.

In the forest, she found flowers of every size and color. Red, yellow, white, and orange blooms were scattered among the vegetation in a glorious array of colorful hues. Wild orchids grew in abundance among the towering bamboo shoots, some stretching as high as one hundred feet to blot out the sun and leave the forest cool on even the hottest days.

Much to her surprise, Lynna slept soundly at night, waking unharmed and in one piece. She heeded Rob's dire warning and didn't venture too far into the jungle, only skirting the edges and never failing to be amazed at what she saw.

Giant trees stretched toward the sky, their tops creating an umbrella that kept the sun from falling on a forest floor littered with rotten tree trunks, scrubby plant life, and roots. The cool green of the forest was broken often by a vivid array of flowers, blossoming trees, and vines.

One tree was more unusual than beautiful, with fruit that reminded her of hanging sausage links, although Rob warned her that the tree grew poisonous fruit. Flourishing among the trees, wrapping and twisting endlessly, were the ever present vines. The vines were nearly as thick as a man's body, and twined through the forest like giant ropes.

Soon the forest gave way to breathtaking hollows, as tall elephant grass swayed in a landscape dotted with colorful wildflowers. She could sit for hours and watch the parrots, cuckoo birds, pelicans, and ever present hummingbirds that fluttered around the wildflowers. She found herself laughing at the same piercing screams that had filled her with terror on her first night in this tropical paradise.

The shallow ocean waters were alive with exotic tropical fish and giant tortoises. Oftentimes, she noticed fins protruding from the water and decided to stick to swimming in her pool that day, and, as always, she was alert for the monstrous pythons Rob had cautioned her about. He warned her that even though their bite was nonpoisonous, they could easily squeeze the life from her.

She felt suddenly cool and shaded, and glanced up to see thick black clouds rolling in threatening masses over the mountains, and heard the now familiar rumbling of thunder. In the Caribbean, afternoon thunderstorms were a frequent occurrence, usually brief, but often accompanied by heavy downpours of rain. For this reason she hurried down the path toward the cave.

Preoccupied with her thoughts, she failed to notice the tall ship anchored just off shore.

Chapter 33

Lynna reached the clearing just as fat drops of rain soaked her from head to toe. She stood in the mouth of the cave for several minutes and watched the leathery tree leaves bend under the weight of the rain, before feeling a chill and changing into her dry sarong.

She lit the wall torches and prepared a delicious lunch of oyster stew, using coconut milk. She felt safe and warm in her cozy hideaway, and curled up on the bed to listen to the steady dripping of rain in the forest, while wishing for the thousandth time that she had a good book to read. She decided to write her own story in her mind, featuring a dashing sea captain with sea green eyes, as she drifted into a dreamless sleep.

The rain had ended, and the sun was shining brightly after her nap. The forest smelled fresh and alive, and the massive canopy of trees still trickled water long after the rain had ended, drenching her as she walked beneath it.

With no direction in mind, she eventually found herself at the pool. Since she was already wet from dripping leaves, she dove into the water and swam to her lily pad, pulling herself over the side to sink into the cushioned bottom. Her arms and legs dangled over the edge as she kicked her feet to propel mother nature's raft.

A butterfly, the biggest she had seen, landed on her knee. Its wingspan was as broad as both her open hands, and the vivid colors were flamboyant gold, red, green, and shimmering violet. "How lovely you are, dear butterfly."

She remained motionless, watching the dazzling insect crawl over her knee, until a startling noise from the bushes caused it to flutter away.

Lynna was at once alert, peering into the dark jungle and willing herself not to be afraid. She relaxed as she recalled her terror when the giant lily pad had bumped against her back, and chided herself for being paranoid.

She closed her eyes, and was soothed by a gentle rocking motion as she drifted over the rippling swells created by her kicking feet. She convinced herself the noise was nothing more than one of the jungle's small furry creatures at play, only it wasn't a small furry creature.

Three men watched Lynna from behind the bushes, speechless, afraid to move a muscle lest the vision before them should disappear. For two of the men, she was an ethereal golden goddess for their love starved eyes. For their Captain, she was the answer to many devout prayers.

Joshua watched in disbelief as the tremendous weight he had carried for so long was miraculously lifted from his weary shoulders. Happiness swelled inside his heart until he thought it might burst.

After months of desperate searching, he had found her. She was tanned and healthy, so he knew she had been well cared for on this deserted island, but by who?

She appeared petite and vulnerable in the lily

pad, as her golden hair spilled over to float on the surface of the water. Her sarong had slipped high on her thigh to expose the length of her shapely golden legs to their hungry gaze.

"Lynna," Joshua whispered.

Her eyes flew open at hearing a stranger's voice, before her heart dropped as she witnessed her worst nightmare come to life. Three strange men stood in the shadows, soaked to the skin, with wet hair plastered to their heads. To her terrified eyes, they were the epitome of evil, causing her to leap from the lily pad to swim to the opposite shore, uncertain of which way to run.

"Don't be frightened, my love." The tallest man stepped forward with a soft smile curving his lips, and a questioning light in his sea green eyes.

She backed up as he began walking around the pool toward her. "Stay where you are," she warned.

"Lynna, my love…" Before he could finish his thought, she took off running at breakneck speed through the jungle as if she were being pursued by the devil himself.

"Dear God, help me," she beseeched, praying for guidance. Where could she hide? Who were those horrid men chasing her? Why did one of them call her Lynna? Suddenly, the answer was clear.

The pirates.

They weren't dead as Rob had assumed. They were very much alive, and determined to kidnap her and return her to the pirate ship. Rob would return to the cave and live out the remainder of his life wondering what happened to her. "Rob, please, come help me," she whispered, more terrified than she could ever remember being.

No!

Rob wasn't here to protect her. She would be forced to fend for herself.

She couldn't hide in the cave; they would follow the trampled path just as she and Rob had done, but her weapons were in the cave. The spears she had become so adept at using. She would need them if she was to survive the sea rovers' attack. She raced blindly through the forest, clutching her side as sharp talons of fear stabbed her.

Inside the cave, she grabbed two spears and turned to make a hasty retreat, having no desire to be cornered by the men.

What she witnessed standing in the entrance of the cave caused her body to go slack. She contemplated using the spear on herself, but lacked the courage. Instead, she faced the men blocking her only exit, and dared them with a savage glare to make a move.

"Why did you run from me, Lynna?" Again, the tallest man stepped forward, with a look of genuine hurt and bewilderment marring his handsome features.

He was almost convincing, but Lynna recognized it for what it was, a ploy to make her lose control of the situation. She raised the spear with her right hand and aimed it directly at his heart, as she held out her left hand to stop his progress.

"Stay away from me, or I will use it," she ordered. "Now get off my island."

"Your island?" Mystified, Joshua could only gaze at her in complete befuddlement before turning to the man beside him. "Return to the ship and give the crew leave to come ashore." As he spoke, his eyes never once left her exquisite face. "I can handle this."

Lynna gasped, horrified at his words. Perhaps she could defend herself against the three of them, given the weapons in the cave, but not his entire crew.

"Are ye sure, captain?" The crewmember sounded unsure about leaving him alone with the wee lass, beautiful though she may be. With her deeply tanned skin and curve hugging sarong, none of the men had ever witnessed a more breathtaking sight, and saw little comparison to the timid girl they remembered so well from her time on the *Windjammer*. "I feel certain she wouldn't hesitate use that thing," the crewmember mumbled, pointing to the sharp tip of the spear.

The taller man was the captain of the ship.

A deep chuckle rumbled through Joshua's chest. "I won't hesitate to summon help should the need arise."

The crewmember chided himself for being overprotective, and left the cave. He had seen the captain do battle with several men at once and come out the victor. He should be able to hold his own against this slight wisp of a girl.

Alone with Lynna at last, Joshua casually strolled over to the table and sat down, knowing full well that to get close to her would be his undoing.

From a safe distance, his eyes traveled greedily over her scantily clad form. Her shining golden locks fell in silky waves over her sun bronzed shoulders, and a lavender orchid was tucked behind her right ear. The sarong molded to her alluring curves, causing her unfettered breasts to swell enticingly against the thin material.

He would give all his worldly possessions to take her in his arms and make sweet love to her for the remainder of the day and night, but first he must get to the bottom of this charade.

Lynna cast a wary eye toward the man seated at her table as though he owned it. Still, she had to admit he was a rather magnificent man. His shining black hair spilled over his forehead to be carelessly brushed aside. His eyes were the very color of the sea, and seemed to strip away her sarong and leave her naked beneath his searing gaze.

A deep longing shone in the emerald depths of his eyes, and for some strange reason, Lynna had the urge to toss the spear aside and rush headlong into his arms, confessing to him how terribly frightened she had been. She longed for this strange man to hold her, and ease her fear. While she had no memory of the past, she felt an overpowering attraction to him. That's when it finally clicked in her brain.

He must be Michael.

Her husband.

Of course. Why else would she feel so drawn to him? He had survived the shipwreck and searched until he found her. Happiness and relief washed over her in a flood as she followed her heart and lowered her guard. She asked in a breathless whisper, so close Joshua could feel her warm breath on his lips, "Are you Michael?"

Anger flared deep within him as her words ripped through his soul. "What childish game do you play, Lynna?" he stormed, grabbing her roughly by the shoulders. "You know who I am, cease with this senseless charade."

She had been wrong. Dead wrong. This man was

not her husband. He was a bloodthirsty pirate. Stark terror was her only emotion as his fingers bit cruelly into her shoulders, and his eyes probed hers for answers.

Joshua witnessed the terror that registered on her lovely features and his anger immediately evaporated. He was alert when she turned to run, and caught her easily before she could make her desperate escape. As he pulled her around to face him and their eyes met, he noticed the questions mirrored in her tortured gaze.

Her slight body trembled beneath his hands as tears glistened on her sooty lashes. He cupped her chin and forced her to look at him when she would have turned away. "You don't remember me, do you?"

The soft words tugged at her heart so that Lynna again felt the urge to be held and comforted by this man. His breath was warm against her ear as he pulled her close, and their bodies collided to ignite a fire in her loins that left her shaken.

"I can make you remember me, Lynna," he whispered huskily. "Never doubt that for a moment. We shared too much to forget."

His lips touched hers, gently at first, then urgently demanding a response. Lynna's fingers circled his neck to entwine in his hair and draw him closer. His hands on her body scorched her through the thin material of her sarong, fanning flames that demanded to be quenched. Joshua lifted her reverently and carried her to bed.

"My darling, Lynna. I have been to hell and back these past months, not knowing whether you were alive or dead. Yet, I refused to give up, and searched

island after island until I found you." He planted soft
kisses on her eyes, nose, and finally her mouth. "I
could not accept the possibility of never holding you
in my arms again." His strong hands closed over her
buttocks as he pressed her softness fully against him.

Lynna.

That must be her first name, but her last name
was Devereux. The word penetrated her brain and
had the same effect as ice-cold water being thrown in
her face. She was Lynna Devereux, Michael
Devereux's wife.

She couldn't allow this man, this scum of the
earth pirate, to take what belonged only to her
husband. No matter how badly her body craved his
touch, or how strong her desire was to find the
release her trembling body yearned for.

"Stop," she cried, pushing him away. She
quickly retied the sarong and rushed outside, hoping
the cool evening air would clear the confusion in her
head. She followed the path to the pool, eager to
wash away the feeling of his hands and lips on her
body.

Once there, she stopped dead in her tracks.

The forest was alive with the sounds of shouting
and robust laughter. She moved as stealthily as a cat
to peer through the thick undergrowth, only to
discover her pool filled with naked, frolicking men
enjoying their first baths with fresh water in months.
Her face was a bright shade of pink as she turned and
ran headlong into the broad chest of the one she
sought to escape.

"I should have warned you, my love." He
chuckled, holding her ensnared as his gaze roamed
over her enchanting features. "The men have been at

sea for many months, and unless you prefer their company for the night, I would suggest you return to the cave with me."

"I will return to the cave," she gritted. "However, I will go alone."

"As you wish," he stated simply, walking past her to join his men for a much needed bath.

She lay in bed wide awake as shouts from the men's camp carried through the jungle, making sleep impossible. If only the cave had a door, with a latch. What was to prevent the pirate captain from taking advantage of her while she slept? She had no doubt as to him being entirely capable of such a brutish act.

She went to the corner and found the sharpest spear to tuck under her mattress. Feeling reasonably safe, she was finally able to drift into a fitful and dream laced sleep.

She awoke feeling gloriously happy and looking forward to a day on the beach, having momentarily forgotten the events of the previous one.

"Good morning," Joshua greeted, from his vantage point beside the bed.

Lynna gasped, and tugged the cover up to her neck, giving him a look that she hoped accurately conveyed her true feelings. "What are you doing here?"

"Seeing that no harm befell you during the night," he replied, puffing lazily on a cheroot.

She leapt from the bed to stand before him, outraged by his possessive behavior. "I can assure you, sir, that I do not need nor want your protection. Since I have managed to survive quite nicely thus far without your assistance, I have no reason to doubt my ability to do so in the foreseeable future."

Joshua seemed to enjoy her angry outburst as he sipped from a cup, from which drifted a most delicious aroma.

Coffee.

Real coffee.

How her mouth watered for a taste. Lynna couldn't draw her eyes from the steaming liquid as she suddenly realized how tired she was of drinking water and coconut milk.

He handed her the cup. "Forgive me, my love. It slipped my mind that you have been deprived of the luxuries most of us take for granted." A slow smile curved his lips as he watched her drain the cup. "Tell me, Lynna. How have you managed here, alone?" He made a sweeping gesture with his hands. "How did you acquire this furniture? Surely you didn't carve it yourself."

She decided it wouldn't hurt to answer a few of his questions, since he had shared his coffee with her. She moved closer to the edge of the bed where her spear was hidden, just in case he had another volatile mood swing.

He had built a fire in the fire pit just outside the entrance to the cave, and walked outside to refill the cup.

"The cave was like this when we found it," she answered over her shoulder, while making the bed. "All Rob and I had to do to make it livable was clean it up and chase out a family of..."

"Rob?" Joshua's voice was low, almost a growl. "Excuse me, Lynna, but did you say… Rob?"

"Yes, Rob," she murmured, inching her hand

toward the spear. It was obvious that the man was barely able to control his rising temper. He appeared livid, ready to explode at any given second. What had she said to make him so angry? Whatever it was, she had to keep him talking until she could reach the spear. "We have been blissfully happy here, Rob and I."

In one violent motion, Joshua threw the cup, sending the remains of the coffee splattering against the wall. He grabbed her by the shoulders as his eyes bore into hers. "Who the hell is Rob?" he ground out, as an indescribable pain stabbed at his gut. "Have I been replaced by this Rob so easily?"

Lynna wondered if perhaps the man was mentally unstable, or possessed by hidden demons? Then again, if he thought her and Rob were more than just friends, perhaps he wouldn't attempt more intimate advances towards her. She had to convince him that they were indeed lovers. "Rob?" She offered Joshua a beaming smile. "I can't tell you very much about him, because I honestly don't know."

"You don't know?" Joshua seethed. "You set up housekeeping with a man you know nothing about?"

"Of course, I know him," she hedged. "We... met on the ship."

"And?"

"Rob tells me the ship was attacked at sea and sank, and we were the only survivors. As luck would have it, we washed up here on our lovely island." She remembered her ploy, and sighed with longing. "I couldn't survive on this island if Rob wasn't here to protect me."

"Where is this Godsend now?" Joshua spat, as his voice filled with the anguish he was unable to hide.

"Who?"

"Rob," he snapped. He spoke slowly as he would to a small child. "Where… is… he… now?"

"Oh, he left a few days ago to explore the other side of the island. He should return any day now."

She turned around just in time to watch the furious man storm out of the cave.

✺⋆ *Chapter 34* ⋆✺

Joshua returned to find Lynna kneading what looked like bread dough. He entered without an invitation and seemed somewhat calmer, although she had been fooled by his mercurial mood swings before. He leaned against the wall with his arms crossed, quietly watching her. "Where did you get the ingredients to make bread on a deserted island?"

"From a breadfruit tree." She glanced toward the corner to make sure her spears were where they should be. "Rob spent some time on a plantation in the Caribbean, and was taught which trees and fruits are edible. He taught me to soak breadfruit in seawater until it softens. Then you peel it, and mash it into a pulp. Next, you knead it like this, roll it, and bake it as you would regular bread dough."

"Amazing," he had to admit.

"Look at this." She held up what looked like a chunk of ivory. She sliced a small piece and offered it to him. "Taste it."

Joshua was surprised to find it had a pleasing nut taste. "What is it?"

"Palm cabbage. Rob taught me the cabbage is the buds on the trees."

Joshua had long since tired of hearing her tout Rob's numerous accolades. "Aren't you just a wealth of information?"

"Rob is a very good teacher." She instantly regretted mentioning Rob's name again, after watching Joshua's knuckles whiten under the pressure of his clenched fists. She hadn't meant to provoke him. "Since neither of us remembered my name, he calls me Buttercup."

"How touching, I'm sure." Joshua moved to the entrance of the cave, to peer outside as he massaged the tension from his temples. "Do you ever leave this cave?"

"I did, before you and your men intruded on our privacy," she answered truthfully. "We spent most of our evenings on the beach, having clam and oyster roasts, building bonfires, or just watching the sunset. I have never witnessed a more breathtaking sight as when the moon hovers over the island." Lynna cut her eyes at him. "Now I'm afraid to leave the cave at night."

Joshua returned to the table and crossed his booted feet at the ankles, nodding toward a neat row of seashells lined up on a shelf. "I see you've found a few shells to add to your collection back home."

She had no idea what collection he spoke of, but she knew a discussion of shells was not what he had on his mind. She waited patiently for him to get to the point of his visit.

"You need not fear going out as long as you accompany me, Lynna."

Which danger was greater? Facing his men, or being alone with him?

They were silent for a long time, both lost in thought. Joshua was the first to break the silence. "Am I to believe you have no memory of anything that happened before your happy little island adventure with Rob?"

"Believe what you will." She shrugged. "What I

have told you is the truth."

He ignored her. "And that you landed on an island with a man you met only briefly, and the two of you immediately set up housekeeping together?"

"Did you expect us to live in separate caves?"

"I sure as hell did not expect you to share his bed." Joshua's chest heaved with anger as he scrubbed a hand over his face. "I find it hard to believe you have been living in a cave all this time with…with…"

"Rob," she supplied, since he seemed to have some difficulty with the name.

"Have you no explanations for me, Lynna?" Joshua was begging her to make him understand. "How did you go from loving me, to marrying Michael, to this tryst with… with…"

"Rob."

He opened his mouth to say more, but thought better of it and fled the cave in a huff.

Lynna smiled at his retreating form, going over in her mind what he had said. He certainly painted her as a woman with a colorful past. Thankfully, he wasn't aware of her giving herself to the pirate captain to save Rob from being flogged, or he would have surely added that offense to his long list of grievances.

Lynna sat on the beach, digging in the soft sand with her toes as she watched a ship with the name *Windjammer* rolling and dipping with the ocean swells. Heavy clouds rushed over the mountain to make the midday heat bearable as a cool breeze caressed her heated skin.

The beauty of the island left Lynna awestruck,

and had been hers and Rob's alone until those awful men found it. Still, if she admitted the truth, the men weren't so bad.

She no longer believed them to be pirates. The few she had come in contact with had gone out of their way to be nice to her, always polite and offering assistance should she need it. As for Joshua, what did she know of this man who claimed to love her?

Absolutely nothing.

Still, it was nice to have her freedom back after being cloistered in the cave. Joshua had ordered his men to move their encampment further down the beach, now she rarely happened upon a member of his crew. Little did she know that each man had been issued a personal warning by the captain, and had taken his words to heart. "The lady is mine, and I do not share what belongs to me. Any man who fails to heed my words will answer directly to me."

"May I join you?" His sultry voice startled her.

Lynna turned to find Joshua watching her intently. "It would be pointless, as we have nothing more to say to each other." She brushed the sand from her legs and made to rise.

"I can answer most of your questions about your past." His soft words caressed her like silk. "Aren't you curious, my love?"

She turned to face him, since she had many questions about her past, but she was also afraid of discovering she had been little more than a shameless hussy. She was happy here with Rob, on their island. Would knowing the truth about her sordid past make her miserable, and force her to live the remainder of her life in regret?

On the other hand, it might be best to learn all

she could, while she was being offered a chance that might never come again.

She was still debating over what to do, when the decision was made for her. Joshua seemed determined for her remember everything as he divulged all that he knew in great detail.

As he spoke, Lynna felt the cooling ocean breeze, smelled the salty sea brine, and heard the wind billowing the sails on the *Windjammer*. She envisioned Aunt Judith sitting at the table in the small cottage behind the great plantation Magnolia House, stitching a new ballgown.

She imagined Crystal running down the beach in Jamaica, and her heart constricted painfully as he told her about the darling little girl. She fought desperately to fit the missing pieces of the puzzle together. "What part did you play in my past, Joshua? Do you live in Georgia as well?"

"My home is in Charleston. We met onboard the *Windjammer* when you originally sailed from France, and we were recently reunited after three years apart."

Lynna peered across the harbor to his ship, hoping for a memory, but none came. Although she felt a quickening in her stomach when she gazed into a window below deck.

Joshua decided not to mention her father, it would only cause her more grief. A mischievous grin curved his lips when he recounted her first night of passion on his ship, and rapidly vanished as he continued with Suzanne's treacherous schemes. Pure hatred shone in his eyes as he recalled the pain on Lynna's face the night of the Harvest Ball, when he had been tricked into believing Suzanne carried his child.

"I couldn't have loved you." Lynna tried to reason with him. "Would I have married another man so soon if I had?"

"You married Michael because you thought we could never be together. You believed, as did I, that Suzanne carried my child. I convinced you that I couldn't leave my child to be raised by a madwoman, choosing to suffer the consequences of my own actions for the sake of my innocent child."

"You have my utmost respect for your decision to remain with your child, had there been one."

He held a handful of sand and allowed it to sift through his fingers. "We are both free now, Lynna. We can start fresh. Your memory may return in time, but if it doesn't, I can make you love me again." He winked. "Trust me, it won't be difficult."

Lynna wanted to believe him, and prayed that his words were true. Still, she couldn't push the nagging thought from her mind that he was a complete stranger, and could be filling her head with lies. Rob was aware that she had lived on the plantation with Michael. Why had he never mentioned this child named Crystal? She wondered if any of what Joshua told her was true.

He took her hand, and she didn't resist when he led her to a grassy knoll where colorful wildflowers fluttered in a gentle breeze. He bent to pick a handful and present her the fragrant bouquet as an offering of peace. When she refused to meet his eyes, he tilted her face and read the confusion in her azure gaze. "You question the truth of my words, Lynna?"

With their mouths only inches apart, it was an act of sheer willpower that kept him from tasting her dewy lips. He was certain beyond a shadow of doubt that if given half a chance, he could make her remember him. He was sorely tested now each time he was near her, as it grew harder and harder to leave her. The only solution to the problem was to put some distance between them, until she found it in her heart to trust him.

"I'm not sure what I believe. I need time to think, and sort out my feelings," she whispered. "You must try to understand how confusing this is for me." Her eyes swam with unshed tears as she pleaded for understanding.

"You will have the time you need." Joshua made a spur of the moment decision. "I will return to the camp with my men."

Lynna's pulse quickened. "Will you come back?"

Her response filled him with a small glimmer of hope. "I will be back, Lynna." He planted a tender kiss on her lips before she could voice an objection. "I will not leave the island without you."

She watched him walk away until his tall shadow blended with the trees.

A day later, she awoke to find him watching her. "Don't you have anything better to do with your time?"

"Better than watching you sleep?" Joshua shook his head, having found it impossible to stay away. "Since I was denied the pleasure for so long, I can't imagine a more agreeable past time. I find watching you in the flesh far greater than imagining you in my dreams."

Why did she have such a strong desire, an almost

overwhelming urge to hold back the covers for him to join her? When her blushing cheeks betrayed her, Joshua needed no more encouragement. He moved toward her slowly as their eyes locked, so close they could almost touch.

When she felt his warm breath on her lips, she panicked. "I can't betray my husband. Even though I have no memory of him, there must have been love between us or I wouldn't have married him."

It was entirely possible that Michael had survived the shipwreck, just as she and Rob had. When she raised her hands to stop Joshua's progress, he easily brushed them aside with a steely glint in his emerald eyes.

"Don't fight me, Lynna. My patience has worn thin, and I will have for myself what you so eagerly give to Rob. I cannot bear this torture another day."

The past few days had been especially difficult for Joshua, as sleep had been impossible. He hadn't meant to mention the other man, yet he couldn't rid his mind of him, in this same position, holding the woman he loved. The thought of them together, making love, burned his mind like a branding iron, and left him possessed by a blinding rage.

He ripped the sarong from her shoulders with a rending tear, drawing a ragged breath at the sight of her naked loveliness. He prayed she would come to him willingly, without a fight, but fight she did. She clawed at his neck and left four bloody trails.

He took her hands in one of his, and held them above her head as blood from the wounds she had inflicted dripped on her neck and chest.

Lynna fought with all her strength not to succumb to his lust.

She remembered the spear hidden under her bed, but it was impossible to reach with his heavy weight atop her. With no other weapon available, she sank her teeth into his shoulder, causing him to pull away so fast he almost took her teeth with him.

"Does Rob have to fight you when he takes you? Is that how you like it now, or do you go willingly to his bed?" He hated her for the pain she was causing him. No, that was a lie meant to justify his depraved actions. He could never hate her.

He glanced into Lynna's terrified eyes, and his heart melted as he realized one truth. If the only way he could have her was by force, he didn't want her.

Overwhelmed with tenderness, his mouth descended and he drank from her sweet lips one last time before leaving the cave.

Chapter 35

Lynna was in the midst of a good cry when Rob returned. "Buttercup, who is all dem mens' out yonder?"

At the sound of his voice, she wrapped the spread around her and flew into his welcoming arms. She heard his sharp intake of breath, and felt his huge body tremble with rage as he glared at the blood smeared across her neck and chest. "Who done dis to you?"

She hesitated to tell him, since she had no desire to see Joshua suffer. "As you can see, I'm unharmed, Rob." She tried to sound brave. "This is his blood, not mine."

"Buttercup, you done give yo'self to save me from bein' flogged, an' long as I live ain't no man gwine hurt you an' live ta brag 'bout it." He left her helplessly clutching the canvas spread as he strode determinedly toward the beach.

Rob had hoped and prayed to never deal with another white man as long as he lived. Still, he had a wrong to make right, and he would see it done.

Lynna quickly donned her good sarong and followed him.

Joshua and Rob were face to face when she reached the beach. Rob's huge form towered over Joshua as he stood at the water's edge, washing smeared blood from his neck and chest. "Is you da man whut done rape Buttercup?" Rob demanded, with his fists clenched tightly by his sides. He was ready to take on the entire crew if they dared interfere.

"Did she tell that you I raped her?" Joshua had no idea who Rob was, nor the depth of his anger.

"She ain't gots ta tell me," Rob snarled. "I done seed de blood on her, so is you gwine answer me or not?"

It was slowly dawning on Joshua just how angry this behemoth was. "I certainly wouldn't describe our encounter as rape."

"What evah you calls it, I aims ta kill you fo' it," Rob warned, just before his meaty fist connected with Joshua's jaw and sent him sprawling backward in the sand. When Joshua tried to stand, Rob kicked him viciously under the chin, snapping his neck back with enough force to break it.

Rob lunged again, but Joshua grabbed his legs and was able to bring the goliath down. They exchanged blow for blow, rolling in the sand until Rob won the advantage when he landed on top of Joshua and wrapped his hands around his neck. Joshua clawed at the massive paws to no avail, as blackness rapidly closed in on him.

"Stop!" The scream was torn from Lynna's lips as she raced across the sand. "Stop! You will kill him!"

"He need ta die fo' whut he done to you," Rob raged.

Lynna made to throw herself on Rob's back, at the same time as Rob drew back his fist to pummel Joshua. Rob's fist caught Lynna below her left eye and knocked her out cold.

Joshua's men heard Lynna's scream and came

running. It took four stout crewmembers to subdue Rob and tie him to a coconut tree, and two of them would be incapacitated for days. "You need me to get the cat-o-nine-tails, Captain?" one of them asked.

"Yes," Joshua croaked. His bruised throat burned like the fiery flames of hell. He hoped to intimidate the giant who had almost sent him to an early grave, and keep him still long enough to find out what the hell was going on.

Lynna opened her eyes to see Joshua kneeling over her. "Lynna, are you hurt?"

"I's sorry, Buttercup. I sho' nuff is sorry," Rob muttered sorrowfully, struggling ferociously against the ropes that bound him.

"Nonsense, it was an accident," she replied, still dazed. "I should have made my presence known. You would never intentionally harm me, or anyone else."

"Here's that whip, Captain," the eager crewman grinned.

Whip?

At that moment, the fact that Rob was tied to a tree with his back exposed, sank into Lynna's spinning head. She leapt to her feet and forcefully shoved Joshua aside to shield Rob with her body. "Bring me your knife, Joshua. If you inflict one lash on this man, I swear I will murder you all in your sleep."

Joshua took the distraught girl into his arms and held her against his chest until she stilled. "Calm down, Lynna. I will untie him if he gives his word that he won't try to kill me again." He had never seen Lynna so distraught, her slight figure trembled with rage.

Joshua ordered six of his most able bodied seamen to stand at the ready before issuing the order to untie the giant.

That voice.

Lynna knew that voice. Words, images, and faces scrambled in her mind like a jigsaw puzzle. She left Joshua's embrace and cradled her head in her hands as she walked the beach. She needed to be alone, to sort through what was happening in her mind, but it didn't help.

The mad chaos left her dizzy, as hundreds of images swirled in her head, her childhood with her mother and father by her side, setting sail on the *Windjammer*, Aunt Judith, Tobias, Suzanne, Aunt Gypsie, Aunt Bertie, Crystal, jumping over the side of a burning ship and, finally, Joshua. A tornado was in her head, spinning and spinning, faster and faster until she fell to the sand with a blinding headache.

This must be what insanity feels like.

After several minutes had passed, and the headache slowly began to ease, Joshua helped her to her feet and into his welcoming arms. She longed for his comforting embrace, fearing the mass confusion in her head would return, but it didn't.

Suddenly, her mind was clear.

Joshua?

With a cry of delight, she leapt into his arms and sought his lips for a smoldering kiss that didn't end until one of the crewmembers cleared his throat. "My darling, Joshua," she whispered, lowering her lips to his again. "It really is you. I remember now, I remember everything."

"It's about damn time." Joshua grinned,

spinning her around and around in his arms. "I thought I would have to kidnap you off this damned island." He nudged his head toward Rob. "Who's the behemoth?"

"Rob, of course." She grinned at his shocked expression. "I wouldn't be alive now if he hadn't taken such good care of me. I owe him my life."

"Rob?" Joshua glared at Rob, marveling at his own stupidity. He had been a fool to jump to such harebrained conclusions, without first finding out the details. With a nod toward Lynna's champion, Joshua spoke from the heart. "I am forever in your debt, sir."

Rob returned his nod, and in a tone of voice that left no doubt as to the seriousness of his words, he warned, "I knows no black man ain't 'pose to threat no white man. But out heah on dis island, dey ain't no law to speak of, an' Buttercup done said we was equal', so I's tellin' you now. If'n you, or any otha' man touch her agin, an' she ain't want you to, I rips you apart wit' my bare hands."

No man there doubted the sincerity of his words as he disappeared into the forest.

Lynna and Joshua were eating their last breakfast on the island when Rob entered the cave. Joshua stood to shake his hand. "My ship is ready to sail with the morning tide, Rob. Are you sure we can't persuade you to join us?"

"Naw sir, I's stayin' heah. Dey's huntin' fo' me back in Jawga."

"Nobody will find you at Sea Grove, you have my word," Joshua assured him. "You will have your own cabin, and live life as leisurely as you please."

"Please, Rob?" Lynna pleaded. "Come home with us."

"I's happy heah, Buttercup." Rob shook his head sadly at the thought of being all alone on the island, without her. "Fo' de firs' time in my life, I's happy."

"I understand, Rob," Lynna moved toward the big man and into his waiting arms. She turned to Joshua with tears swimming in her eyes. "Could we come back to the island next year for a visit? Perhaps by then he will have changed his mind and be willing to return home with us."

"Of course we can, and I will send a ship periodically to bring supplies." Joshua extended his hand to the huge man. "I owe you a debt of gratitude, my friend. One that I will never be able to adequately repay. If you hadn't thrown Lynna over the side of that pirate ship, odds are great that both of you would have perished along with the others. And if you hadn't been with her here, on the island..."

Joshua could only shake his head, refusing to give thought to the horrible possibilities of Lynna being completely alone on a deserted island. "Thank you again." He turned to Lynna with a beaming smile and held out his hand. "Come, my love, the *Windjammer* awaits."

Epilogue

Four months later, Lynna found it impossible to be still. "Aunt Judith, this is absolutely your most stunning and fabulous creation yet," she marveled, as she twirled in front of the cheval glass.

Judith smiled radiantly, silently agreeing with her niece's assessment.

Lynna spun around the room excitedly. "Oh, Aunt Judith, can you believe I am finally marrying the man of my dreams?"

Judith was almost as elated as her niece. "Your dreams have at long last become a reality, my darling."

The wedding gown was a magnificent work of art. Off the shoulder creamy organza, with row upon row of lacy ruffles cascading over the wide flowing skirt, and hand sewn crystal beads that caused the gown to glitter. Her tulle veil fell around her face, and a ten foot train attached to the skirt to trail behind her.

Lynna stood at the top of the mahogany staircase at Sea Grove, with family and friends gathered below. Her fondest wish was that Joshua love the gown as much as she did, and believe her to be as beautiful as she felt in it. She heard the music begin downstairs and knew it was her cue.

She lifted the skirt of her wedding gown and slowly descended the stairs as the soft strains of a pianoforte filled the air. She paused to draw a calming breath when she reached the bottom, and watched a wide grin curve Joshua's lips on first sight of his stunning bride.

Lynna walked past Aunt Judith, who was swathed in widow's weeds. Her uncle had met with an early demise in a drunken brawl in one of the taverns he frequented, shortly after their return.

Judith smiled a secretive smile, noticing the slight rounding to Lynna's stomach. Just yesterday she had altered her wedding gown, again.

Lynna had loving smiles for Aunt Gypsie, Aunt Bertie, and Uncle Cliff, who returned her smile with tears of joy.

Jeremiah, Patricia, and Malinda sat next to a beaming Samuel and Beth.

Everyone she loved was in attendance, except her beloved father. She couldn't allow herself to think about that now, and spoil her wedding day. Instead, she smiled a beaming smile as she walked down the aisle toward the man she would love until she drew her final breath. A man who was unbelievably handsome in his wedding raiment.

At last, she stood in front of the pastor and Joshua took her hand.

The pastor intoned, "We are gathered here today..."

Lynna barely registered his solemn words as she met Joshua's loving gaze.

"If there is anyone here who objects to the joining of Lynna Makenzie Mathison and Joshua Daniel Jordan, let him speak now or forever hold his peace."

"I object!" came a loud voice that was easily

heard over the music. "And her name is Lynna Makenzie Rhodes."

Lynna's heart skipped a full beat as a hush fell over the assembled crowd.

Could it be?

At the sound of the familiar voice, she turned. "Father!" she cried, as her trembling legs threatened to give way beneath her. She left a grinning Joshua at the altar and rushed down the aisle to fill her father's outstretched arms. "Father, where have you been? What took you so long? I have so much to tell you. Oh, Father, you have made me the happiest bride ever."

"My own darling daughter is about to be wed, and I wouldn't have missed it for the world." Nathan Rhodes struggled to maintain his composure as he held his daughter close. "Here, my child. Let me look at you."

Joshua breathed a deep sigh of relief. Months earlier, just after he and Lynna had become reacquainted and he knew he would conquer all odds to make her his wife, he sent a ship to France with orders to bring Nathan Rhodes to Charleston, hogtied if necessary.

Then, he had instructed Judith to proceed very slowly with the making of her wedding dress, and prodded his mother and sister to invent any problems necessary to postpone the wedding for at least three months.

After several minutes of holding his cherished daughter in his arms, Nathan brushed a betraying tear from his cheek and cleared his throat. "As the father of the bride, I have but one objection. I was not permitted to give my daughter away. Therefore, I would request that the wedding be started from the beginning, so that I may have the honor of escorting my precious daughter down the aisle."

"Of course, Father," Lynna's emotions bounced from laughter to tears as she walked with her father to the bottom of the stairs to begin the wedding march anew. "Father, why didn't you write to me? I've been so worried about you. It has been so long since you sent me away, and why didn't you send funds as you promised?"

"Why didn't I send funds?" Nathan Rhodes blustered. "Why, you were given a monthly allowance that should have kept both you and my sister living like queens. What is the meaning of this? Are you telling me you did not receive your monthly allotment? Who else had access to my sister's account?"

"Tobias." Finally, Lynna knew the answer to a puzzle that had vexed her for years. "I should have figured it out sooner. One of his relatives owns the bank."

"You have my word, that as of tomorrow, the bank will no longer be in operation." Nathan held his daughter as though he would never let her go. "Each and every day was torture for me, Lynna. I simply could not risk corresponding with you, my darling. I refused to leave a paper trail leading the villains straightaway to you."

"I understand, Father."

"Nevertheless, when I received word from Captain Jordan that you were to be married, I had to come. I couldn't miss the wedding of my most beloved. Now that I'm here, I find that I enjoy having my feet planted in Georgia soil again. Who knows? I just might decide to stay a while."

"I have something to tell you, Father, that might help with your decision." Lynna blushed prettily as she patted her stomach, and whispered in his ear.

Nathan's fists clenched at his sides as he gave his soon to be son-in-law a quelling glance, before relaxing and taking a deep breath. What was done was done, and his daughter had never looked happier.

He placed his daughter's hand in the crook of his arm, as he walked her down the aisle and handed her over to Joshua with a broad grin. "Again, I implore you, Captain Jordan. Guard my most treasured possession well."

"With my life, Mr. Rhodes," Joshua promised. "With my life."

The End

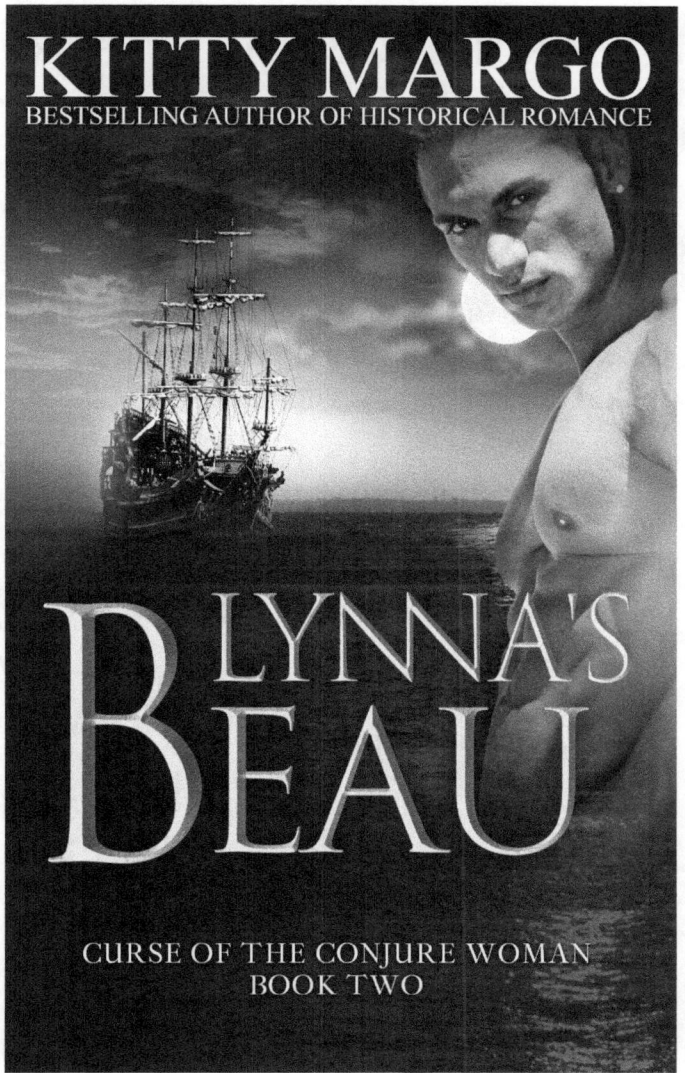

KITTY MARGO

BESTSELLING AUTHOR OF HISTORICAL ROMANCE

Lynna's Beau

CURSE OF THE CONJURE WOMAN
BOOK TWO

A NOTE FROM THE AUTHOR

A few facts about the earthquake mentioned in Lynna's Rogue.

To my knowledge, there wasn't an earthquake in Charleston in the 1850's. However, in my quest to find a reason to send Lynna to Jamaica, I invented one.

The Great Charleston Earthquake, as it would come to be known, struck the city on the evening of August, 31,1886 at 9:50pm. It had an estimated magnitude of 6.9 to 7.3.

The earthquake caused 60 deaths and between $5 and $6 million in damages. Over the course of the next 30 years, there would be more than 400 aftershocks to add to the damage.